The Red Priest

The Red Priest

by

WYNDHAM LEWIS

METHUEN AND CO. LTD.
36 ESSEX STREET, LONDON, W.C.1

First published in 1956

CATALOGUE NO. 186/U

PRINTED IN GREAT BRITAIN BY
THE CAMELOT PRESS LTD., LONDON AND SOUTHAMPTON

Contents

1. The Red Priest passes through the Mews   *page* 1
2. The Ritual of the Gutter   14
3. Land of Hope and Glory   30
4. An Efficient Secretary   36
5. An Appointment in Difficulties   46
6. Jane Greevey at the Church   50
7. A Luncheon Party   62
8. A Strong-minded Conversation   71
9. Norwich   75
10. The Vicar's Party   85
11. A Cup of Tea in a Cell   92
12. Hambledon College   97
13. The Miniature Recommended   106
14. Mary Alerted   116
15. A Special Service with Three Russian Priests   122
16. The Ghastly Girl   129
17. To Hell with the Earl of Ames   138
18. A Stone-Age Man   148
19. A Debate   155
20. Kenya   166
21. Messrs Dodds, Smithers and Yorke   173

22.	A Proposal	*page* 184
23.	Marriage	196
24.	The Beginnings of Married Life	203
25.	The Ghastly Girl Again	210
26.	Meeting of Mothers-in-Law	217
27.	Address on the Indian Religion	224
28.	A Stretch of Months	234
29.	The Ghastly View of It	248
30.	The Trial	251
31.	Hartnell and Horridge have a Deep Look	272
32.	The Trial Continued	277
33.	The Plantation	284
34.	The Birth of Zero	288

I

The Red Priest passes through the Mews

The graceful and grey, long-legged and small-headed Jane swung back to caress the famous names lined up upon her shelves. She had been talking, a toll number, to her sister, Ida Greevey, as long-legged and almost as small-headed as herself, but a little older. Her head now was full of the fierceness of the marmalade cat, who had again raided the roofland marked out for itself by Ida's cat —a gentle creature, unaggressive in colour, who must have its hands full with the neighbour's ginger beast. However, from the small pile of books Jane had removed for dusting, she took up a copy of *Antic Hay*; expelling some of the dust from its small precious body, she thrust it into the shelf beside the famous names of thirty years ago. She sat musing for a moment before picking up a second Huxley; but, out of the corner of her eye, she caught sight of Hughie. His censorious face was hovering about in front of her window.

He had slipped along from the garage door, from the place he rented from her. Jane rose and moved over towards the window, for Hughie's face had warned her that something 'outrageous'—something 'abominable' was occurring, not far beyond the walls of her house. She could well believe this, for she observed the lid of her dustbin held on high, used, as was customary, as a shield, rushing past her windows, screams of savage defiance coming from behind it. There were indistinct sounds of battle to left and right, and she was about to investigate when her telephone rang violently upon the desk at her side. It was Hughie, who obviously had slipped back to his hide-out, and was calling her.

'I say, they are behaving very badly, Miss Greevey. It is a new gang. The lids of all the dustbins have gone—they are being used as shields. I thought I had better tell you. It is a perfectly new gang, Miss Greevey.'

'Thank you very much. . . . I will attempt to rescue my dustbin lid.'

'I shouldn't.' Hughie's voice sounded very grim.

Jane hastened towards her front door. She must not allow this new lot to get away with it. As she threw open the door a fragmentary tomato flew past her face, exploding against the wall at her back, a missile of suitable size for a small fist. This imposed caution, and Jane protruded her head. There was an infernal racket all around her, composed of the harsh pipings from about thirty little throats, and a half-dozen larger ones, as Hughie had warned her—the 'new gang', obviously. She could not see her dustbin lid. She called out 'Hi . . . you!' But the new gang continued its advance down the Mews; what looked like a hundred midgets were in aggressive retreat, throwing anything they had at the invasive new gang, and snarling and squeaking defiance. Empty meat tins, boxes full of refuse, forks, pipes, broken glasses, cricket balls crashed against the dustbin lids. There were bellows from open windows; the hysterical barking of dogs from behind garage doors, the horn of a stationary car, a police whistle, a drum beaten by a mnnikin and a hundred contributory noises added to the hullabaloo. 'Hi! Give me back my dustbin lid!' was a pale contribution of Jane's to the uproar, as she thought she detected the lid. Her protest was quite disregarded by those crusading with the lids, and those resisting the new gang.

Jane withdrew, closed her front-door, moved back into her room, and threw up her window. Hughie hailed her with a shout from his half-open garage door, just beyond her front door.

'This is too much! This time boyhood and nipperhood have exceeded the limit. . . . Oh! serve you right! A casualty! I am going out to see what it is.'

Hugh Bestens-Corbett came out into the Mews, crossed it and stood beside one of the taller boys, who had a dirty handkerchief held against his eye-socket. They came back towards the garage. When they were quite near, Hughie, speaking as seriously as he knew how, supplied her with the latest news.

'Young Arthur Pastor has a piece of glass in his eye. I am taking him round the corner to Harrison's.'

'Can I be of any use?' Jane screwed her face as if she had a piece of glass in her eye.

'I don't think so, thank you.'

Jane looked uneasily down the Mews. Hughie backed his car out and moved slowly out of sight. Smoke was coming from the bombsite, at the end; it blew across the Mews; she watched it dismally, everyone seemed suddenly to have disappeared; some or all of the midgets were camping in the bombsite, the new gang having retreated from the Mews, she supposed. Jane left the window and returned to the cleaning of the books.

Funny how they all had vanished, Jane pondered. Evidently they had been frightened by something; she wished they had been crows, then a scarecrow could have been stuck together . . . or two, one stationed at either end of the Mews. She wished there were some way of frightening them. The exodus past her window had, for some reason, frightened her. She thought of the mothers of those dirty infants. As soon as their birth had been compassed, it almost seemed, they were shot out into the streets to join a marching gang of their own height, and with the same sewage smell. They marched off, sometimes never to be seen again. Their birth might have been the thirteenth or fourteenth bad dream of that kind to the hag responsible for them. Their faces—she meant the brats'—bore a very odd expression which never seemed to leave them. What was it? Jane was unable to analyse it. She thought it was like an old woman's watchful scanning of a coffin on its way to the cemetery speculating as to how much it cost to be stuck underground with that medium dignity. Usually their faces hung by their eyebrows from a roof of cloth, a twisted cap. Jane had been attempting to track the existence of such a frail little being with a large face, wondering if they slept in the gutter, fighting with the sparrows, or with the rats in a paternal dwelling at the river-side. She wondered if their little white bodies were ever pulled out of their garments and cleaned.

At Jane's back was the succession of towering city blocks of that steamrolling avenue headed for the rear of Buckingham Palace. Ebury Square was the southern extremity of one of the wealthiest and smartest areas of London, centring, in London's heyday, in Belgrave Square and the Lowndes estate. Ebury Square was in fact not a square, but a huge causeway, or what in America would be called a boulevard. To the north of it was now to be found a moribund stagnation of nineteenth-century palaces, with the Mews behind them no longer resounding with the jingle of harness, but rather with the practice notes of B.B.C. instrumentalists, or with the bang and rattle of second-hand cars. A nest of lesser embassies was supplied with a still respectable area—the Iraki, Abyssinian, Bolivian, Gold

4

Coast, and so forth ranged along the north fringe of Ebury Square.

Marten's Mews, where Jane Greevey had her house, was a product of the war—although the little dwelling in which she lived had been converted considerably earlier. There were a number of chauffeurs, but these had nothing to do with the street behind which the Mews lay. There were an equal number of residents, pure and simple, half of them aristocratic refugees, as it were, from neighbouring streets. A millionaire, Sir Philip Mortlake, whose house in Ebury Square the government had possessed itself of during the war, was a conspicuous resident. Jane Greevey had, for six or seven years, lived there with an inconspicuousness which did her credit.

One or two of these residents behaved in an irregular way. Sir Philip Mortlake, for instance, frequently parked his Rolls-Royce outside Jane's front door at night, without asking leave. Sir Philip was well acquainted with Jane's habits, and just before eight o'clock in the morning the Rolls would disappear. Once or twice she had arisen a half hour earlier, at seven-thirty. Looking out of her bedroom window she had caught Hughie's censorious eye from the garage, fixed upon the Rolls-Royce, and had been able to surprise the prowling figure of her next door but one aristocratic neighbour, the Hon. Eustace Holderness. The Hon. Eustace, as he circumnavigated the Rolls-Royce, gave it a reproving scowl or two, and once or twice protested elsewhere at the bullying of Jane that went on by the millionaire Mortlake. It was the habit of Holderness, at that hour, in a once superb silk dressing-gown, to escort his dog to a hogbin, maintained public-spiritedly by Jane. The animal would leave signs of the intermittent character of its bladder upon this metal cylinder; Jane saw with regret the visitations of this incontinent dog, but, so long as the

5

hogbin was able to hold its ground outside the yard door of the ex-Countess of Scilly's backyard, Jane was satisfied that dogs will be dogs. She was the backdoor neighbour of the beautiful but irritable ex-Countess, who, in conversation with her cook, on her arrival back from the Continent, stared in surprise at the hogbin, asked what it was, and subsequently commanded that it should be removed. Jane, sympathetically informed by the cook, stood her ground; the canine licence of the early hours she accepted, provided the bin withstood the expulsion orders of the ill-tempered Countess, who stalked about, in the rear of her fashionable mansion in Blessington Street, behaving like a wicked Countess in *Alice in Wonderland*. Besides, Mr Selby, chauffeur to the Duchess of Bristol, assured Jane that it was quite in order to station one's hogbin in the territory of a neighbour if they should omit to have supplied a public-spirited hogbin themselves. In any case, *he* would not hesitate to put the Duchess's hogbin up against the back door of no matter who. The district council was supposed to supply the hogbins, but, in this Mews, there were only two, Jane's one of them. All the more did she resist a raid on hers.

So much for the Mews in which Jane dwelt.

It was about an hour later that the telephone bell rang. Hughie was ringing again, this time from his basement flat in Blessington Street.

'Just thought I'd tell you. Took Arthur Pastor to hospital. For some reason his eye is full of glass. They've kept him there . . . are going to operate. Poor Arthur. Really rotten luck.'

'Poor little boy. It was very decent of you to take him to the hospital.'

'Of course it wasn't. Could I let the little beggar go home —with that eye? Have you recovered the lid of your dustbin, Miss Greevey?'

'No, I have not looked round yet. . . . I do not expect . . .'

There was a growl of protest in the telephone. 'You mustn't say that. We'll come across it somewhere. I will come round and have a look.'

Jane rose and drifted across to the window. In a few minutes Hughie's car nosed its way into the Mews, and stood outside the garage which he rented from her. He left his car, and crossed the Mews, bent down, and in a minute turned around and was swinging what appeared to be a dustbin lid in his hand. He held it up in the air, shouting 'Your lid I think.'

'Oh, good show! Thank you ever so much, Mr Bestens-Corbett.'

He brought the lid back smiling, placed it on the dustbin, and said 'Fits beautifully.' Hughie was a very mature six-footer; his double-breasted serge suit had also seen a great deal of life. But Mr Hugh Bestens-Corbett held himself pretty well, and his face was up to scratch also, if it would never be like that of a young man again. As it appeared at the window of his car, observing some scandalous misdemeanour, it had a comic severity, but his mind did adhere to life seriously, and, a good part of the time, sternly. Beneath the shadow of Victoria he was born to command, in a small way, and was being trained to acquit himself adequately in any latitude when the great Queen passed away, and other Monarchs succeeded her—less and less in tune with this sternly built subject of Victoria.

He now leaned against the wall beside Jane Greevey's window. He seldom got nearer to Jane than that; but they shared that part of the Mews which connected the garage to her home, with this in common, that Jane had been born in the Victorian Age like himself, and conformed with the sexual thus far-and-no-fartherishness in which she and Hughie had begun to grow up.

7

She knew her Hughie very well, she thought; and she noticed him sticking his chest out as he lay against her wall, and that, with other almost inperceptible signs, made her understand that males were in the neighbourhood (for had it been females the chest would have been stuck out but the expression on the face would have been softer and more inviting). While she was noting a host of signals she leaned upon the window, as silent as he was; and, to her amazement, the space between his doorslit and her gaping window was temporarily occupied by a tall, clerical, but rather queerly costumed figure. The newcomer stepped along daintily, guiding his feet always to the crest of the cobbles, not allowing himself to sink into the little valleys between the protrusive stones. His powerful body was sheathed in a cassock, balancing as it seemed his biretta on the crest of his forehead. A little later Hughie observed that his movements reminded him of a footballer butting at a ball. And his eyes seemed to be thrust upwards, as if in the act of poising an uncomfortable object upon his painfully rigid head. ('He's afraid of its falling off,' was Hughie's explanation.)

Jane needed no prompting to realise that this stranger was the 'Red Priest.' There he was at last—the scandal of the neighbourhood, one of Hughie's outstanding bugbears, the Rev. Augustine Card. The moment he had passed Hughie turned to her, pulled down his upper lip, and gave a heavy wink.

The reaction of Jane's heart was quite violent enough to announce the presence of a mettlesome hippogriff: but, at the very moment of the wink, the notorious young clergyman turned back towards them and started to retrace his steps. Her heart stood almost still, as the ocean blue of the inquisitive eye became plainly visible, and was, she thought, fixed upon her. The forehead, the colour of fresh raw beef, now revealing itself in the light of the milky sun, rolled up to halt the descent of his biretta. But for some reason or other Jane felt convinced that, if the headdress had been removed, the furrows of the forehead would remain in exactly the same position; he was one of those men whose face is ploughed up into a perpetual enquiry.

She had not realised how tall he was; instinctively she turned towards Hugh Bestens-Corbett to communicate her surprise. She found Hughie, however, sprawled out at her side, lounging back against the wall of her house, almost with a shoulder thrust forward into the embrasure of her window. Noticing his extremely unceremonious position she turned from him with a slight frown of annoyance, for she was made to share in his rudeness, and she drew away a little.

She was certainly the objective of the blue eye, and it was to her that the authentic accents of what had once been England's ruling class were addressed.

'I wonder if you could tell me where Lord Francis Bellamy lives,' he asked her.

'I am sorry,' she answered and hesitated.

'The other end of the Mews . . . last house on the left,' barked Hughie, unceremoniously intervening.

The priestly figure received this unsolicited blast by allowing his eye to drift over the lounging form of Hugh as if he were not really there, the centre of his face, especially the nostrils, suggesting the impact of an inexcusable effluvium. Then he turned upon his heel and hurried away, the cobbles imparting a fastidious air to his rather tip-toeing gait, probably not intended to be offensive. But Hugh cleared his throat in a challenging manner, as if it were intended to be followed by expectoration.

'He is tall,' Jane observed.

'Six-foot three,' Hughie spoke with professional masculinity. 'I know someone who was at Eton with him. He was apparently an athlete. He was the public-schools boxing champion. Very swish, oh, fifteen years ago.'

'He looked rather as if he might have knocked you down. He is an aggressive man.'

Mr Hugh Bestens-Corbett pushed himself off the wall, and gave his six-foot of manhood a defiant shake. He had not liked the implication that he could be 'knocked down'. He strode into the middle of the Mews and displayed himself to Jane. Then he strolled back towards her and unburdened himself.

'The Rev. Augustine Card is a clown,' he asserted. 'Poseur! In a country parish he would probably get himself thrown into a duck pond or tarred and feathered.'

'Many people rather like their parson to be a little romanishly picturesque,' objected Jane, who had been favourably impressed and relished the spectacle of her peppery tenant Hugh working himself up into a rage.

'Don't I know it!' Hugh exploded. 'The Chillinghams . . . General Chillingham, you know, and his family go to his church. They have always been Anglo-Catholic. The last man there, Seed, who died last year, was quite bad enough. But he didn't stalk about the neighbourhood dressed up like a Catholic priest in full war paint. Nor did he fill his church so full of incense that you can smell it in Victoria Station. At first you think it must be floating over from Westminster Cathedral, staging a supermass to celebrate the arrival of a new Papal Legate or something. But no—you discover it is merely Canon Card's offspring flooding the neighbourhood with incense from the celebration of an exceptionally high Mass, with St Catherine's doors wide open, a little knot of gaping charladies watching the ceremonial genuflexions from the pavement, a white jacketed acolyte conducting late arrivals to their pews.'

'What fun!' commented Jane, with a high-pitched little

peal of girlish laughter, which succeeded in causing the
sorely tried Mr Bestens-Corbett to throw a sneer into her
open window.

'It may seem extremely diverting to you, Miss Greevey. I
am not devout I know, but I do not like to see the Church I
attended in my youth used for performances of this sort.
The Bishop of London ought to insist on his keeping the
door of his church closed. I consider it disgraceful.'

If Jane had heard her tenant and friend exclaim 'disgraceful!' once she had heard him do so five hundred times.
Few days passed without his familiar voice on the telephone,
delivering explosively this idiotic vocable; or, his eyes
blazing, shooting it from the garage into her front door.
Hughie, as she called him in her private mind, had been
drawn away from his watchtower over the garage door, and
across her gazing figure, to stand at her left elbow in a
bellicose position, to face, groupishly, the clerical intruder
—to present a hostile Mews—one in which trespassing was
noted with disapproval. She leant on the windowsill, gazing
after the inquisitive-looking cassocked gentleman—observed
him track down the young lord; but Lord Francis' black
garmented man informed him, it was apparent, that his
Lordship was not at home. And, twirling a little a white
evening paper he had acquired on his way down, he directed
himself towards the main street. Suddenly a covey of little
brats scuttled across the Mews vacating the bombsite.
Evidently they considered the birettaed figure some new
kind of policeman. As they rattled into an alley on one side,
he passed out of the Mews on the other, without noticing
the commotion his passage had caused.

Jane looked up towards Hughie, but the latter had
believed he had surprised in Jane a feminine weakness for
the cloth, and he left her, moving towards the entrance to
the Mews, with an expressive failure to wind up the episode

in some more formal manner than with the snort of disgust which actually reached her. With a hint of abruptness Jane pulled down her window and stepped over to her settee to prostrate herself at full length upon it. She could hear the clumsy fingers of a neighbour toying with an elegiac melody of Grieg. The Mews was at peace.

After the passing of the Red Priest, and her disagreement with her tenant, Jane lay for some time in the deep peace of the Mews, when not being raided by children, or except for the goings and comings in the first hours of the morning. At last she rose and moved towards the telephone. She dialled Matilda Tidings.

'Oh Matilda, are you still an Anglo-Catholic?'

'Certainly. Why do you want to know, Jane?'

Jane wished to know more about the Red Priest, and she suggested to her friend that they should have dinner at Blackenbury's restaurant that evening. Matilda, who lived in a flat in the King's Road, over an auctioneer's, said she would meet her about seven. Jane dashed at one or two of the famous names which had not yet got themselves replaced in their customary rank, but she had not time to do any more just then. She recognised in her charlady a proletarian aversion from the Book. This flattered her. She used (secretly boastful), with much display of peevish dissatisfaction, to complain about Jennifer's omission to dust the books. Jane would say to a friend, 'I do the books myself,' rather in the tone that, speaking of a laundry, a lady may remark, 'I attend to my personal linen!' Jane began to tidy up—being so tall she was almost able to see the dust along the top of picture frames, and, in any case, specialised in lofty spots for her correctings of her Jennifer's handiwork. Her way of growing old was to be washed out more than anything else. Her ash-blonde hair, for instance, was just grey; but it was an ash grey which was very delicate and attractive; and her face, similarly, had hardly changed at all, but lost all its colour, and, peering about beneath the still thick hair, might have been that of a girl. Her eyes were of a pale blue-grey, she chose for her lips a minimum of colour.

So she cultivated the faded appearance, aiming at the aesthetically genteel with great success, as, sadly willowy, she plunged, with a wilful awkwardness, about her cluttered house.

2

The Ritual of the Gutter

Facing the Victoria Station enclosure in which the taxicabs and buses assemble, and outside the large semi-circle of iron railings, is an island of shops. Among these is the best fishmonger's in London, Blackenbury's, and attached to it a small restaurant. At this Jane Greevey and Matilda Tidings had agreed to meet for dinner.

This was the nearest civilised spot to Marten's Mews, and on her way to it Jane debouched into the extremity of Ebury Street. There were a hundred holes and corners, a crisscross of lanes and gulleys south of the Mews, through which Jane had threaded her way. Beyond Ebury Street she crossed into Buckingham Palace Road, and across to the Grosvenor Road Hotel entrance, in front of which she and Matilda met.

'I have been passed by two armies of midgets,' Matilda said, pointing over her shoulder towards Ebury Street.' The second were aged about five or six up to eight or nine. They seemed to have no object, but these dirty little men march along very fiercely, kicking out their little feet. What astonishes me is that they are quite unselfconscious. These gatherings of elderly infants, appearing at any hour of the day all over this district, are assembled with some meaning. They do not fight or brandish wooden swords if they meet; they have no interest of that sort. Anything purposeless, marching fervently ahead into nothingness (this place is full of them), is vaguely disquieting. They are accepted as "little soldiers" by the police. But is that what they are?'

Jane laughed darkly. 'No,' she said, 'they are not aimless innocents, they are swarms of little pests created by the trashbins, which never existed before the war. You are lucky to be able to think of them as *purposeless*. Their tiny minds are full of the rubbish of the Mewses.'

The two women were standing where the station traffic flows outwards, waiting for it to stop. When the last taxicab rattled its way out, they crossed towards the island of shops, and at last reached the Blackenbury restaurant. This was completely full, and would be so for at least an hour, they were told.

'Come home with me for dinner,' said Jane Greevey. 'I have some asparagus and a bottle of wine. Look, I will buy that enormous lobster, what do you say?'

Matilda agreed voraciously, showing all her large teeth.

The lobster was purchased and, with it under her arm, Jane led the way back to Marten's Mews. After crossing Buckingham Palace Road they met with a couple of filthy little creatures broken off from some gutter legion headed for an Op. in some rich Mews.

'There, for instance, are two of the warriors in question,' said Jane Greevey, 'the kind we were talking about just after you had put in an appearance. I know all about that midget tribe. They will suddenly burst into our Mews, and within a flick of an ass's tail the lids of all our metal rubbish bins are flying everywhere. The lids removed, the contents seem to fly out as if by magic—empty sardine tins, magazines, old shoes, every kind of refuse. All our waste products seem to come to life. Around the Mews are the empty, dignified streets. Although the houses seem unlived in, they are, in fact, fuller of people than ever. The rents are higher than ever, but the fashionable life is gone. These lonely streets and squares seem to have burst into a kind of sewer life by the agency of their daily refuse, which is not incinerated as happens in the States—not collected, as the city supposes, by an army of dustmen, but marched away with by an army of brats.

'Perhaps you remember our Mews is blessed with a bombsite. Our domestic refuse collects there, or a good deal of it. A hideous uproar issues from it, our cans and broken crocks fly across it, smoke rises from the bonfires, composed of what we have discarded. Our private letters are read with storms of cackles, garments we have said goodbye to clothe a fiercely marching Tom Thumb, trailing in the gutter behind. Sometimes an ambulance dashes down the Mews, headed for the bombsite, and speeds away, carrying one or more bleeding midgets—material for the Casualty Ward. A drunk, one night, come from a party at one of the minor legations which swarm in our neighbourhood, lay down and died. Well, the corpse found its way on to our bombsite. A reptilian rat was seen squatting on his chest attempting to light a cigarette he had stuck in the dead mouth. As if it had been picked by vultures, one-eyed, and the grinning head a mass of tiny holes, the dead man was rescued by the police.'

'Your Mews is a Grand Guignol, my dear,' said Matilda.

'It can offer that, certainly,' Jane replied. 'We live in the midst of what was in 1939 the most inaccessibly exclusive district in London. If one of its inhabitants could have been shown, in a prophetic dream, what it is like now he might have taken an overdose of a sleeping drug.'

As they approached the top of the Mews where Jane Greevey dwelt, there was the familiar sound of gang warfare. Entering it at a hastened pace, it was apparent to Jane at once what was happening. The gang of larger boys was attacking the mass of midgets swarming in the centre of the Mews. This was a retaliatory visit, but it was unsuccessful, and they were retiring, hurling heavier missiles than the usual brattery was used to. There were howls of tiny pain, and the infant class were answering back with anything sizeable they were able to find. Jane inserted her key in the front door and dived inside, followed by Matilda, whose dress had been spoilt by some unlovely combination of rubbish, thrown by a quarter man a yard or two away.

'You loathsome imp!' she protested, over her shoulder.

Hugh Bestens-Corbett slipped out of his garage, loomed behind Matilda beaming but dignified, slid into the hall a dustbin lid, with a considerable clatter.

'Here, Miss Greevey, your lid once more. You had better keep this in here. Your dustbin is empty, but they can't run away with that.'

Hughie vanished, and Matilda slammed the front door with a thunderous bang.

'So your gallant tenant has got back your dustbin lid for you!—well played, sir!' Matilda added sardonically.

'Good show, isn't it? Brave little Hughie,' Jane chimed in, coming into the living room.

'What on earth,' Matilda enquired, 'are all these goings on?' She was almost as censorious as Hughie.

'Hughie,' Jane told her, 'says it is a new gang. The Knights of the Dustbin Lids do not seem to be making much headway against the hordes of the three-foot tens. That is a very virulent gang and absolutely numberless.'

There was a sudden rush outside in the Mews, and, choked with emotion, a hundred squeaks of triumph. The two women went over to the window. Swarming like ants, the little faces of the Great Unwashed (a name found for them by the Victorian middle class), excited, and alarmingly unsmiling, continued their Victory parade; two or three of the strongest of the gutter midgets staggered in their midst, holding aloft a soot-black banner. They had worsted the dustbin lids.

The telephone bell rang hysterically—or it seemed to do so to Jane. Picking up the receiver, Hughie's voice was as solemn as the diminutive massed faces without.

'You see what has happened. I dare not show my face at the door.'

'Why?' asked Jane.

'I am the Shelterer of the Defeated. You remember Arthur Pastor? Well, *they*, the Undersized, remember too.'

'I should lie low if I were you. There are swarms of little brats just outside the garage.'

'And *you*, Miss Greevey, *you* keep under cover too! Are your curtains drawn?' Hughie's voice was in a crisis key.

'No,' Jane answered. 'But would that not attract the fire of the enemy?'

'Perhaps it would—perhaps it would. You're right—I think you're right. I say, Miss Greevey, should anything . . . er disagreeable . . . occur, ring me at once. I would dial 999. Better if it came from me!'

'I will. Thanks most awfully, Mr Bestens-Corbett!' Jane hung up on a solemn note. She sank back dramatically in her chair, fanning herself with her handkerchief.

Matilda said 'Well?'

'Well, well,' Jane echoed. 'Earlier in the day the rabble of undersized brats you noticed, who practically own this Mews, were unexpectedly invaded by bigger boys than themselves, who took possession of our dustbin lids to use as shields. My tenant (who has just telephoned me) took one of the bigger boys, whose eye had been badly injured, off to the casualty ward of the hospital. This act of kindness was noted by a hundred little eyes. He is now afraid to come out of his garage, for he is identified with the Knights of the

Dustbin Lids; he, with some reason, believes he would be attacked.'

'What nonsense!' Matilda threw up her head in disgust. 'Do you mean to say that that grown man is afraid of those wretched little creatures!'

'They are more formidable than you think—because of their very smallness. Have you never realised the many advantages of being small?'

There was a silence. Matilda sat there looking at her friend. She thought it might be a case of being *de trop*.

'I could not help overhearing . . .' she began, with a significant hesitation.

Jane laughed. 'Such exchanges on the telephone are a daily occurrence. Do not run away with the belief that Hughie and I have more than a business relationship. I am his landlord. It is because we have been able to remain so remotely "neighbours"—so near and yet so far—that he and I see so much of one another—through the window, or at the door. Now he seems to be engaged to a most beautiful young woman, and she is often in the garage with him.' Matilda's disgusted 'The Wolf!' broke in. 'They chatter away in there half the morning,' Jane continued, 'while he is pottering about with his car.'

'You do not manage that man at all well,' said Matilda. 'He is your tenant—occupying a small space, with quite a sizeable space crushing down upon him. You should speak with an authoritative ring. If you do not, he will end by being your master.'

'You amuse me,' said Jane. 'Your plans for me, bossing it over the Mews, leave out of count my shrinking disposition. I have no appetite for domination. I do not aspire to the mastery of the Mews.'

'All right, be sat on if you prefer it,' said Matilda.

'It would be quite impossible for Hughie and me to do any

sitting on one another. All he does is a little tiresome protection. He is my officious guardian. But, if he holds an umbrella over his landlady, is not that rather Chinese? Matilda darling, I am not a man-manager.'

'More fool you,' said her guest.

'What on earth do you mean?' Jane demanded.

'Were you not aware that I am a man-manager?' Matilda looked severe.

Jane shook her head, looking up reproachfully at Matilda. She looked at this managerial type, a little like a frightened animal.

Matilda glared up at her pale friend—so great a contrast to that grey and drooping figure, she with her dark red cheeks and her dyed black hair, and her black eyes.

As Jane grew more and more alarmed, she showed signs of resistance.

'Tilda, I am very angry with myself for allowing you to think that I am criticising Hughie by my silly protest. He and I have great fun together. But to be an old woman is a perfectly bloody thing to be.' Jane laughed with a streak of hysteria. 'When a woman has passed a certain age (mine and perhaps yours) she should be obliged to wear a uniform with trousers, so that there should be no misunderstanding.'

Matilda had listened with a sort of glare, tight-lipped and accumulating something destined to explode.

'A uniform! This is not *you* speaking, Jane!' she protested. 'I should like to wring that fellow's neck! A uniform! I should like to force Mr Hughie to wear an *Old Boys'* uniform. . . .'

Jane Greevey rose hurriedly and crossed the room to close her window.

'It is evident that you are absolutely *cowed*,' cried Tilda. 'He should be invited to listen to every word of what I have to say. . . .'

Jane returned to her chair, a little shame-faced at what she had done, and more 'cowed' by her woman friend than by the man with a long ear so near her open window. 'The trouble is, he is a *listener*. The picture of Hughie in an Old Boys' uniform is terrifying, it is so insulting. He is, for instance, engaged to be married, as I said, to a wonderfully attractive young woman, who can't be more than about twenty-two.'

Tilda sprang to her feet.

'How disgraceful,' she exclaimed: 'the old wolf! The banns should be challenged, or whatever it is happens. At what church should one enter one's protest, Jane?'

Matilda stood, grandly combative, in front of the mantel-piece, her eye fastened bellicosely upon the closed window.

'Tildy, you are grand!' her friend assured her, and then Jane, in order to feed this fine anger, produced another fact to swell the indictment.

'I ought not to tell you, but Hughie is at great pains to hide up the fact of his engagement from me. When the beautiful girl fetches him in the Mews, standing outside the door, and calling softly "Hughie" . . .'

'I'd Hughie him!' burst in Matilda. 'The monster!'

Jane's amusement knew no bounds. She sneezed in her excitement.

'I always call him "Hughie" now myself,' she gleefully confided to her champion.

'Does he know you do?' Tilda enquired. 'But I bet the allusion would escape him.'

'He is very trustful. . . .'

'He trusts you to act as a fool in all things,' Tilda corrected.

'That's about it, I am afraid, if one accepts the cynical view.' Jane smiled indicating that she only half accepted the cynic.

It soon became obvious that Matilda was not prepared to accept the rôle of the 'cynic'. When Jane proposed to change the conversation she was not co-operative. She leaned forward and fixed a very serious eye upon Jane. Then she plunged back into the controversial topic Jane had wished to slide away from.

'I am not inviting reciprocal confidences, believe me; but, although I remain Miss Tiding, I am anything but a virgin'—Jane shrank from her—'I am not married, because . . . how shall I put it? I have a taste for men, and I had enough money to be independent. Don't look embarrassed, Jane. That will be the extent of my confidences. Now, Jane, I have got to know a good deal about men. I know what I am talking about when I generalise about men. Big "strong" types like Hughie, arrived at the age of fifty. . . .'

'Forty-nine' smiled Jane.

'That will do just as well. No woman should marry if she is the happy possessor of a "temperament". What is the percentage of "temperamental" women?'

'I have no idea,' Jane hastened to repudiate any *expertise* where her sex was concerned.

'Certainly not as much as fifty per cent have a "temperament".'

'Oh,' Jane looked a little alarmed.

'As for myself, for instance, I like pulling a man down on top of me. A confession!' (What a beastly woman, said Jane to herself. I must see much less of Tilda. Because, in Jane's romantic sexology, the man impended apologetically. The only thing about the man that the woman might 'pull down' was, in moments of extreme boldness, his darling head).

As bold as brass, Matilda did not hesitate to throw herself about a little before her nauseated friend. Then she uttered, in a richly clamant voice, 'But I regard myself as a bit of an exception. And men, I believe, may be classified in rather the same proportions. You think this is all rather disgusting? I know, but it is most necessary not to be squeamish. To which classification does the young lady in question belong? After the honeymoon, will your Hughie be very sexually attentive? Of course not. I doubt if he would even give the poor girl a proper honeymoon. They are, I suppose, at present chaste?'

This was a side of Matilda which Jane had never surmised. She rose rather abruptly, glided across the room to where some hyacinths had been placed in a large vase. She gave them a new position, pulling one or two of them up with her long delicate fingers, as if to enable them to get a little air, which they must surely need in the proximity of this woman, who, it suddenly seemed, would devour more oxygen than would the normal person of her sex, and she put her face nearer to them to smell them.

Matilda had watched this with a smile. It was plain that she regarded Jane's flowers as symbolic. She evidently thought that Jane experienced the desire for a *pure* contact —how illustrative the approaching of her cheek to this congested-looking blossom.

As Jane returned to her seat, she murmured 'How jaded those flowers look.'

'Yes,' Matilda gazed at the flowers. 'How shamelessly sexish those thick flowers are, don't you think so, Jane? Some flowers really make me feel shy.'

Jane arranged herself in her chair, as though she, like her flowers, would be the better for a little fresh air. But she showed that she had no intention of discussing flowers along the lines suggested by Matilda.

'You think like a man, it seems to me, Tilda.'

Matilda smiled indulgently. 'Once I nearly got married

—have I told you that, Jane? I had a fiancé. But before the marriage my young man persuaded me to rehearse the honeymoon. I did not think much of his performance. I did not go on with the marriage.'

'I am glad of that,' said Jane. She rose, and said, 'I don't know about you—but I am getting hungry. Shall we go into the dining room, as I call it?'

'Why not!' demanded the guest, rising.

As they crossed the passage, Jane caught sight, for the first time, of the back of Matilda's head, or the lack of a back to Matilda's head. People who grew straight up from their backs to a flat top of the head, at right-angles to a flat top— this, Jane regarded as expressive of the absence of most pleasant qualities. She had never yet known a person with that kind of head who was anything but a brute of some kind. She had never suspected Tilda of an ugly weakness for men. They were neither of them young, neither married: the assumption was that 'men' was a closed book—Matilda had always given her to understand that it was shut beyond recall. The warm personal sympathy she had experienced for this woman, situated rather like herself, was rapidly disappearing. However, the change from one room to another happily permitted her to make a fresh start with Matilda at least to some extent; and she was now looking at her friend's face rather than the back of her head.

So they sat down, and they had the lobster between them to devour as well as some asparagus. Almost at once Matilda said, 'Tell me more about those warlike children, who seem to infest your Mews. How about the police?'

Jane sighed. 'Well, that is not easy to answer, but you have heard of the "gangs" of biggish youths in Clapham, Battersea, Wandsworth and so on? It has come to your notice that Youth lifts its ugly head in the purlieus of Britain?'

'I seem to have seen,' said Matilda, eyeing the aggressive-
ness of her hostess, 'that a nasty teen-aged flowering of the
suburbs has attempted to imitate New York.'

'I am glad that it was not entirely with surprise,' Jane
remarked, 'that you saw the gutter exploding in our Mews,
and a handful of commandos of the teenage variety smacking back at the mildewed midgets produced in such profusion by the squalid wombs of Westminster. . . .'

Matilda raised her eyebrows. Jane showed her spirit in a
survey of the gutters which spat all around her. This valkyrie
came to life in the smoke of battle blown up from the
sewers. As she sat there above her portion of the lobster,
the very tall colourless woman plunged on, in spirit like
some apocalyptic horseman. Matilda had not crushed her by
her tendency to insist too much on sex. When sex was the
subject she had had poor Jane underneath her, as it were,
battering away at this prostrate specimen of the English
middle class. But now it was different; Jane was an authority
on the bombsite brat.

'You certainly dwell in a place which one has to know to
understand . . . and this is England after all,' Matilda told
her hostess.

'That is very important to remember.' Jane had her
head tilted back a little, and was introducing into her
lengthy body a seemingly interminable piece of asparagus.
'Yes, this is England, and the police are the police—eight
thousand understaffed in London. And those who have been
persuaded to join this unpopular force, crouch in their
stations, and apparently never poke their noses outside,
even as traffic cops. There should be a policeman every
two or three turnings out of Sloane Square. Perhaps there
is one, but I know it is amazing how far you have to go
in London now to come across a police constable.'

'Yes. Where the devil are they?' Matilda looked angrily

around as though a police constable should have been standing at attention in each of the four corners of the room. 'They don't pay them enough!' she snapped.

Jane had finished the last of her pieces of asparagus. She yawned deeply; her vitality was very low, thanks to the attempts to shine of Matilda. After the yawn, she allowed her eye to rove around that square, dark body.

'Matilda,' she exclaimed, 'I had an adventure today.'

'Oh?' Matilda was rather startled. She thought that perhaps the chaste giantess, Jane, was about to unburden herself of something really coarse. 'A wolf?'

'Not a wolf exactly; it was a clergyman.'

'Oh!' Matilda's tone drooped into the tempo of the parish magazine.

Jane began describing how the Rev. Augustine Card had made an unexplained appearance in the Mews. 'Can you tell me anything about this extraordinary individual? He almost clashed with Hughie Bestens-Corbett, you know.'

'Augustine Card?' Matilda concentrated. 'My mother knew his father, Canon Card. He is a very brilliant man. His wife, Lady Imogen, is, or was—it's some time ago that I heard people speaking about the Canon—Lady Imogen is reputed to be a woman with a great deal of character. Her father, the Earl of Craigliven, you may have heard of. Craigliven is an historic castle. The present Earl has been prominent in politics.'

Jane shook her head; she was offering her friend a large dish full of fruit *compote*. They paused a moment while these little bodies were being transferred to their plates.

'I was saying,' Matilda said smiling, 'I was telling you, about the Earl of Craigliven, was I not? He is reputed to be intelligent as well as rich.'

Jane Greevey saw, in memory, the arrogantly puzzled face of the much-talked-of priest: she understood how such an ancestry as Craigliven might make it difficult for him to tolerate the rudeness of her Hugh. Matilda, of course, wondered if poor dear old Janey was a victim of the showy, still not very old clergyman.

'I wonder if you read at the time,' she said, 'about Canon Card's son?'

'No, I don't think I did. What was that?' Jane searched in her mind, but she felt sure that she had never heard of him before.

While Matilda had been speaking, Jane had realised the true meaning for her of this not exactly attractive woman, why she valued Matilda as a friend—perhaps why she had, in the first place, come to know her. Her 'county' pretensions were her long suit. The Tidings managed to keep their end up within range of the snobbish bark of several packs of hounds, and their muskets could be seen on the fringes of two or three shoots. That was the great attraction. How disgusting! Gazing at this imposture—what snobs we all are, even the best of us! thought Jane.

'Well,' said Matilda as she gently stirred up her memory, 'it was just a schoolboy's prank. In his last year at Eton, Augustine Card did something which made a great sensation. On some public occasion, I forget what it was, Canon Card's young hopeful pulled a mounted policeman off his horse, jumped up into the saddle, and gaily rode away. As far as I can remember this occurred just inside the park, near Hyde Park corner. He was pursued by several mounted policemen in front of Apsley House, down Constitution Hill, past the Palace, and so on towards Parliament Square. The original policemen were joined by others, and in the end there was quite a cavalcade. The young man was overtaken in front of the Houses of Parliament. He was interrogated, and it turned out who he was. It was apparently the outcome of a bet—no politics were involved. That was twenty years ago. Augustine Card, it seems, did not take Holy Orders until just before he became Vicar of St Catherine and the Angels. From the start he was very "high". He announced that he was an Anglo-Catholic. At the time of that announcement his escapade was recalled, when, for a bet, he unseated the mounted policeman. There was a bit of discussion about Anglo-Catholicism. You didn't see it?'

'No, I didn't see that either. I was away at that time.' Jane paused, then she said, 'Well, thanks. I think I see more clearly now. If at the beginning of life a man behaves in a very sensational manner, anything that he does at a later period will, of course, be referred back to that.'

'That is exactly what happened,' Matilda agreed. 'When he launched out into Anglo-Catholicism they suggested that, symbolically, he was jumping on to a policeman's horse.'

'Yes,' nodded Jane. 'Naturally.'

'And as to the "Red Priest" . . .'

'Ah yes, I wanted to ask you about that title,' said Jane.

'He is a fellow who has an appetite for the limelight. It must make things rather uncomfortable for the Canon. The Cards are a great church family. There was an Archbishop Card in the last century. Well, I have seldom been to St Catherine and the Angels since Augustine Card has officiated there; but I am going next Sunday.'

Jane looked excited. 'Next Sunday?' she repeated eagerly, 'I wish I could offer to come with you; but I have to go down to Bath, where my mother still survives.'

Matilda nodded politely. 'I see,' she said. 'Let us go there together some other Sunday.'

'I should love to. That would be wonderful,' Jane cried.

'Well, about the "redness"; not long after he became Vicar, he invited some Polish Bishop to come over and preach at his church. He then joined the socialist party. And a few weeks after that a photograph appeared in the press showing him drinking a cocktail at a party at the Soviet Embassy. Well, that made him "red". There was not much else. He had dinner on a Soviet ship in the Port of London with the "Red Dean" and J. B. S. Haldane. Let me see. I cannot remember any more eccentricities of that kind. I do not think his "redness" goes very far. He is a self-advertising man, and redness is one of the obvious ways of getting advertisement—especially for a parson.'

Jane considered what she had been told, associating it with the beautifully dressed, handsome cleric she had seen in the Mews. In a minute or two she laughed.

'He does not look very proletarian. He came to our Mews in search of Lord Francis Bellamy.'

3

Land of Hope and Glory

I n the Bath to London train the following Monday morning Jane had a surprise. She had bought two papers, the *Mirror* and the *Express*, before going to the train; a few minutes after the train had left the station, she tilted her hat a little forward to protect her eyes from the light, settled herself in her corner seat, and picked up the *Daily Express*. There stood before her upon the front page of her newspaper a full-length portrait of Father Card—for so he was described. The headline above it read: 'PRIEST AS BOUNCER. MARQUESS TURNED OUT OF CHURCH.'

Her heart beating a little quicker, the paper trembling slightly in her hands, she read eagerly. The so-called Red Priest had dragged out of his pew, and then, with two sidesmen, had thrown out of his church the Marquess of Keltingbrook. The Marquess had resisted expulsion; but the boxer priest had had no difficulty in overcoming his resistance.

Then came a detailed account of how this happened. The Marquess, who had regularly attended St Catherine and the Angels for thirty years, objected to Father Card's liturgical habits and other things. He had stood up and interrupted the service while Father Card was in the pulpit, just beginning his sermon. In a loud voice he denounced the young Vicar who had only been there for about a year, and had 'Painted the Church Red,' as the Marquess described it.

Next the paper outlined how Canon Card's son came to be known as the 'Red Priest'. After that came a great deal about Anglo-Catholicism. Finally, the genealogy and political history of the Marquess of Keltingbrook was sketched, and then came a great deal more about the background of the Reverend Augustine Card. In another part of the paper there was a photograph of Augustine at Eton, when he was interviewed about his escapade with the mounted police. There was another larger photograph of Card, the boxer, knocking out a very immense young man, and becoming Public-Schools Champion.

In the *Daily Mirror* was a photograph of Father Card with his grandfather, the Earl of Craigliven, upon the battlements of Craigliven Castle. There was also a small photograph of Lady Imogen, his mother. This paper played up the family side of the Red Priest, whereas the *Express* confined itself to Father Card as a schoolboy. Jane carefully folded up the two newspapers, as she wished to preserve all of these photographs, and study them more carefully when she got home.

When she was at her house in the Mews she telephoned to Matilda. That lady had seen all the papers, but had herself actually been in the Church. In reply to Jane's anxious enquiry she answered briefly. 'The Marquess of Keltingbrook is an irascible old man. He seems to think that he owns the Church. He stood up and made a speech, while Father Card was preaching his sermon; so, as Father Card said afterwards, what was he to do? Give up his pulpit to the noble Lord, or get rid as quickly as possible of this interrupter?'

Jane was an enthusiastic supporter of her friend's account of the matter. The Marquess was expelled expeditiously but really very gently. Jane asked what her friend thought would happen to Father Card. 'Happen to him!' exclaimed

Matilda contemptuously. 'Nothing at all. Why should anything happen to him?'

Jane rather sheepishly said 'Oh I see.' She saw, and that ended the matter. After a few words more she said 'Goodbye', and left the telephone.

Deflated, disappointed, a little annoyed with Matilda, Jane went to the window and flung it up. Mr Hugh Bestens-Corbett had just entered the Mews, and was regarding her, she thought, somewhat derisively. But her dander was up. She simply stepped back and pulled down the window. A few minutes later the telephone rang. She picked it up and, in a full authoritative blast, what she heard was that full-blooded name, 'Hugh Bestens-Corbett here.' Coldly she answered, 'This is Jane Greevey, at your service.'

There was a pause, and then the other spoke.

'I say, Miss Greevey, are you offended with me?'

'Oh no, why should I be? Do you mean because I shut the window? A sparrow flew in. I closed the window hoping that I might comfort the little bird.'

There was a laugh that carried in its bosom a sneer. 'I did not see any bird.'

'No?'

'Well, Miss Greevey, how about the Red Priest? He has become a bouncer; he is a top-drawer bouncer, too. Marquesses!'

'If someone prevents a clergyman from performing his sacred duties, what is he to do? He has to turn him out, hasn't he? If he allowed a man of whatever rank to dictate to him what he should do, from the body of the congregation, what do you suppose would happen to such a poor-spirited clergyman?'

There was an angry clearing of the throat which succeeded in producing a cough.

'There is such a thing, you know, as being too high

spirited a clergyman. I can see, Miss Greevey, however, that you are a stout defender of Father Card. But I do not suppose that the Bishop will take the same view of the matter as you do.'

Jane Greevey knew very little about Bishops, but that did not stop her. 'A clergyman, in keeping order in his church, is on perfectly safe ground. The Bishop has no authority . . .'

'Miss Greevey, Miss Greevey, you evidently are not very well acquainted with the power possessed by the Bishop. A Bishop . . .'

'A Bishop, Mr Bestens-Corbett, has a very limited power. But since neither of us knows much about the intricacies of Church government we had better stop contradicting one another. Besides, I have some letters to write, so I must say good day to you, I am afraid.

'But, Miss Greevey . . .'

Jane hung up the receiver; then she proceeded to the rear of her house, and began pattering about in her kitchen, for she knew that Hugh Bestens-Corbett might come and tap on her window (calling out 'I see you, Miss Greevey—I can see you quite well') and she knew that she might be unable to refrain from answering him without having words, or something or other.

But as a matter of fact her authoritarian neighbour was so outraged by what he called her 'attitude' that he contented himself with humming 'Land of Hope and Glory' (he was in the garage, and Jane heard him quite easily—it was a song she particularly disliked); and he swore that Miss Greevey could settle her own Mews problems in the future—and God knows there were enough of them. Then he stamped off to his basement flat without glancing at her windows.

Two or three local men had visited the Bishop, and an evening newspaper bore the headline 'WILL BISHOP ISSUE

REPROOF OF RED PRIEST'. A copy of this paper was slid into Miss Greevey's front door. Shortly afterwards the bell of the telephone rang. She took no notice of the telephone for some minutes, but at length she sauntered towards it, and removed the receiver.

'Have you noticed, Miss Greevey, the headline in an evening paper, and do you believe that the Bishop will expel Father Card?'

'Mr Bestens-Corbett, I have seen the copy of the evening paper which you so offensively slipped into my front door. I have no views upon the probable action of the Bishop. I think of sending a note to the evening paper, informing it that an idiotic tenant of mine thrust its tonight's copy in at my door. I am amazed that you should ask so silly a question. I shall ask you to vacate the garage if you continue to annoy me.'

The receiver was banged down, and the conversation ended.

Shortly afterwards a note was dropped into Miss Greevey's letter box. It ran as follows. 'Dear Miss Greevey. It perhaps is not necessary to say that I shall refer no more to bishops or to anything relating to the church. I do not wish to lose the garage. But I think it was very unkind to threaten me in that horrible way. You have always been so considerate to me, and we have been such good friends. Do not let the thing which I shall not mention alter that in any way.

Yours sincerely,
Hugh Bestens-Corbett.'

Jane smiled as she put down the note. Her threat, her woman's threat, being taken so seriously by Hughie amused her. When they next met in the Mews, Jane was very gracious, there is no other word to describe her regal manner.

34

'A pleasant morning after the rain,' Hughie remarked, and she answered, 'A most engaging weather, I agree. I hope that it continues so balmy and accommodating.'

'Indeed, so do I,' answered Mr Bestens-Corbett, slightly raising his hat, as he moved onwards.

4

An Efficient Secretary

I n what he described as his 'cell', Augustine Card lay at full length on a chaise-longue, which was so luxuriously upholstered as to be practically a bed. He was wearing a blue silk dressing-gown. Five newspapers lay upon the floor at his side.

The closing of the front door shook the Vicarage. That was Horridge. The Rev. James Horridge was his curate, who, with his second curate Herbert Wimbush, shared the Clergy House with him. Horridge, or 'Horrid', as he was known in the Clergy House, mounted the stairs three at a time. He must have some news. Then he burst into the 'cell'. The 'fighting' face of the curate wore a smile. 'Hope I do not intrude? I have news. My article for *The Fashionable Woman* has been accepted. They want two photographs—one practically naked.'

'That is excellent,' said the Vicar.

'I thought so too. I picked the wrong career.'

'I perhaps should have stopped in Publicity,' the Vicar suggested. 'I hope they never get hold of that part of my past!'

'Teeny! I now know how to blackmail you. I know— I will write a second article for the *Brassière*, and I know what the title will be!'

'Horrid! Have a care!'

'I think the new Saint Augustine must be portrayed in his chaise-longue.'

'No, sir. I shall be seen saying my office in that empty room at the back.' Augustine pondered. 'As to the nudity, how about this?'

He pulled open his dressing-gown, and his heavy muscular body lay there completely nude, except for a short pair of pants.

'That will do splendidly.' Horrid nodded.

Augustine, pulling the dressing-gown round his body again, fixed his eye upon his curate. Employing the tone of command he announced, 'Heute ist Freitag. Gute Nacht. Today is Friday.'

'Incontrovertibly,' Horrid replied.

'If Herbert does not return by five o'clock tomorrow, I shall have to get a man to fill his place. It's High Mass, and that can't be done without three of us. If I can get no one else, I must dress William up as a Deacon.'

Horrid succumbed to a spasm of laughter at the idea of their policeman friend wearing the humeral veil and a dalmatic. If Bill realised he was to be dressed like a bishop he would probably decline. Augustine would be furious. What would he do? He was quite capable of going out into the street and addressing the first man he met, saying probably, 'I say, would you like a job? We are going to elevate the Host at the High Mass, and I'll give you half a crown if you will help us out. One of my curates is away sick, and we can't do High Mass without three of us officiating.' He might pick on a rather beery customer, who would turn up tight on Sunday. And then—oh anything, he might do anything. Horrid clearly foresaw the terrible mess they were liable to get into. So he adopted a business-like manner, was brisk and humourless.

'I believe, sir, that we have to be very careful about this,' he said to Augustine. 'I will try shortly to put my hand on some clergyman or other. As we do not know whether Herbert will be able to turn up, we ought *at once* to secure a substitute.'

'What would a real clergyman cost us?' Augustine sounded a little alarmed.

Horrid surrendered to his customary levity. He had foreseen what the Vicar would say at the idea of securing 'a real clergyman'.

'About the expense,' said Horrid, 'I don't see why we couldn't get one for about twenty shillings. Bradshaw's is sure to have one.'

Augustine was silent. He obviously relished the idea of dressing up a street-hawker, disguising him in a tunicle and dalmatic, placing him in the required position, in front of the high altar and trusting to the dumbness of the congregation not to notice the odd behaviour of this clumsy fellow.

However, he decided to leave the matter in Horrid's hands. He lighted a cigarette, picked up a writing pad on which he had scribbled a few notes, and visibly dismissed the problem of the High Mass.

Horrid pulled out of his pocket a shabby book, and threw it down upon the papers at his chief's side.

'*A Theological Revolution*. All about St Augustine.' Horrid pointed towards the book, then sat down, and removed his pipe and pouch from his pocket.

It in no way diminished the attractiveness of the massive face of Augustine Card that his forehead had been blessed with a superfluity of skin. The head remained furrowed like a large dog's, the soft folds converging in frowning lines at the centre. The expression of his face was consequently one of unremitting enquiry—a look of juvenile puzzlement was what it seemed to the eye of those favouring the augustian personality. For instance, as he invaded the Mews, seeming to thrust up his biretta like the footballer butting at the ball, he had certainly seemed adorably puzzled (wondering and questioning like some innocent child) to the bewitched Jane Greevey. Now, the mysterious book thrown there by his curate lying at his side—announced as a theological revolution, and associated with a name not unfamiliar to Augustine Card—the natural puzzlement deepened upon his brow, while very slowly he revolved his head in the direction of the book, very indolently picked it up, and with an appearance of arrogant indifference directed his eyes upon the name and title engraved upon the spine.

'Allin . . . Allin? What's all this? You startled me for the moment. This is not about me.'

'No.' Horrid was unsmiling. 'It is the other Augustine, he of Hippo.'

Augustine's interest having been abruptly and automatically extinguished, the book fell from his hand back on to the newspaper on the floor at his side.

'I did not realise the uncanny originality of St Augustine,' said Horrid, picking it up, and returning it to his pocket.

'Oh yes, most extraordinary. My father wrote a small book on the subject.'

'How stupid of me. I had forgotten.' Horrid sat sucking at his pipe with an unconscious persistence.

'You are doing yourself no good with that awful pipe.' Augustine looked severely at the young curate.

'I can't afford cigarettes, and I must smoke *something*.' Horrid drew another book out of his pocket. 'I'm a walking library today. This book has two pages missing, so I got it for sixpence at the same shop.'

'At Mendelssohn's?'

'Yes.' Horrid held it up. '*The Vision of Glass*. It looks very interesting.'

'It was sixpence too much,' the Vicar stirred angrily. 'I never read an emptier book.'

'Oh, it's no good then.' Horrid slid it back into his pocket beside the other book.

Augustine Card jumped off the chaise-longue, threw off his dressing-gown, and stood nude, except for his elastic-belted underwear. He looked superbly gladiatorial, heavily muscled from head to foot.

'Come along, Horrid. Let's do a bit of self-defence.'

Horrid jumped up, dragging his jacket off and throwing it over a chair.

'If you promise not to knock me down—my usual proviso.'

He slipped his shirt over his head, and looked alarmingly slight by the side of the other man. They walked down a short passage and entered a quite unfurnished room, which they used for their exercises. Each picked a pair of boxing gloves off a shelf, and soon were both dancing about in front of one another, exchanging smart token blows, rather for exercise than anything else. They were so ill-matched that Augustine preferred this pretence at boxing. Twice a week William, their athletic policeman friend, came round, and that was sometimes more like a fight than boxing. Once Augustine, who was a little the heavier, gave the policeman so rough a time that he was sent home in a taxicab, feeling unable that day to perform his duties as a policeman.

The two clergymen, at a sign from Augustine, called a halt to their gymnastics, replaced their gloves upon the shelf, and left the room. Horrid had not realised how near exhaustion he had been. He panted out a few words to his chief, and disappeared in the direction of the bathroom, Augustine going to his own bedroom. He could be heard massaging himself to the vigorous crooning of John Brown's Body lies a-Mouldering in the Grave. Their exercise had not in any way left him without breath. After that he dressed, and returned to his 'cell', where Horrid joined him. The chaise-longue was pushed aside, and they both sat down to attack the business of the day, Horrid acting as secretary at a table facing the window, and Augustine, in a more comfortable chair, at his right hand side—the rearrangement, on paper, of the pew-seats for next Sunday, things related with the recent disturbance, diocesan matters to be attended to, bills to be paid, and letters to be answered.

'What is this?' asked Horrid. 'General Chillingham to give up his pew-seat, but there is another letter from Mary Chillingham, same address, requesting that her seat will not be changed.' Horrid held up two letters.

'That was an old fellow and his wife,' Augustine told him. 'The daughter is a girl who is so ravishingly pretty that before now I have made an ass of myself. When I ought to have given her the wafer I just stood lost in amazement at her beauty.'

'Oh yes, I know her,' said Horrid. 'She ought to be charged for reducing the efficiency of the staff.'

'I agree,' Augustine assented. 'Send her a letter saying she may come, occupying same seat, if she pays us a fine of ten shillings a week to compensate for reduced efficiency of the clerical staff owing to her beauty. Sign it "Management" '. Horrid was shaken with laughter.

'I had better leave that to you,' he said. 'I will deal with the General.'

'Right. Or you type it, and I will sign it.'

'Entendu. Teeny, here's another lady wants a seat!' Horrid called out. 'Jane Greevey. Marten's Mews. That's where Bellamy—Lord Francis Bellamy—lives. What tariff for Jane?'

Augustine scratched his head.

'Oh, tariff B. I think,' he said.

'We have almost as many new ones as those who said goodbye,' Horrid said, turning over a number of cards in a folder.

'Yes. Mostly attracted by scandal,' Augustine was of opinion. 'We will, on the whole, increase our audience.'

'My fee,' said Horrid, 'will improve accordingly.'

Augustine nodded. 'Ten per cent of the enhanced pew-rents. . . . I say, Horrid.' This was a new voice speaking, and Horrid jumped to attention.

'Yes, sir,' he said briskly, half looking over his shoulder.

'Here is one letter, Horrid, one very serious letter which I must answer.'

'Yes. Would you like to do that now?' Horrid turned round, and looked at the Vicar.

'Well, look. It is my father.'

'Ah, I see, sir.' Horrid knew that this was a very different matter.

'I think you have guessed, Horrid, what is the difference between the Canon and myself. What it really amounts to is that my father prefers to think of the newness about me as the newness of a boy at Eton. For some time it remained like that; I grew up late. But it happened very suddenly—and ever since my father has thought that he was dealing with one kind of offensive person, when he was dealing with another. You understand?'

'Yes, sir,' the secretary nodded, frowned and smiled.

'Horrid, I have seen the fangs of the Welfare State, I have smelt its breath. I know that Craigliven Castle will in a few years be a national monument—at present it is a seaside boarding house presided over by a one-time gamekeeper— I know that absolute taxation will soon have abolished everything above the level of the charlady or the railway porter. England is not on the way to being a second Sweden, with the beautiful houses of working men, whose rooms glow with the inside of forest trees—not that, but a sort of Methodist's model of Russia. Well, Horrid, I know where power is, and power is where I must be. It is no longer a matter of waving a red flag with a schoolboy fierceness, but the necessity of getting as near as possible to a vodka-tippling diplomat—near enough to the Black Throne to get a little straight news from the other side of Nowhere. Well, in a letter I have received this morning, my father asks me "Was that large slice of a sermon, published April the third, characteristic—the 'Sermon on the Mount' passage?" This was a sermon in which I spoke as a Christian. You understand his alarm?'

The young face of the secretarial-curate looked almost haggard. It was his way of being *very* polite.

'Yes, sir, I understand,' he said.

'When Christianity leads to the Black Throne—when it is power—that is ungentlemanly,' the Vicar insisted.

'That is superbly true,' said Horrid.

'All the same, Horrid, the Canon has paddled his own canoe very near the verge of the cataract. He never understands why I have shot over the top. Let me dictate this note. "Dear Father. I am skating on very thin ice—I am a Christian and may fall in. How deep is the water?" Oh, "Yours ever".'

'I wonder if he will answer "far too deep to be comfortable". Excuse me, sir.'

'See that goes tonight, Horrid.' Father Card sprang to his feet. 'I say, do let us at once do something about the possibility of finding ourselves on Sunday without a third hand for the Elevation of the Host?' He strode up and down in his cell, at the thought of the terrible mischance, his frown deepening at the image of that 'casual' beast Wimbush, responsible for it. 'That fellow Wimbush is really behaving as if he paid me, and not I him. He might at least have sent a telegram.'

'Yes,' muttered Horrid. 'I think he might have done that.'

'Might have done that! Surely he knows that we have our hands full. It is very unkind of him just to disappear like this.'

Horrid was well aware that probably the Vicar's main complaint against his second curate was that they had several hours reading of the Fathers to be got through every day, and he deeply resented this being held up. He could not ask Horrid to take Wimbush's place, because that gentleman, willing as he would be to do anything for Augustine Card, unfortunately knew only just enough Latin to get him through with the responses and other things in the services (when they were being very Roman), and knew no Greek.

Horrid held up a half-dozen letters, and said, 'These, sir, I can easily handle. They are the nonsense letters that arrive every day.'

'Thank you, Horrid. Waste a stamp on one or two of them.'

'Yes, sir.' Horrid crouched over the table, addressing himself to his nonsensical activities. Father Card flung himself down on the chaise-longue. He proceeded with what he called his 'office'. He had not been engaged in this way for more than two or three minutes when the telephone bell rang. Horrid took off the receiver. 'Yes? Father Horridge speaking. Oh, it's you. Oh, you are, are you. All right, I will tell him. . . . Father Card?' (turning towards his chief), 'this is Wimbush. He has hurt his ankle, riding a bicycle. He says it is a great bore, but he thinks he will be all right for Sunday, perhaps hobbling a bit. Is that good enough?'

'No, it is not,' answered Father Card. 'Ask Wimbush if

he is certain to be here on Sunday morning, limp or not. He usually does limp, in any case. Where is he?'

Horrid made a few enquiries at the telephone, and then, in a tone of disgust, answered, 'Shepherd's Bush.'

'Shepherd's Bush!' exploded the Vicar. 'That is nowhere. It is not even in the suburbs. Why has he not telephoned before? Ask him that, Horrid.'

Horrid muttered away at the telephone, in a to and fro of what appeared to be a rather disagreeable conversation. Then he turned to the Vicar, placing his hand over the receiver.

'I cannot gather why he has been so silent. He is rather surly. What shall I do about him? Shall I give him the What For?'

The Vicar nodded.

Horrid took his hand off the mouthpiece. 'It is obvious, Father, that you are uninterested in your duties. Father Card feels that, unless you are prepared to promise us, limp or not, that you will present yourself here this evening, at five o'clock, we had better say that you are no longer a curate at St Catherine and the Angels.'

He listened for a moment to a great outpouring in the telephone, said, 'O.K.?' and turned towards Father Card. 'He will be here at five o'clock, sir.'

Horrid watched the Vicar until he nodded; then he nodded himself and returned to composing what he regarded as meaningless letters to idiotic people.

5

An Appointment in Difficulties

The next morning, at about eleven, Augustine was as usual recumbent, but he was gazing in a rather discontented way before him. Horridge was out on an errand, and he had an appointment with someone he had not seen for some time. He lay there, musing about this man. He did not feel very sure whether he really liked him, although they were meeting as very intimate friends.

A minute or two later he heard Emma answering the front door bell. There were many sounds proving to him that she had done so. A flurry, and then someone jumped the stairs, next came a well-known rat-a-tat on his door. He admitted six-foot of good-looking manhood, with a face he had not seen for three years.

'Harty—darling! Well, this is a great pleasure.' Augustine lifted his right arm in a roman salute.

'Gusty!' Hartnell stood near the door. 'I am afraid to shake your hand. You look too muscular!'

'Very well then, be seated.' Augustine waved his hand towards a chair. 'Harty, I am delighted to see you. What is the news?'

'Well, I will not disguise it, I am full of news. First, I have the College, but—I am not in it. There is someone else there who thinks he should be Principal, and so he remains there, and carries on as Principal.'

46

'A pirate!' roared Augustine.

'A genuine pirate,' agreed Hartnell. 'He has persuaded some of the students and most of the teaching staff to carry on.'

'Yes, but who owns the place?' asked Augustine.

'A sort of a Committee. And this "Board", it is called, asks why I do not take possession. I answer that there is a Man in Possession, and that it is not part of my assignment to expel the Man in Possession. Their reply is that they will not pay the Man in Possession, or his staff.'

Augustine lay laughing on his chaise-longue. 'You often used to ask me, up at Oxford, why I was wasting my time developing my muscles,' said the recumbent Padre. 'Here is the answer, is it not?'

'I do believe that you have found the answer,' said Hartnell. 'My academic attainments cause a Board of Guardians to confer upon me the title of Principal of Hambledon College. But there is the end of the matter. A Doctor of Divinity, like myself, was already on the staff of the College—see?'

Father Card pondered deeply. 'Let me see. Where is your College?' he asked.

'Hambledon College is just the other side of the river,' said Dr Hartnell.

'Wonderful!' cried Father Card. 'We will be able to meet quite often. Now, about this predicament of yours. It seems to me that the solution is for the Board to appoint an entirely new staff. Then you and your Staff should move in together. Who is the guy who pays all the salaries in a College? He would move in as well. *Numbers* is what you need. Muscles alone is no good. My muscles have only been useful for a strictly limited number of things.'

'Yes.' Hartnell nodded his head. 'My little study of you—

my "Living in a Room with a Man-Eating Man"—has to be revised.'

'You jumped to conclusions. . . .' Augustine yawned. 'Well, that is that! Before you leave this house, however, you shall be in touch with a first-class, fighting solicitor. That is all that will be necessary. Let us turn to other matters. Are you properly provided with money? That is all right. If you had had no money, I could have given you the address of an agreeable moneylender. Now, has anything else been happening to you, Harty?'

'Really nothing. I can think of nothing,' protested Hartnell.

'And I have been doing no fighting since I became a skypilot. I have felt inclined to sock a good many people in the eyes. But I have refrained from doing so.' Augustine beamed. He sprang out of the chaise-longue, and stepped over to the telephone. Before picking up the receiver he turned towards his friend.

'Harty, I am about to put you in touch with Andrews, Spencer and Blockett.'

He dialled the appropriate number. 'Charles Blockett? This is me. An Oxford friend is here. We lived together in Oxford, as undergraduates. A most extraordinary thing has happened to Doctor Hartnell! . . . No, he is not a Medico, but a Doctor of Divinity. . . .' Augustine turned to his friend. 'Harty', he said. 'The papers are full of your case, did you know it? Well, they are. Mr Blockett has been discussing with one of his partners what steps you should take. But there is no time to waste. According to Blockett you should go to him at once and get into action immediately. May I tell him that you will obey, that you will go to him at once?'

'Of course I will,' said Hartnell, getting up. 'Here and now.'

Augustine turned back to the telephone. 'My friend, Doctor Hartnell, will be with you in five or ten minutes. What fun! Goodbye!'

Augustine stood up. 'It's too bad that you have to go away, Harty. Telephone me and tell me what has happened with Blockett. Where are you staying? As soon as you have got this straightened out, you will come and see me again won't you? But if you get into that college, do not move out of it until the place is in full working order under your direction. Goodbye!'

They shook hands and Hartnell's goodbye followed Augustine's. Laughing and waving, Hartnell passed out of the door and jumped down the stairs.

Augustine returned to his chaise-longue and took up the *Express*. There, in the largest type, was PRINCIPAL UNABLE TO TAKE POSSESSION.

6

Jane Greevey at the Church

olding her note from Horrid in her hand, containing a pew number, Jane Greevey entered the Church of St Catherine and the Angels as the bells were beginning to ring. Matilda was at her side. As she was an old member of the Congregation, she thought she would have no difficulty in being allowed to sit next to Jane. As a matter of fact the sidesman did not remember her. He had to communicate with his colleague on the other side of the church, who at once identified Miss Mortlake. They then went forward and settled down in the seats allotted them. The sidesman whispered to Matilda Mortlake that she must write to the Clergy House asking to be confirmed in possession of the seat now being granted to her—giving her the number. Jane found that they were in a position more than half-way up the aisle on the left-hand side of the centre. It was not very long before she perceived the girl who remained in her mind as Hughie's fiancée. She was ushered into a pew about three rows ahead of her, by a man who handed her back a letter, just as her sidesman had returned the letter of identification to Jane. She thought that the girl (the 'fiancée') was very nervous. She seemed timid. She cast a sharp glance at her neighbour, who sat beyond one intervening seat. He was a young man, with thinning hair. He appeared quite at home. The proximity of so dazzling a person seemed to leave him unmoved.

Jane did not continue to look at the 'fiancée', for she did not want to be noticed, and Matilda was whispering to her about the number of seats unoccupied.

'The row has thinned out the seats up here, hasn't it? This is where all the Big Shots used to sit.' Matilda looked around her. 'Oh, here come some more. Here is Lady Stonewood.'

It is a common experience that, if you stare too fixedly at someone, even from behind, they are apt in the long run to turn round and look at you. That this telepathic reaction is more than an occasional occurrence was proved before very long. As Jane's glance wandered here and there she quite suddenly discovered her eyes and those of Mary Chillingham, for that was the name of the beautiful girl, staring into one another in a manner deeply embarrassing to Jane. The girl gave a curious half-smile of recognition, and turned away.

Jane started; for, as she was dragging her fascinated eyes away from Mary Chillingham, they dilated in amazement. But what she saw was not a phantom; Hughie floated in to the aisle, then he bore down upon his supposed fiancée. Moving with him, but slightly in the rear, was a sidesman holding one of Horrid's notes. When Hughie reached his destination, he bent down and spoke to Mary, who gave a violent start, and looked up, speaking quickly, and, seemingly, with unusual determination. Hughie expostulated with the angry girl, but almost at once he and the sidesman walked away, stopping about six pews behind where Mary was sitting.

Jane watched or spied. The beautiful 'fiancée' appeared very displeased. She eventually turned round, ascertained what seat Hugh had been allotted, and almost immediately she rose and left the church.

Jane, still excitedly spying, saw Hughie quickly follow. She had of course no accurate idea of what had happened.

In view of her romantic misconception of the relationship of these two people, the way she interpreted it was a lovers' quarrel. When, five minutes later, the girl returned alone, since there was no sign of Hughie, Jane concluded that the two had had a showdown resulting in Hughie's return home with a flea in his ear—miserable, discomfited Hughie! Then an idea occurred to her; did the 'fiancée' wish, for some reason, to remain alone—oh *why* did she wish to remain alone? Jane could not imagine, except that perhaps Miss Chillingham was devout, and old Hughie scoffed at religion, which was displeasing to her.

Then Jane was obliged to admit that someone made his appearance beside whom the trivial misunderstandings of the two background figures from Jane's Mews life were supremely insignificant. Indeed, the images of Hughie and Mary were instantaneously blotted out. For the superb and so obviously very devout figure of Augustine (as she now called him) surged up from the vestry, and stood aside for the passage of his procession, his lips moving as if in prayer. Two altar-boys swinging censers, swaying from side to side as they walked, a beautifully dressed choir, and in the rear two curates—two because this was High Mass—behind whom the Vicar placed himself, composed a very fine procession.

The Reverend Augustine Card was now a notorious public figure, and a week earlier, as he had moved across the church, genuflecting as the altar made its appearance, he was not that. No. It appeared to Jane that a consciousness existed in the church of a great alteration. They had all seen this hero of Jane's on the historic battlements of Craigliven Castle, with his grandfather, the Earl (a magnificent kilted Highland Chieftain), and they also had been shown Augustine *desnudo* delivering the winning blow upon the chin of a giant-like figure.

As Jane had her eye fastened upon the Vicar, she noticed (at first without a tremor) that, for a long moment, his eyes rested upon the young woman, known to her as her tenant's 'fiancée'. Then, as she happened to glance at one of the curates (actually Horrid), just ahead of him, she saw this man indicate Mary Chillingham to a sidesman—saw him hand to that official a white envelope, and saw the sidesman move quickly around, until he was standing beside Mary, saw him bow and hand her the envelope, with a smile. To say that she was scandalised by these proceedings would in no way convey what Jane felt.

Her mind was in a tumult of surmise. She then noticed that here and there, where the seat was not yet occupied, there was a white envelope propped up on the shelf beside the books of the pew-renter. But there were not many empty places in the church, which was now almost full.

Hectically retracing the events of the last few minutes, Jane was constrained to admit that in the glance of Augustine there had been nothing but the merest glance of recognition. As to the curate, his face had remained even solemn. She was sorry, but there was no trace of such expressions as one would expect to detect in the case of intrigue. Jane, in her young days, had spent some months in Spain, and she had a very vivid recollection of the atmosphere in a Spanish church—or as seen by her. In her romantic old-maidish memory the atmosphere was much thicker with intrigue and clandestine amorousness than in fact had ever been present. But, until the significance of these white envelopes was revealed to her, they grew and grew in her imagination, until she actually could see the kisses visible through the white of the nearest envelope. This was only a momentary obsession. 'Silly old fool,' she scolded herself almost aloud. She shook herself a little, and fastened her eyes upon Augustine—so tall and massive, so solid a rampart of good sense.

Her mind dashed back, and converted into unequivocal humdrum objects the white envelopes. Suppose the envelope handed to Miss Chillingham was exactly the same as the other envelopes placed here and there, what would it be? Would it be a reminder of some special service? Or would it be a note asking for subscriptions? Or what? Perhaps General Chillingham's family played a rôle of some kind in the organisation of the church?

She almost turned to Matilda, and asked her, as an expert, to tell her what she supposed the white envelopes were. But she refrained; for she was determined not to admit her friend to any of this interior life, which kept her mind in a perpetual tumult.

Now, however, the service was beginning. The introit was quite strange to Jane. Speaking in music, the choir on the near side began the solemn statement. The antiphonal response from the small cluster of choristers facing the glittering little nest of singers on the other side of the chancel gave a vocal answer that was raw and deep and trembling, as though from captive children; this indeed was the impression created in an untutored mind of some vivacity. The bowed head of the priest, as he approached the altar, was musically assailed by the questioning of the youthful voices. The hero she had tremblingly come to watch had begun the story of his fabulous life, among the choiring voices. She watched the curled head of Father Card with a little anxiety. These choirs were acting as choruses in a play of Sophocles. But his head, as it was turned upwards, showed the deeply lined forehead. This strongly furrowed brow was what Jane had first noticed in dear, dear Augustine—disdainful and questioning now; before, sorrowfully submissive.

A hoarse whisper came from Matilda. 'This is the introit. Father Card has improved the music beyond recognition. In Father Seed's time there was nothing like this.'

Jane pushed her ear to catch the whisper intact. She nodded her understanding.

The emptiness in the pew ahead was solidly filled. Three rather ancient members of her sex had occupied all the space in front of her. The service now had to be seen through the barbarous silhouettes produced by the scarlet and gold headdresses of these savage old maidens. Female elderliness was contorted into three separate systems of coping with old hair—of building it up into strangely coloured monoliths, of smoothing it into cataracts of dirty silver. Father Card's adventures were now to be followed between two moving structures of fantastic chevelures, the crowning glory of lady parishioners. Jane imagined her own pallid wispishness converted by some coloured glue into an unreal foliage drooping beneath her ear, and shuddered.

She watched Matilda out of the corner of her eye; but it was easier, in the long run, to watch those immediately ahead; and so she stood, or knelt, or sat down, sang or was silent, in imitation of the three ladies forming the horizon beyond which the gorgeously clothed clergy and their satellites performed. She muttered rhythmically when they emitted rhythmical sounds—singing of hymns she could do nothing about, except to move her lips up and down. These embarrassments interfered with Jane's concentration upon Augustine Card's personality; among the obstructions immediately ahead she had even lost sight of Miss Chillingham.

It was in a great confusion of images, of first this happening and then that happening, that Jane came upon the crisis; she saw the splendid figure of Augustine near the high altar, with the two curates kneeling at his side, with several other figures behind him swinging censers and crouched in abject humility. Augustine was genuflecting—Jane held her breath as she saw Augustine raising something into the air, and there was the sound of a small bell. Then there was a patter of Latin; but she had noticed that nothing but Latin was spoken in this strange Anglican Church.

Gradually this great central event was at an end. And it was not very long before this pre-eminent figure mounted into the pulpit, and Jane shrank as she felt that the youthful furrowed face had levitated above her and was bending over in a meaningful way in *her* direction. A slight smile played around on her lips, keeping her mouth a little open. It seemed to her that he remarked how her peering face was fastened upon his, tirelessly watching him. However his voice rang out, and he was announcing that he really was obliged to make some reference to the events of last Sunday. He would be very brief. There was nothing for it but physically to eliminate that person determined to prevent him from proceeding with his service. It deeply grieved him to have to behave in that way, all the more so because the Marquess of Keltingbrook was a member of the congregation who, for many years, had worshipped in this church. His sabotaging of the service had been preceded by a correspondence, in which, in letter after letter, he (Augustine) had done his best to persuade this most devout old gentleman to overcome his doctrinal objections. But he could not be moved to do so. He considered that this difference of opinion could be settled by nothing short of a test of strength. He (Augustine) was placed in a position in which either the Marquess would drive him out or Augustine would remove the Marquess from the church. It was the only thing to do—a predicament, the congregation would agree, for a man of Augustine's cloth.

Leaning forward upon his forearms he spoke in a voice of deep emotion. 'Let me say with the sincerest humility that if I did not feel myself entrusted with a mission I would give way to the prejudices of this well-meaning member of my congregation.'

Jane saw that this attractive man was staking everything upon the dynamism of his personality. He was saying to this considerable collection of persons 'I am engaging in this enterprise to re-create your faith; if my personality inspires you to believe, let us worship together here.' Or so Jane saw it. It was that kind of offer, with whatever words he found to clothe its nakedness, that she, Jane Greevey, was abjectly willing to conform to. She would follow this teacher wherever he wished. But how many Jane Greeveys there were in the body of men and women behind and around her she could not guess. It seemed to her like a magnetism emanating from a Pied Piper, which commands you to follow. A door opens in the mountain, and you go in. Jane hoped it would be a great magnetism felt by everybody, and, all together, they would enter that door, singing some hymn she did not know.

Oh—yes, she saw, indeed she did—as he was speaking she saw the eye of the preacher fastened upon—fastened upon—*what*? Her eye flew with his eye, in sympathy. And where did it alight? Oh! She was watching Mary Chillingham opening her envelope, and drawing out from it what looked like a card of some sort. Her eyes were not good enough —she was too far away. She rose, almost without knowing what she was doing. She slid along the pew, she reached the end and turned, she took a step or two, and, tall as she was, she had almost to double up to do it. Her face was thrust down quite near to Mary's and her eyes were riveted upon the card. (The sermon continued, but Jane was conscious of his eyes fixed upon *her*.)

There was a start of surprise.

'You are looking at my card? It is an invitation to a Party at the Vicarage. Have you got one?'

Jane blushed so deep a crimson that Mary smiled up at her.

'No. No, Miss Chillingham. I have no card,' she whispered back.

'Well, if they do not give you one, come with me . . . will you? Shall I come and pick you up,' Mary asked her in a voice as low as her own. 'I know where you live. Hugh Bestens-Corbett rents your garage, doesn't he? I've seen you in the Mews. Very well, this says Sunday the twentieth. Eight o'clock. That is next Sunday. . . . Shall I come and fetch you at eight o'clock? we can get there in a few minutes. Settled? Fine or rain. I am sorry to say I don't know your . . .'

'My name? Jane Greevey,' she whispered, so low that Mary could not hear it. Noticing her new friend's bewilderment, she said in a louder voice, 'Jane—Jane you know, like Jane Eyre.'

'Yes, yes. I've got it. Jane.'

'Greevey . . . an ugly name, think of gravy.'

Mary smiled up at her. 'I like gravy.' They both smiled and nodded, and Jane glided back to her pew, her ears burning—so terribly red—she was sure they must be one of the reddest things in the world, and a tell-tale beacon, assailing the eye of the Preacher.

As she sank down beside Matilda, she smiled guiltily, and whispered, 'I *had* to see what was in that envelope! Excuse me, Tilda, for my bad behaviour in your church.'

'I was a little surprised when I saw you floating away. But I'm glad you floated back again.' Matilda smiled indulgently.

Jane sat with her eyes down, and determined not to raise them again until He had left the pulpit. She would know when He had left by the solemn invocation coming back to her ears through the mists of half a century, 'Now to God the Father, God the Son, and God the Holy Ghost, be ascribed all Power, Might, Majesty, Dominion,' . . . something like that announcing the end of the sermon. There would be a scarcely audible 'Amen'.

Matilda sneezed, and Jane nearly jumped out of her skin. Matilda's sneezes were so personal. After that, Jane sat with her head bowed; she began turning over in her mind exactly what had happened. Would she ever be able to forgive herself . . . would she ever be forgiven? Would the blazing red face of the stupid old woman bending over her ever be washed out of Mary's mind? Now Mary knew her secret. It was terrible . . . it was inexpressibly awful. That lovely young girl knew her silly old secret—so impossible to understand when one is young and beautiful. Yet Mary seemed very understanding—very, very understanding. Why was she so . . . how could she be so infernally understanding? So horribly understanding? She was a horrible girl to understand so much. To understand so bloody much, as Hughie would put it. Hughie! She would tell Hughie all about it, they would both of them scream with laughter about it. When next she saw Hughie, she, Jane, would say to him one of those things she had never said—the kind of thing Matilda would say. She breathed deeply. She saw Hughie's face distinctly, and she prepared to speak to it. She suddenly felt herself spitting . . . and, deeply ashamed, she found herself offered a plate full of money. The offertory.

Again very red in the face, she began fishing about in her bag for a half-crown. She found it, pulled it out swiftly, and jangled it in among the other coins. Then Matilda's hand darted towards the plate, and she heard a sound less clangorous than her half-crown. . . . The plate receded.

'Mercifully grant peace in our days.'

She distinctly heard him saying these words, as she had heard him say so many other things in a mist of prayer and of singing, with the incense in her nostrils, the incense that was taken, along with the invocation, to God's own distant presence by bowed angels.

'In the beginning was the Word, and the Word was with God, and the Word was God; the Same was in the Beginning with God. All things Were Made By Him, and Without Him was Made Nothing that was Made.'

It was *His* blessed voice.

She fell into a reverie. She thought of a great many things, with singing and praying interwoven with the thoughts, but never interrupting them. She knew now that she should never have come to this church. When Mary Chillingham came next Sunday to fetch her she would not find her there. No. She would not be made any more of a fool of. She began to develop a very great aversion for this disgustingly beautiful girl. It was only for a year or two, it was nothing to be proud of, it was just a stupid condition common to all women for a short time. No one but a cad woman, a fool woman, took advantage of it. She knew it was only loaned her by nature as a dress for a moment to trick some man. She, Jane, did not mind the deceit . . . so long as it was not used to deceive *her*.

She went on and on thinking in this way belittling this loathsomely beautiful girl, trying to extract herself from the web she had become entangled in, wishing that Matilda was somewhere else. Then suddenly she felt cold. She had not looked up since the episode of the burning ears. No one was in the church . . . or, rather the two or three last members of the congregation were fading out of the door, and a sidesman was scuttling along the aisle towards her. She rose guiltily and hurried to meet him.

'I thought you were asleep, Miss.'

'No.' Jane shook her head with a shy smile. 'Just offering up a final prayer.'

'I beg your pardon, Miss.'

As she turned round and started towards the door she realised that Matilda had disappeared. She was nowhere to be seen. Outside it was raining—she was thankful to say. She hurried back to the Mews preparing an answer for Hughie, if he happened to pop up, as she passed his basement flat in Blessington Street, and if he were so unwise as to snigger. But the rain kept him indoors.

7

A Luncheon Party

General Charles Chillingham, C.B., D.S.O., and his family lived in a very smart house, near the Sloane Square end of Ebury Square, not in the giant block of palatial houses, but where the monster parade of mansions breaks up. Dazzling with new lemon and black paint, and daily spit and polish, the house stood out in a terrace of beautifully kept villas. This old cavalry officer was supposed to parade the shining black railings along the front of his house every morning. And the women too—his wife, two daughters, and his servants, seemed to be obliged to live up to their residence. Of these two daughters, one was a war-widow. The younger, Mary, twenty-seven, was the young woman known to Jane Greevey as 'Hughie's fiancée'. She was not that; she would have laughed if she had heard herself so described! A very spruce young officer was almost affianced to her—no qualification such as this would be necessary if it were not for her extreme disinclination to admit to it. Mary Chillingham was so accustomed to the society of older people—her father and his friends, of whom Hugh Bestens-Corbett was one; then her mother, and her sister (who was nearer to forty than she was to thirty)—that she found it difficult to take Arthur Wootton seriously. He was a child-like Grenadier, as dumb as his busbies.

Mary was fond of dancing, but she wanted to go to what Arthur called 'highbrow' plays, and read books which to him seemed mad, or written for people so clever that they dwelt in some arcanum, situated perhaps on the farther side of Hampstead Heath. His parents were 'rather nice people', his family was county, he would have a little money—she was constantly told at home that, if she let Arthur slip, she might never get another chance. So she *supposed* she was engaged; she found it very difficult to resist the imputation that she was affianced; but the lowness of Arthur's I.Q. caused her to shrink from admitting it. As for such time as she passed with him, she behaved as if she had been asked to look after a child of six, and conversed accordingly. Her real companions were still the elderly; that dear old thing, Hugh Bestens-Corbett, was a useful escort for the highbrow film, or the Picture Gallery and so forth.

There were young men, too, who went around with her, with whom she could discuss the latest book by Charles Morgan, the latest Ealing Studios films, or music by Michael Tippett. But she was a loveless girl, except for Arthur's unclassifiable kisses.

The day following Mary's first lonely visit to the Chillingham pew at St Catherine and the Angels, both Hugh and the young officer were lunching at the Chillinghams. They went in to lunch discussing the events of a week before, when Father Card had expelled the Marquess.

'I shall go there no more,' said the General.

'That is the General Officer speaking,' said Mary. 'Because a vicar chucks out an old gentleman who tries to sabotage his service. . . . How would you have liked it, Father, when you were taking parade, if one of the senior officers had ridden forward and attempted to take your place—loudly denouncing your way of performing that military ritual?'

They all took their places at table.

'A parade is not a church service,' as he was sitting down, the General said. 'But why I shall not go there again is simply because I take going to church seriously, and I like worshipping quietly, not in the middle of a brawl.'

'Charles, as that puts the matter in the right light, it must end the debate.' But the General's wife was wrong, the debate did not end.

'I am so sorry, Father, to disagree with you,' said Mary.

'Evidently you like a rough house to say your prayers in,' the General told her. 'I hardly knew I was in God's House when Father Card was chucking out Lord Keltingbrook. Even the organist played the wrong kind of music. Beethoven's *Eroica* is not church music, is it?'

'Did they play that? Preposterous!' broke in Hugh.

'Oh, when I go there now I expect the organ to break into jazz at any moment,' the General assured him. 'They don't seem to have any church music. They just seem to play whatever they happen to think of, Massenet . . . Chopin . . . Puccini.'

'You obviously go to the wrong church.' Mary beamed pleasantly upon her father. 'If all you want is a nice quiet place to pray in, you can get that by going up to your bedroom, leaving orders that you must not be disturbed. But you go to a church to take part in a service. A good deal of noise is unavoidable; but the quietest of all services is to be found in the average Low Anglican church. Sleepiness is the dominant characteristic: that's where you should go.'

'We all know, my dear, that you are an excellent debater,' said her mother to Mary. 'Trained at Newnham and so on you can easily beat us in an argument.'

'Very well,' Mary looked a little annoyed. 'What you especially dislike is sarcasm, isn't it? Then we will bar what you call sarcasm. I will gladly admit that Father is more serious about worship than I am: but the Anglo-Catholic theory of worship I am really rather interested in.'

The General seemed to shake himself a little.

'I am too, I suppose,' he said. 'But, all the same, I would rather go to the sleepy old Low church you recommend, Mary, than be present at brawls stimulated by questions of theory.'

'I think Mary must inherit her skill in debate from her father,' Hugh observed. 'What Charles has said upon the subject is by far the most convincing. I don't often go to church myself; but if I did I would pick a quiet one.'

'In order to have a nice sleep,' Mary laughed.

'Not at all,' bellowed Hugh humorously. 'If I went to church I should be serious about it: and I should not want my mind to be taken up with the antics of a self-advertising charlatan.'

'Your type of man, Hugh, always classes an intelligent man as a charlatan,' Mary told him. 'He has a hard and fast idea as to what everyone should be.'

Hugh had been really annoyed, and had it not been for Charles he would have been less than polite. 'I am sorry that you do not think I possess intelligence, Mary,' was all he said.

'I humbly suggest that Newnham accounts for Mary's gift of the gab,' came from Arthur, who had not noticed her mother's reference to that college, and thought this was a good opportunity to have his own little say. 'But she seems to have over-reached herself this time.'

'You know an intelligent man when you see one, don't you, Arthur dear!' Mary's eyes shone bellicosely.

Mrs Chillingham looked over at her daughter with a severity which was never failing when Mary, in 'throwing her weight about', came down too heavily upon Arthur Wootton. Mary knew what was coming.

'Mary, because Arthur is a soldier you high-hat him, don't you; but that, after all, is your father's profession. In a certain College which was mentioned just now, the prig was manufactured . . .'

'Why you sent me to that prig-factory I cannot imagine.'

Arthur had been grinning sheepishly in the direction of Hugh; but now he said, 'I must say, Mrs Chillingham, that I am rather partial to a prig.'

'Bravo, Arthur!' exclaimed Mary.

There was a general laugh. Arthur's defence of the prig won every heart. There was a pause which threatened to lead to a change of subject. But Hugh was not going to allow that to happen.

'About that church,' he began aggressively. '"The essence has not been touched on—the personal character of the charlatan. I for my part would not step inside a church where Card presided.'

The General smiled at this typical piece of 'bulldogery' of Hugh's. 'You have never seen this disturber of the peace,' he remarked.

'Oh yes I have!' Hugh exclaimed. 'We had a conversation. I brushed him off. He approached me in Marten's Mews as if he were a Pasha and I a shoeshine wallah. I did not conceal my contempt for cheapjacks of his kind. If he tried to stage a papist racket in a church I had always gone to I would write to his Bishop.'

The General smiled indulgently at his vociferous friend. 'I am a peaceable kind of man,' he objected. 'I shall merely go to another church.'

'I propose to back up Augustine Card,' said Mary. 'I shall continue to go to church as usual. I was there yesterday, and he preached what I considered a very fine sermon. He made us all feel a lot of worms.'

'May I be your escort?' Arthur suggested.

'No, thank you, Arthur. He would eat you if you opened your little mouth.'

Arthur had a belligerent grin.

'I should not like to disillusion you with your hero.'

'I will show up there again next Sunday,' Hugh told her. 'You ought not to be quite alone.'

'Don't be an idiot.' She spoke angrily to Hugh. 'I insist on being alone. If you go on like this, all of you, I will offer my services to Augustine Card.'

'We had better allow her to have her own sweet way,' said Mary's mother. 'She will very soon get tired of Father Card. Do not let us exaggerate what can happen to Mary in a church.'

'I am glad to hear that you are going to give up treating the church as if it were a bull ring,' Mary retorted.

But the party drifted away from that particular topic, though other subjects seemed rather tame beside the outrageous Vicar. Hugh had come in to discuss stamps, which both collected, with his friend the General: they spent an hour or so after lunch talking perforations and postmarks.

Arthur, on the other hand, bore Mary off to Lord's almost at once. When Bestens-Corbett left he made a stately progress almost the entire length of the cyclopean Avenue. At last, turning down Blessington Street, he entered the Mews. He approached the garage, his hands in his pockets. Jane was on her doorstep, conversing with the milkman, trying to find out exactly *who* her new neighbours were. The milkman realised this, and was quite willing to satisfy her. 'Her Ladyship is a widow—*very* rich. She shares the house with another lady. The cook says this other lady is a very wealthy woman too.'

Hugh (not recognised at first in his beautiful clothes by Jane) marched up jingling his money, with a sarcastic smile.

'Ah, Miss Greevey, I hear you are a great churchgoer.'

'It is my business, Mr Bestens-Corbett, if I go to church.'

Hughie, when he went out in that outfit, was always a little above himself. He snubbed the milkman, and Jane thought that, at any moment, he would be a little fresh with her. She kept a cold sharp eye on this Froggy who had been a-wooing. The milkman knew that the Savile Row suit and brand-new light Homburg hat came up from the basement flat out of the little old house around the corner. Usually this fine gentleman was in his shirt sleeves, taking in the milk, or cleaning his car in the Mews. Mr Bestens-Corbett spoke. And the milkman scowled as he wheeled his rattling electric truck round in the rear of Hugh, saying to himself 'He fancies his luck, does our Mr Bestens-Corbett. Don't let him ask me for a double-cream! Not if I bloody well know it, comin' his fine gentleman over me!'

'As you stand on your rights, Miss Greevey,' Hugh was benign, 'it is *allowable* for anyone to go anywhere they please.'

'You are very accommodating.' Jane's graceful features expressed nothing.

'I, on my side, Miss Greevey, am allowed to express an opinion. I am a little shocked to hear of you, an intelligent person as I supposed, consenting to listen to such a charlatan as Father Card. A self-advertising parson like that ought to have his church taken away from him. He is quite free to embrace Roman Catholicism; he ought to be told to do so.' Hughie was bullyingly indignant.

'That is your view, but Father Card's answer to that kind of remark would be to tell you that he prefers to remain in the Anglican Church, and to convert it from within, so that it returns to Rome after its long separation. . . .' Jane looked at him firmly.

'Do you propose to crusade with this bogus roughneck of a man?' Hughie demanded.

'Having duly interpreted your fantastic way of expressing yourself,' Jane squared up to her neighbour as she had never done before, '*Yes*, I shall follow with my sympathy the "Crusade" (if you like) of this very sincere man.'

The representative of the privileged sex, and the submissive, no-longer-young, spinster lady eyed one another silently, the former expecting a climb-down; but it was gradually sinking in that something had changed the colourless maiden lady.

'Evidently this hero,' said the discomfited Hughie sullenly, 'evidently this maiden's-dream-of-a-man, shown us by the newspapers strolling on the battlements of an ancestral Castle, or becoming champion of England by defeating a terrifying-looking giant—evidently this gentleman-parson—this pugilistic Vicar, is going to be fluttered around by a bevy of women. That usually happens. It is not very much to your credit, Miss Greevey; you have usually shown such very good sense. And here you go, making a fool of yourself. A big swaggering priest, who professes to paint the town red . . . it is a purely automatic feminine reaction.'

But Hughie was treading on dangerous ground. Jane's dander was continually rising. At last she said, her breast rising and falling a little faster than usual, 'Mr Bestens-Corbett, if you were talking to a man you would choose your words more carefully. I am a woman, and if you speak insultingly of my feminine—er, tendencies, you tempt me to speak of some of your all-too vulnerable male eccentricities.'

Hughie flushed angrily, but he said, in a sneering voice: 'Oh? What are these laughable frailties of the male nature, Miss Greevey? Please do not show any mercy, or tone anything down.'

Jane looked at him for rather a lengthy moment— perhaps a minute. She was on the verge of telling him what a bumptious idiot he was. Instead she tossed her head and smiled.

'Captain Bestens-Corbett,' she included his rank as a wartime Ordnance Captain. 'Let us remain friendly neighbours. You are a very dashing intelligent, handsome man. How lucky I am to have you just here, in my unworthy garage.'

Ostentatiously holding himself in check, his eyes darting insulting fires, Captain Bestens-Corbett very slowly moved away, as if he expected to be called back.

Jane went inside her house, closing her door very firmly, and stepped quickly into her sitting-room, to have under her malignant eye her mortified, growling neighbour, passing her window, on the way to his basement. Soon she sat down and remarked to herself, 'What a good way that is of doing it! I have sent that "intelligent, handsome" (what was it) man skulking back into his burrow, a very sore little Hughie. What has happened to that little Mouse? he asks himself.'

She knew she had improved her status. And she was compelled to admit that it was the influence of Matilda's stimulation. A rather sneaking bully like her tenant had to be met with a little more toughness than was hers by nature.

8

A Strong-minded Conversation

M ary sat with her mother in her modest 'den', in the early evening of the day of the luncheon party. 'You are a problem child, Mary,' her mother said. 'Of twenty-seven?' was Mary's reply.

'That is the age of my problem,' the mother said.

'Rubbish. How can I be a problem?' Mary asked firmly. Dressed for Lord's (by Jacqmar) she stretched out her beautiful legs, nyloned as France dictates, a mass of youthful perfections. Gazed upon by Mrs Chillingham, that lady cogitated grimly: 'As if such a terribly marriageable woman were not a problem to a mother, with all that on her mind!'

'You have no right to have a problem,' Mary told her. 'You are quite right when you say that you ought never to have sent me to Newnham; it was an idiotic thing to do. I am inclined to think that you wanted to make a school marm of me—a drudge, of an inferior class. Then, since I have left there, I have lived with you and Father and an older sister— always with people much older than myself. The result of my education, and of my association, presents *me* with a problem—not you. Arthur is about my age; but, in my eyes, he is an irritating child. Marriage with him would be awful. My husband should be quite different in education, in intelligence, and fifteen years older. I go to Lord's with Arthur as I should with a young brother (say fourteen), and as to the books we discuss, the theatres he talks about! He quotes me what he has read in the newspapers, and really believes that these judgements are his own. Usually they are idiotic. Yet I have to get married, and, a few years hence, that will be much more difficult. That is my problem. . . . You are partly responsible for it. But do not lay claim to my problem. If you feel *guilty* about it, *it is too late.*'

Her mother sat looking at her, inhaling her cigarette smoke, and rather arrogantly exhaling it, in her eyes an amused, superior look. For she did not see how to make a verbal answer. Retiring behind an amused look, she surrendered to her laziness.

'You wash your hands of your problem, and have nothing to say about mine,' Mary protested. 'It is your fault if I outlined my problem. What are you prepared to do about it? Let me suggest something. I know that money is short; but, if I could have a change of scene, I could escape gracefully from Arthur; then I could set my cap at any man who eyed my nylons with interest, who was educated, and who might be able to keep me. The scene is the problem—Rome, Paris, Monte Carlo? How long will you keep me hunting for a suitable man?'

'I am afraid that the exchequer would not run to that. That is the trouble.' Her mother frowned. 'Please believe me, Mary.'

'I am getting dangerously old, I know. Twenty-seven.' Mary jumped up and took up an envelope. She drew out a photograph and handed it to her mother. 'My latest photograph. I have a good deal of colour in my face, but without that bloom, I look about . . . six years older. . . . Don't I?— I doubt if people who had never seen me would believe that I was only twenty-seven. That is your responsibility again. Newnham took its toll of years.'

Her mother was becoming extremely irritable. As a child

Mary used to indulge in arguments of this kind. For hours she would go on building up a quite consecutively logical, but quite nonsensical grievance. Mary might soon, she felt, accuse her of being responsible for some slight rheumatic affliction, which she once said prevented her from climbing on to a bus. Fundamentally it was a childish retaliation for her mother's good advice. This blooming girl who possessed that kind of wonderful youthfulness which stops when the twenties end was now trying to convince herself that she had already lost those miraculous good looks—because she had been given an academic training for one thing; and then had not been afforded the conditions to satisfy the needs produced by the training. As to Mary, she continued to see two or three of her college friends, and being with them was a tremendous relief. But after a spell of the old life, to have to meet Arthur, and spend an evening with him, was such a maddening experience that it required a great deal of effort not to be offensive. His Guards talk, episodes at manœuvres which he regarded as terribly funny, was almost more than she could support. If they played tennis, rode in the park, or did any of the things he was good at, and knew it, he was so self-satisfied and patronising that the effort needed not to hit him over the head with a racket exhausted her inexplicably.

Her mother now suddenly got up with an impatient frown. 'Well,' she said 'I will leave you to weave any nonsense you like.' She made a bustling exit.

Mary rose and walked violently about. Her mother never discussed it with her, but she must have known that this radiant scented body required some satisfaction. But sexually to have some foolish fellow 'messing about with her'—rather than that she preferred sterility, loneliness, death. Her mother did not apparently know what it meant to be a lovely, intensely desirable creature like herself. She was hopeless. She continued to excuse Arthur, that dull dog. But she could see her mother thinking: 'I don't see why this self-willed young woman should be supplied with the money to transport herself where she could find some university don, or some actor fellow, and bring him back to us—to bore and to despise us—because we do not act, or have not been to Newnham.' More and more, Arthur, a typical young Guards officer, appeared to her mother to be too good for Mary, who would make him very miserable. She hardly any longer could control herself, her patience was wearing very thin. The mother and daughter both suffered the same emotions, but one of them in reverse.

A small French piano, not very well in tune, stood in the corner of Mary's den. There was an hour or two before dinner. Mary could not play very expertly; but she thought she would try and fatigue herself. She opened Chopin's Preludes, sat down at the piano, and began laboriously picking out these musical messages. She did her best to follow these sketches. In about an hour she was thoroughly tired. She left the piano, and threw herself down on her divan bed. She was sufficiently exhausted to bear with her mother during dinner.

9

Norwich

Mary was superstitious, but, crossing her fingers, she started to make a journey up to Norwich on a Friday. She was going to pay a visit to a young man to whom, at Cambridge, she had fallen a victim. Love of that kind had not been a habit with her, and so this particular relationship had impressed itself very much on her mind. Harry Ritchie had been a rather seedy six-footer. She had felt always, at the time, that his eyes were beautiful, and his face was not bad looking, but, apart from saying that, he was not easy to describe. She had determined to go down and see him, to find out what it had been that had made her go as far as the bed with this young man, and discover what the years had done to him.

Harry lived in Norwich, where it was not quite clear to her what he had done after leaving Cambridge. He had answered her letter of a day or two before very sensibly, and with no embarrassing references to their past at Cambridge. All he had said was, 'I wonder if we shall ever have as grand a time as we had up at the University.' He was rather fond of women, and she wondered whether he had got himself entangled with one in particular. There was nothing in his letters to suggest that, and it might be concluded that he was not married. All that she could remember clearly were the beautiful eyes; and that really was what she had come to check on.

Their rendezvous was at one of the oldest hotels in the city. It had not too noisy a lounge, aligned on the street, and with a slight excitement she stepped into this low, long, rather dim place. There was a cry, 'Mary', and before she knew quite what was happening she was shaking his hand. It was almost exactly the same young man as she had known at Cambridge. There were the beautiful eyes, not quite so attractive, but still, nice eyes. He had filled out a little, and this suited him. His tweed suit was not very new, he did not give the impression of great prosperity. He was in a small law-business, of which his father was the senior partner. She had forgotten what he did, and now she remembered— solicitor.

They sank down beside one another in a lonely corner of the lounge. Mary's sensations were mixed; but on the whole she did not wish to be the wife of a country solicitor, and not this particular solicitor. That was final. How she could ever have got into bed with him she did not understand. But there she was for a day, and, possibly, as the day passed, it might produce more agreeable sensations.

'Is there any woman you are very attached to?' she asked bluntly. What an awful thing to have said to him, she thought. He will think that I have come down here for one purpose only, to resume a past relationship, or whatever it was. But, she added to herself, what *am* I down here for? It all seemed idiotic, and she cast a sort of reproachful look at Harry.

But before he had time to answer her question, she laughed and said, 'All I mean is, do we have to avoid a certain part of the town, on account of some tigress being there, who might spring out and make a scene.'

Harry smiled slowly, and slowly shook his head. 'No one

very dangerous, Mary. I have known one or two women, as you may imagine.' He smiled again. 'But at the moment I do not belong to anyone of the other sex.'

'I am afraid I shall alarm you by these questions. But of course they were not really necessary, I do not know why I enquired about that.'

'Oh, I don't know. If you don't see anyone for several years it is quite natural, I think, to put in a question about sex. I was just about to ask you, as a matter of fact. Have you a bloke? or anything embarrassingly disposed to complicate your freedom?' Harry was quite an intelligent young man, and got through these preliminary enquiries very suitably, she thought.

'No,' she said, 'with me, sex has done nothing distorting or fundamental. I have known a few men since our Cambridge days, yes. But I am not deeply entangled with anyone.'

'I am glad to hear that,' said Harry. 'We were such friends. I should not like to think of some big, bristling chap hanging up his hat inside your door.'

'I am glad too, that there is not some big, jolly girl thinking of you first when she wakes up in the morning.'

He laughed lazily, and as he did so he squeezed her hand. 'That is all right then, neither of us has succumbed to the many temptations of sex. You have not changed in your appearance naturally, indeed you are better looking, and I am sure that a whole battalion of nice young men besiege you with sexual intents.'

Mary laughed—she was pleased at what he had said about her appearance.

'No,' she said, 'there is one young man in the Grenadier Guards who asks me to marry him once a week. But he is very stupid, and I have not taken long to discover that most men up to thirty are apt to have a real age of about fifteen.'

A waiter came in, and Harry asked her if she would have a cocktail. They had cocktails, he White Lady, and she Old Fashioned.

As they sipped their drinks, Harry said, 'I am a provincial, and Cambridge was for me, of course, a great adventure, a marvellous period in my life, after which I sink back into the home-town, and I grow duller every day. I think that you must consider yourself very lucky to live in London, and to be near all the new plays, and new books, and new everything. Do you keep up your music, Mary?'

'Oh yes,' smiled Mary. 'I hammer away at my piano. I have a den, as we call it, in our house, and there I have a little French upright. Its tone is so gentle that I can play it up to any hour without complaints.'

'How do you like the Festival Hall for concerts?' he asked.

'I'm afraid I'm too lazy to go there very often,' Mary said. 'And I really have no one who shares my interest in that sort of thing—except one family friend, and he's not always available. So I generally make my own music in my attic.'

'I wish I could go up to Cambridge more often. I do miss the inspiration of Ord.'

'Oh, that wonderful King's College choir! I hear it sometimes on the radio,' she said.

'All my memories of music at Cambridge are bound up with you, Mary.'

'And let me say that I am constantly turning up pieces of music which I bought in Cambridge to play to you. They still are very good.' She smiled.

'Talking of music brings our life in Cambridge back to me.'

Mary looked at her friend's beautiful eyes. As he talked about Cambridge they became slightly more beautiful. She wondered if he meant them to do that. She instinctively moved away from him a little.

'Let us go into lunch,' he said, getting up. She rose also and they moved together in the direction of the handsome restaurant hall on the other side of a central court. It was a little late, and they easily found a table. After they had ordered their lunch, Harry leant forward and said, 'Let us go up to my little flat afterwards. It is in an old part of the town. Rather jolly.'

'I should like to see your little flat,' said Mary.

So that was settled, but it did not mean love—she was determined—simply a place to be in for a short time. After lunch they walked around to his flat. When they got inside Harry took her in his arms and they kissed. But she then pushed herself away from him, and said, 'I did not come here for that. I like you very much Harry. But we are older now, and the risks we ran at Cambridge send cold shivers down my back.'

'What *did* you come here for, Mary?' Harry laughed. 'I experience the same retrospective alarms as you have. But it is no use going about so cautiously as you suggest one should. What is the use?'

She thought he had a rather offensive light in his eye, as if it was too late to be cautious, once you have, for a long time, been incautious.

'You have a nice little flat here, haven't you. And a radiogram!' she exclaimed.

'Come and look at the whole establishment,' he said, leading the way through an intervening door.

She went through this door a little timorously, and was not surprised when, the other side of it, he seized her, and dragged her down upon a bed.

'No! Look here, you must behave—none of that!'

She slipped out of his grip roughly, and sprang away,

very red. She walked quickly back into the first room. Smiling sheepishly, Harry strolled after her. 'You are probably right,' he said. 'My apologies.'

He lit a cigarette, and sat down. Mary sat down too, took one of the cigarettes he offered, and lit it.

'I am a lawyer. What did you come down to Norwich for?' he asked.

'Do you want to know?' She asked this aggressively.

'Yes,' said Harry.

'I came down here to have a look at you, Harry. I always had dismissed you as palpably unsuitable, but I thought I would have another look, and see quite how hopeless you were, or not so bad, perhaps—we were quite fond of one another, and if I had been mistaken, about your social incompatibility . . .'

Harry Ritchie's face had grown red, and he looked angry.

'You wanted to insult me, did you?' he said. 'I was up in your Border county recently. Chillingham Chase is a very grand place, and your uncle a great swell thereabouts. You are talking to me now as a Chillingham?' he asked her.

'The last thing I want to do, Harry, is to be rude to you. All this has come out of your pressing me to say why I came down here. I ought not to have answered. I am sorry if I have been rude.' She had embarrassed herself by her outspokenness, which she was not used to doing. It was because she liked Harry that she was embarrassed.

'I quite understand,' the young man said, 'that a woman in your position ought not to marry a little country solicitor. It should have occurred to you that I might have no intention of marrying anybody—even so well-born a person as yourself. If you had ventured a little enquiry you would have found that marriage was the last thing I was prepared to contemplate. If you had come down here with any idea of marrying me you would have been disappointed. Shall we go in the next room and make love? I am prepared to run the risk involved in that—but, on your side, before taking that risk, please remember that giving birth to a child would not lead to marriage with me. I should naturally think, being a lawyer, that you might be in the habit of sleeping with men, and your visit to Norwich might possibly be a way of providing your child by another man with a real sucker of a father.' Harry was looking straight at her, to see if she followed his argument. It was evident that she did.

'My very unequivocal attitude when I was pulled down on the bed just now is a sufficiently clear answer to any theory about my having plotted to entangle you in the kind of way you are suggesting.' Mary was sitting up, erect, and rather forbidding.

'Yes, I suppose we must dismiss that theory to account for your visit,' Harry said. 'But it seems to me rather a foolish little trip, if you will forgive me for saying so.'

'I should call it damned silly!' Mary answered. 'To make a day's journey to see whether a man is not really a bit of an aristocrat—what could be more idiotic? But I am in the kind of dilemma that women may get into, and, damn it all, I was attached to you, Harry.'

'I imagined we were very good friends,' he said a little glumly.

The flat bell rang three times, three little rings in succession. Harry did not move. Mary became immobile too. Neither spoke.

Again the bell rang—and in the same way—three little rings.

'Why don't you answer the door?' asked Mary.

'It is a couple of nuns, asking for money,' said Harry. 'We were saying just now what good friends we had been. It is easy to say that with too little gusto. I shouldn't like you to go away with the idea that I was no longer so warm a friend, Mary.'

'I like to hear you say that, Harry,' she said in a low voice.

Harry rose, and went over to the radiogram. He put on the record of Schubert's A minor quartet. After they had listened for seven or eight minutes, the telephone bell rang. It continued to ring, and he irritably went over to it. He lifted the receiver and listened. 'I did not hear it . . . I am most awfully tired . . . I am going to have a siesta . . . I will ring you about five . . .' He hung up the receiver. 'An old school friend of mine,' he said. 'He is very persistent.'

'So I noticed,' said Mary.

'He seems to think he owns me because we knew one another as small boys.'

The telephone rang again. Harry went quickly to the instrument, and snatched the receiver off its resting place. 'Do you still hear my radiogram?' he almost shouted. 'No. Do not be silly! . . . I can rest with Schubert in my ears, but not with the ringing of this telephone . . . I'm sorry you misunderstand my love of music . . . I hope so.'

As he left the telephone he said to Mary, 'That is a woman friend of mine, Mary. You do not mind my indulging, very cavalierly, in the sex, do you?'

'Harry, will you ring for a taxi-cab?'

'Why? are you going?' asked Harry.

She went towards the telephone, but as she reached it, it rang. She lifted the receiver, and a tender little 'Harry' came to her ears. Mary answered quickly, 'Do you mind leaving the telephone alone for a few minutes? I want to call a taxi-cab.'

'This is not your telephone, Mary.' Harry's voice sounded very annoyed.

'No, it is yours. Would you mind stopping that gramophone, and ringing for a taxi-cab?'

The telephone bell rang. Mary sprang at it, and, seizing the receiver, shouted, 'Will you keep away from the telephone for a minute!' Then, turning to Harry, she held out the instrument, saying loudly, 'Here, Harry, tell your young lady to restrain her impatience. Tell her to get off the line.'

Harry took the telephone receiver from Mary. He said into it, 'As you hear, I have a lady friend here. I would be obliged if you didn't keep ringing this number for a few minutes.' He placed the receiver back on its hook, and turned to Mary.

'That was rather bitchy,' he said. 'But I will get you off the premises as speedily as possible.'

He picked up the receiver and dialled a number. The response was prompt, and he told the taxi caller that he wanted a cab urgently.

'I think your young lady, after a good cry, will behave as she should,' Mary said. She had already begun to arrange herself a little at a glass.

'If she throws me over because of your rudeness, I will quickly get another one, have no fear,' said Harry.

'I thought you would,' answered Mary. 'I would not have risked blasting your latest amour.'

The taxi-cab arrived in about five minutes. Mary walked towards the front door. She opened it, and an attractive-looking young woman was standing in front of her.

'Harry is here,' Mary told her. 'Do not spank him for being so bold as to entertain another woman.' She saw the pretty piece in front of her lift her hand up to the jamb of the massive door, and then it came very quickly towards her, and she felt a stinging blow upon her cheek. Mary simply stepped down and walked to the taxi-cab. She was followed by Harry, laughing. She entered the cab and Harry stood at the window, his grinning face offered to her indignant view. Mary shouted at the taxi-man to hurry himself, and she paid no attention to the 'Goodbye' of the still grinning Harry, who seemed tickled to death at his concubine's excellent marksmanship with her little fist. She saw, out of the corner of her eye, the young woman, who still stood on the top step outside the front door, grinning at her too.

As she moved along in the taxi-cab her cheek stung, and she felt sure it would continue to do so for many a long hour. In the train she found herself alone in the carriage with a man who eyed her with what she believed was lust. She reflected what she should do if this fellow went into action with her; she decided that a very effective thing was a heavy smack.

10

The Vicar's Party

When Mary arrived in the Mews about eight o'clock the Sabbath silence was thick and deep. She stood still, looking to left and right. Jane was in her sitting-room; she was watching Mary, where her curtain allowed her to pull it back a half-inch and observe unseen. At length Mary seemed to make up her mind; she came towards the watching eye.

'All right, young woman,' Jane said to herself, 'I will come to the Party with you.'

She responded to the knock.

'Will you come in and have a drink?' asked Jane.

'I think so,' said Mary, nodding and smiling.

Jane did not know, of course, that this 'smashing' young beauty was in her element with those of Jane's age, though it did not take her long to notice that Mary Chillingham behaved as if she were a sister rather than a niece. She felt that this was diplomatic, but it put her at her ease. She went to her kitchen and mixed a drink, put some ice in a saucer, and returned to her sitting-room.

Her visitor had picked out one of her books, and was looking at it.

'I was looking at your Matthew Arnold's Poems.

"Apollo comes leading
His choir, the Nine,

The leader is fairest,
But all are divine."

She said this in a singing voice. She left the place where she had been looking at the books, saying, 'Arnold used to be my favourite poet. When I pick up "The Scholar Gipsy" or some other thing of his, I feel as I always have. Do you like him?'

'Oh yes, I do,' Jane replied. 'I like "The Scholar Gipsy" as much as any poem.'

'So do I,' said Mary. 'I am not anti-modern but I don't feel the same about the moderns. "Dover Beach" . . .'

'Yes, "Dover Beach" . . .'

'I suppose England has changed,' mused Mary. 'No one would be thinking of Sophocles on Dover Beach today . . . would they?'

Jane felt guilty. *She* would not be thinking of Sophocles. So she did not answer. She pushed the tray with the drinks towards Mary—who knew all about Sophocles! 'I hope you like them sweet?' The smart thing was to prefer them dry, and Mary, she was sure, would like them dry.

'I like them sweet,' smiled Mary.

Jane felt humiliated. Matthew Arnold was the one poet among her books that she knew practically nothing about. Arnold she had always considered terribly dull and mid-Victorian. But she had not been at Newnham. This beautiful young woman *would* pick out the one book that she had been preparing to hide away somewhere as too old fashioned.

She stood up, stepped to the window, as if to do something to a curtain, and saw that there was no light coming out of her garage. Hughie was not there—luckily, according to Jane. His offensive pleasantries would have been rather more than she could stomach. 'Two little church-goers!' that kind of thing.

'It is like a maze, these Mews,' Mary observed as they left the house. 'Please lead the way.' Jane took her into Blessington Street saying, 'This is the best way'.

As they walked silently along Jane was rather startled when her new friend said suddenly. 'How much do you know about Father Card?'

She could think of nothing to answer at first, but, noticing that her words had silenced Jane, more than anything else, Mary laughed.

'Sorry, my question might be interpreted in more ways than one. What I meant was that our Vicar's rôle as Priest of St Catherine and the Angels on Sundays is not where his duties end. He has a sort of school—an adults' school. Have you attended that?'

Jane had flushed, as Mary Chillingham had good-naturedly come to her assistance. Mary had a talent, it seemed, for making her look and feel like a little child. The misunderstanding of her question—such an idiotic misunderstanding; the embarrassed silence that it induced in her! What on earth could Mary's question have meant that should have embarrassed her? The clownish interpretation which Jane had admitted as a possible alternative was so utterly silly that she trembled as she strode along. Mary saw her tremble and understood. And Jane found this young woman, who was so much more mature than she was, looking at her. She was kindly providing this trembling woman with an issue from a silly-billy position.

'Yes,' said Mary. 'Father Card is, I believe, a rather remarkable man. He quite truly says that any average congregation is completely ignorant of what they are doing when they go to church. When they say what they *believe*, they do not understand what they are saying. Take God. We say we "believe", but we have no clear idea of what it is we believe. The God of the Muslims, for instance, is without attributes. In one sense that is more defined an entity than ours; to be without any attribute is to be a kind of Nothing. But our God, for the average churchgoer, is so hazy a Something, that the Great Blank of the Muslim has more definition. Well, Father Card offers us an enlightening dissentation on such subjects as that.'

Recognising that this girl knew so much more than she did, Jane felt insignificant. She was one of those averages spoken of.

'Have you attended?' Jane stammered.

'No. As I said, I have not been to these séances. But a friend of my mother's has told us all about it. I may say that my father, and a number of other people, disapprove. They object that, though they may not be very clever, all the same they do not require instruction . . . as to how to worship. I know one man who says this of Father Card: 'if Father C. attempts to teach me how to worship, I will give him a few simple lessons in how to preserve common sense against the encroachments of smartalec-ery. Some of them are very angry. They accuse him of teaching heresies, and one man, of attempting to introduce Buddhist doctrines into Christianity. During a sermon this fellow shouted out "This is not a Buddhist temple".'

Jane was so confused by the time they reached the Clergy House that she sincerely wished she had been on her way to a performance rather than to a party at Father Card's. She nearly said goodbye to Mary at the door.

'Be brave!' Mary whispered, for she easily detected signs of wilting in her over-tall companion. 'This is a very unorthodox shop. But imagine you are visiting his Grace of Canterbury.' Mary winked, and led the way in.

As soon as they were inside they found they were in a more or less bare spacious studio. It was full of people, standing and moving about. One of the curates, namely

Horrid, posted near the door, approached them smiling, and Mary presented the card, about which there had been such excitement in the church.

'Ah, Miss Chillingham. Delighted to see you. And who have we here?'

'This is Miss Greevey,' Mary announced. 'I was so bold as to invite Miss Greevey. We were having tea together.'

'I am sure your judgement is always superlatively good,' answered Horrid. 'Let us come and drive some of those ladies away from Father Card.'

The room was over full. It had once been rented as a Studio. It stood in the back garden of the Clergy House; and it was here that Father Card was engaged in disseminating heresy, Buddhism and other things when most honest folk had finished work for the day, or so some of his parishioners asserted.

Horrid cut his way through the somewhat adhesive material of the party, with a gay 'sorry', now and then. Father Card's head rose above those in his neighbourhood. There were four women in front of him, but he could be seen to be habited in a cassock, as were his curates, but his biretta grew upon the upper groove of his forehead, and he never failed to butt at it, as if it threatened to invade his face.

Horrid, with *his* party, stood obediently beneath the gaze of his principal, but clearly with no intention of displacing the two women already in possession of the Vicar's full attention.

'Is it true, Father, that Origen was a Buddhist converted to Christianity?' was the question being addressed to him by a very determined-looking woman.

'No, Mrs Sinclair, you have been misinformed,' Father Card told her firmly. 'At one time Buddhist tenets may have been found in his teaching—a very different thing.'

'Thank you, Father. But do you, yourself, believe . . .'

Father Card held up his hand appealingly, with a 'Madam, you wish to fasten on me . . .'

Horrid signalled to his chief, and spoke.

'Father Card, excuse me, I have two ladies here.'

'Ah, good evening, Miss Chillingham.'

Those who had been conversationally in possession of Father Card looked around at Miss Chillingham. Her great beauty at once convinced them that they were *de trop*. They melted away, with smiles and slightly significant nods of the head. Horrid and his two charges stepped briskly into the vacant space.

'Nature abhors a vacuum,' murmured Horrid. 'This is Miss Chillingham *and* Miss Greevey.'

'Excellent. And keep that lady with the green hat at a distance, will you?'

'It is very kind of you, Father Card, to allow us to speak to you,' said Mary. 'Jane Greevey, who is with me, is a great admirer of your work.'

Augustine Card recognised at once that this wonderfully attractive girl was, *par dessus le marché*, intelligent. This was not from anything she had said, of course, but her manner, and the calm self-reliant light from her eyes, instead of the self-consciousness which, as a rule, went with such looks, claimed first place. For such a woman to be able to think was as rare as to find a famous man, undominated by his fame.

Immediately Father Card came to life. The 'sleepwalking thinker', as he had been described by someone, awoke. The thrusting forward of the heavily wrinkled brow, as if sleepily, almost stupidly, searching for something, was transformed—so much so that Mary Chillingham wondered if the customary mask was, in fact, a carefully considered pose. The priest sighed almost familiarly.

'It is terribly stuffy here. There is hardly room for all these people. Please come to tea with us in the Clergy House . . . there we can have a quiet talk. This is rather like a terminus on a Bank Holiday!'

Mary said how much she would like to come to tea; and, looking in a large black diary, Father Card asked if she were free on Wednesday, that was in three days' time, and Mary thanked him with unaffected alacrity.

'I wonder if you are related to Sir Richard Chillingham— you look so like him?' he asked her, with a charming smile, and when she said he was her uncle, he exclaimed, 'I could have picked you out anywhere! The resemblance is remarkable. He is a great friend of my father's.'

At this Jane Greevey drifted away . . . this is almost a family party! she thought. Seeing a portrait of Cardinal Newman hanging on the wall she glided over towards it, and, after that, she noticed a little farther on another striking head. It was Wilberforce. From the noble head of the liberator, she passed to a German portrait of Lord Acton.

By this time Jane was a long way from her friend, whose aristocratic basis had now been established, and, seeing that there was a Sir Herbert Greevey, and that he was no connection at all of hers, she felt that she had better melt into the surrounding obscurity. She was not one of the Family.

Easily evading the watchful Horrid, near the door by which they had entered, Jane departed in a mood quite unlike that in which she had originally approached Mary Chillingham.

II

A Cup of Tea in a Cell

O n Wednesday afternoon, it was in Father Card's cell that Mary kept her appointment. He had been looking at a photograph when she came into the room, and, with a smile, he handed it to her. It was Chillingham Chase that had absorbed his attention, and among the familiar scenes there was Father Card, only younger and differently dressed. This was rather like a dream. She was instantly aware that the man she was now in front of had completely changed from what he had been before. It was as if in public he wore one face, and now he was alone— alone with her. They were alone.

This was very extraordinary. The only mask by which most people knew this unusual man had been dispensed with; and all the time she was there he remained as he must have appeared to intimates. For it was perfectly clear that the face she had always seen in public was one manufactured for his public life, one very rarely laid aside. By this time it was second nature, for it was rigidly adhered to; and, with the public face, went a public nature. Similarly, when he laid aside his official face, there was—quite intact—a private nature, which then, quite visibly, as it were, he summoned from some interior. And he did not trouble to conceal his relief at finding himself able to be his 'private' self. Whereas publicly he 'sleep-walked', as it had been remarked, when he was without his usual disguise, he seemed to come to life. Mary was amazed at the alteration. It was as if he had lifted a mask off his face.

'I hope you will not be offended if I say that you seem quite a different person when one sees you in your "cell"? I have a cell too—I call it a "den". A place inhabited by a wild beast! I shall be wondering now whether I change in so remarkable a way when I enter my den! Whether I become a wild beast.'

Father Card laughed—so natural a laugh that it seemed to surprise him himself. He flushed a little. He said 'I enter a cell—I do not call it a den. A cell is a place for a recluse, but, when I enter, that is the last sort of thing I feel or am.' He smiled again. 'I say, I believe I have changed more than I knew!' he said, rubbing his hand over his face. 'I hope I have not embarrassed you?'

'Almost alarmed me!' she said.

'I must not do that,' he spoke in a subdued tone. She looked up quickly to see if his face had changed. But it still was its free self. 'It is only when I encounter an intelligent person that I am inclined to lay aside the conventions I have assumed. That happens very rarely.'

She looked at him carefully.

'What do you mean by intelligence?' she enquired.

'Ah, I have a meaning of my own, I agree. Something *very much more than* intelligence . . . you, for instance, are sensible enough for a person to be able to be free.'

Mary looked uncomfortable, however.

'Why do you pay me these extraordinary compliments?' she asked. 'We scarcely know one another.'

'It was you,' he said, 'who began to ask me unconventional questions.'

Mary smiled. 'Of course it was,' she said. 'But your last compliment far outweighed that question of mine, didn't it?'

93

'Well, we'll leave it at that. . . . Now, Miss Chillingham, tell me whether religion really interests you. For I am of course, first and last, a religionist.'

Mary laughed. 'Well, as I am picked up and dropped down in my pew again . . .'

'Did I do that?' said Father Card. 'It was unintentional. We were both out of our depth, perhaps, and I climbed back into the Ark. I suppose that was it. And all my catechism meant was this. I—Father Card—am interested objectively about Christianity, in addition to being a professional of religion—you, in addition to being a churchgoing young woman, are *you* curious about the raft on which you find yourself—about the strange bearded gentleman—like the Bishop of Antioch—who, because he was a Christian, found himself looking into the eyes of a man-eating Bengal tiger?'

'. . . to be quite frank, no . . . early Christians . . .'

Father Card clapped his hands. 'Good . . . all that means is that you know nothing about it.'

'I expect so.' Mary laughed softly.

'When you first heard about the Differential Calculus . . .'

'. . . exactly,' answered—and interrupted Mary. 'Or the Milky Way, or anything boring-sounding like that . . .'

'Exactly. All I was about to suggest was that you should enrol in my nightly class, either as pupil or as teacher, which ever you preferred.'

Mary fanned herself, and blew a little. 'That is a very handsome offer. Yes, all right, I will enrol myself. Write me down as a full member. Send me the bill in due course.'

Father Card shook his head. 'Not a bit. I am sure that quite soon you will be interested. If you fail to be interested, then I will send in my bill. . . . Understand?' Father Card inscribed her name in a large book. 'As you say, the Milky Way sounds hideously dull. But billions of constellations must contain something.'

94

'If,' she said, 'one were enabled to examine it—an ants' nest . . .'

'. . . or such strange places as North or South America,' Father Card felt an ants' nest might not achieve interest.

At the door of his cell the Vicar gently and very slightly opened it and listened. Then he pushed it fully open, and said 'I will escort you down to the street door. Father Wimbush might be met with.'

By the time they had reached the front door Mary felt intoxicated, as if she and Father Card, during this brief interview, had been imbibing, instead of tea, some nameless, colourless, but insidious liquid. Looking back upon her visit from the front door Mary seemed to have been engaged in some kind of conflict, but, looked back on from farther off, she seemed to have been with some alarming magician for the first period; then came a second period, during which she felt she had been swimming against the tide, or she and the magician together.

Or, rather, she felt that first of all, the unusual, mysterious Vicar of St Catherine and the Angels had transformed himself—that this transformation had, in its turn, transformed her visit into something else, and she had ended as a member of some kind, in a large book of some sort.

As she was walking away through the cold evening, she remembered at once the photograph he had shown her, of Chillingham Chase, her uncle's north country estate. Father Card, then an Oxford undergraduate, was standing with a lady she did not know, and another lady, Lady Chillingham, her aunt. She had been somewhat embarrassed by the appearance of this photograph. There was a scene, used as background, with which she was extremely familiar, and, introduced into the middle of all this, the man with whom she was having tea, only ten years younger. What was she supposed to say?

95

'Ah, Chillingham Chase! And there are you!' Or should she say 'You as an undergraduate! How very interesting.' Or 'Hallo, I say, this is my aunt!' What she, in fact, had said, 'Ha, the old Chase! and you, looking a shade thinner!' That, apparently, had not been what was expected. Well, what the devil was she supposed to say?

As she moved along Ebury Square a young man looked at her very hard. She curled her lips a little, as if a photographer had said, 'Look pleasant, if you please'. This appeared to startle the young man. She walked quicker. And as she began to walk quicker she suddenly remembered that they had had no tea.

This was most extraordinary and bewildering—What had the Red Priest been up to? Why had he invited her to tea in his cell, and given her no tea? Had he been making a fool of her? This was all very puzzling, and just then (she had been walking very quickly) she reached home.

Established in her den, she flung herself down upon her divan, and decided to rename her den. In future it should be her cell.

At this point it may be said that when, eventually, she was next alone with Father Card, she reminded him that he had invited her to have tea in his cell, and they had not had tea. Father Card laughed: 'Fancy your remembering that,' he shouted. 'The fact is, I was so interested I forgot all about the tea. I apologise.'

12

Hambledon College

'I t is rather a bore, but after breakfast I must go over and see Hartnell. I shall leave you in command.' Augustine was speaking to Horrid. They had just begun their breakfast.

'Very well, sir. Will youth and beauty be around?' Horrid looked towards Father Wimbush, who was busily reading the newspaper.

'No, Horrid. She is away. You will have a peaceable morning. The new organist may turn up, but that will be quite simple. The organ has to be attended to—last week it made an abominable noise—did you notice it? But as we have no money for that at present, tell him to hold on for a week or two the best way he can, and I advise you to give him a cup of coffee and take him on at chess.'

'Right,' laughed Horrid.

When, after breakfast, Augustine stood just outside the Clergy House door, he hesitated, unwilling to engage a taxi-cab, but unable to think of a less expensive way of reaching Hambledon College. A taxi-cab, realising his difficulty, drove very slowly past him, and he called it sharply, as it began to recede.

Hambledon College was an old building, of a considerable size, improbably situated not far from Old Battersea House. Augustine found a kind of commissionaire in the central hall of this building, and was immediately guided to the offices of Dr Hartnell, where his friend sat with a secretary. He was rather boisterously greeted by Harty, particularly elated to find himself in possession, and in working order, so quickly.

'Your lawyer is a conjurer,' said he. 'He sent a clerk with me, and we went into a lecture room where a man was busily engaged dishing out higher mathematics, and I practically expelled him. The Man in Possession was away, and when he came back he was greatly surprised to find me installed in his study. It was great fun. But come through here, where it is more comfortable.'

Harty led the way into an inner office, which certainly had more social amenities, some quite comfortable chairs, and Augustine and his friend were soon very much at their ease.

'I don't know what I should have done without your lawyer,' said Hartnell, producing a syphon and a bottle of whisky. 'Let us have a snort.'

'What is this place?' Augustine asked him.

'You may well ask that—sunk in a Battersea slum. But we are quite well known. We have some two hundred men here all the time. Our diploma is of considerable use in applying for teaching or tutorial jobs. We cater for a number of people who want tutoring in this direction or that, and we have, downstairs, half a dozen large studios, each directed by an all-round man, who takes on half a dozen persons wanting to be trained up in some particular line. He goes from one to the other. That is the real guts of this place. Up here we provide people with a short general training, which fits them to some extent for all kinds of vocations. We are in fact phonies, as you no doubt realise. A man here can learn to pretend to know something he doesn't. We are quite efficient in a phoney way, and that does supply a want. The teaching staff are most of them university men, and we *could*, although of course we don't, supply a man with all the necessary information about life in Oxford or Cambridge, and we *could* arrange him to pass himself off as having been at one or other of the universities. We do not connive at these things, you understand, but we do privately think that a number of crooks pass through our hands.'

'How uproariously funny,' said Augustine, 'and how perfectly suited you are to the job of director.'

'For instance, we have a young man lecturing, quite near to where we are sitting, on *Writing*,' said Hartnell. 'He will take one of the people in front of him, and will ask him if he has had any experience in the last year or two which would make a book, or, less pretentiously, an article, or (somewhat altered and modified) a story. Now, supposing there is someone who believes that he has the material for a book, this fellow is quite competent to go into the matter with him, teach him how to handle it, and, if the man actually wants to produce a book, we will practically write it for him. We then, of course, would hand him over to one of the special men downstairs, one with the special aptitude required for that particular job—and day after day the fellow would be writing a book henceforth. We have about seven, I think it is, writing books,' laughed Hartnell. 'There is one of them who, I truly believe, will make a best-seller. This lecturer I was speaking about trains them very well in writing a detective story—or mystery story, as we prefer to call it—a novel, and a short story. He is very good, quite resourceful, and in fact I cannot understand what has brought him here. Why is he not making a fat living with his pen?'

'Could we go in and listen, Harty?' asked Augustine.

'Why yes,' Harty replied; 'let us go in there now. It is only a step.'

The lecture room appeared to be fairly full. They sat down, and Augustine studied the lecturer. He was an intelligent-looking, dark, youngish man. He said, 'The novel is a long time piece, but it must, from beginning to end, contain the same life impulse. You could not take a character out of it and place it in another novel, it could not adapt itself. These books are creations of a distinct order. If a figure receives a serious bite in the course of a novel, it can only be cured in the pages of that novel.

'This is claiming a great deal of vitality for the novel. But of course I am speaking of novels of a high order. If it is your intention to write this form of composition, drop into its veins on the first page a little ipecacuanha, so that the reader will be sick before he goes to sleep.'

There was a titter in the audience. The lecturer proceeded. 'This form of composition is, of course, to be avoided by beginners.'

The lecturer turned over his papers, and then he said 'We will now turn to the short story. This is a very dangerous form of composition. Because it is short, some people think it is easy. This is a fatal error.

'It is a good thing to have a model. The best model today is Ernest Hemingway. He only deals in the subject of action. But, at his best, he is very perfect. *The Killers* is an excellent example. A short story has the same requirements as an epigram. It is at its best when it is epigrammatic. It has to crack, like a whip. Twirl your story in the air, for as long as convenient, then pull yourself together, inject into it all the strength you have got, and make it *crack*.' The lecturer made this word explode in the lecture room. His voice took on a rather nasal sound.

'It is obviously only action stories that have to crack in this way. Miss Stein gave Hemingway a very good piece of advice. She told him to turn the gas tap down and down——

gently—gently—until it was *almost* out. This is an invaluable suggestion, especially to a writer inclined to throw himself about. It would be a very good thing to tell a proposed short story writer to creep into it on tiptoe, and only reveal himself there once he has really got into the space to be occupied.

'You cannot invest a small area too violently, or you will bang it to pieces. Or it is like getting into a boat; you have to be careful not to upset it. Balance yourself carefully and creep in. That is the best injunction for a short story.

'If you want to know how to twist your phrases into a soft drop, think of the modern method (in imitation of the Middle Ages) of putting cotton wool inside the curl— instead of the rigid effect obtained by a curling iron. Build your curl around cotton-wool—I mean in moulding your phrase. Now, once you are in the boat, do not rock it. Let your movements be cat-like, and develop the graces by means of the effort to balance. If you have a prose that dashes itself about, you will be sure, in the end, to meet with a mishap.

'Let us imagine ourselves writing a short story.

'First, the subject. A fishing expedition, in which one of the young men gets drowned. In a case of this kind you would have to get to know a variety of things. First about fish. Secondly, the technique of fishing. And, three, find out all that you could about drowning. The most important of these is the third. You cannot only write stories about jobs you are familiar with, accidents you have had yourself, or whatever it may be. But it is best to avoid subjects that entail too much discovery on your part.'

A member of the class put up his hand, and said 'Excuse me, but I was writing a short story the other day about a diver. I have never myself done any diving, do you think I should have chosen some other subject?'

'I certainly think,' answered the lecturer, 'that it would have been better to avoid so technical a subject.'

A small and delicate-looking man next wanted to know whether he was debarred from writing, say, a western story, because he could not himself live under very rough conditions.

'Oh no, sir,' answered the lecturer. 'I should imagine that most western stories were written by invalids.'

The questioner looked very relieved, as obviously he was intensely desirous of writing about cowboys.

The lecturer then proceeded. 'The recent questions I have been asked seem to make it necessary for me to take at once the subject of technicality. In the United States, if a person wishes to write about a locomotive driver, he will get himself engaged in some capacity which will give him the opportunity of watching the locomotive engineer at his work as much as possible. Hemingway, in his early life, was a reporter, and evidently spent a good deal of time reporting championship fights. In no other way could he have become so familiar with the fighter; and certainly he has written several of the best stories in existence about a man occupied, from his youth up, in that way. It is the tendency of writing in the United States to be highly technical—just as was that great journalist, Rudyard Kipling. (*Captains Courageous* could only be written in one way, namely by getting to know all about the life of these men.) If you took this principle far enough, a man would only be able to write his own life. I, for instance, am in the teaching profession; all my stories would be about lectures, like this, and all the circumstances of the life of the teacher.'

Someone was saying, 'Is not all fiction to some extent written in that way? I do not mean only such obvious cases as Conrad, or *Moby Dick*, but practically all books one can think of.'

The lecturer answered this question in the following way. 'There is no evidence that Shakespeare had had any experience of courts, or of kings and queens. But he did not have to, because his audience found quite acceptable an unreal dialogue, and behaviour that was completely unrealistic. Meredith, similarly, had no first-hand experience of the life he portrays. It is a question of what degree of realism the audience demands.'

Augustine, speaking quietly, said to Hartnell, 'I think that is a very good point, don't you. Harty? It is a question of the appetite for realism at the time.'

Hartnell nodded. 'Yes,' he hissed. 'Soames is one of my best teachers. Let us walk round, however, and see one or two of the others at work.'

Augustine and Hartnell rose and left the room. As soon as they were outside Hartnell said, 'I was very lucky to get that chap. His lectures are always full, and we have produced two or three detestable short-story writers, and I believe a novelist is coming along.'

'Good man!' said Augustine. 'Have you any parsons underweigh?'

'No, no. I have no budding bishops.' Hartnell shook his head. They entered a lecture room, where a full-blooded voice was calling, '*Faites vos jeux, Messieurs et Mesdames!*' It was a Frenchman giving examples of French delivery in comparison with English or German. Next he was shouting, '*Achtung!*', and then imitating a station porter at Victoria Station.

'The purpose of this is to show that French is an energetically spoken language, whereas English is a rather indolently spoken one,' said Hartnell.

They sat down, and the French lecturer continued to give examples of this same lack of emphasis of the English, from a Guards' Parade recorded for a gramophone, with the singing voices giving words of command which sound so attractive to the sightseer present at these parades. He went on to show how this energetic spirit could also be followed into everyday speech. He illustrated what he wished to say by ordinary sentences such as '*Ne vous donnez pas la peine, mademoiselle*'—'*Votre tactique était mal executée*'—'*Foutez-moi la paix, Monsieur le Président du Conseil.*'

This lecture was rather thinly attended. One of those present held up his arm, saying, '*Monsieur*'; afterwards he was heard to say 'Am I right in supposing that '*Foutez moi la paix*'' is unparliamentary?' To which the lecturer replied, '*Mais oui! on s'en sert de cette expression seulement si on est en colère.*'

The same man asked, 'Would one not be expelled from a conference if one expressed oneself in this way, Monsieur?'

'That would depend on who you were,' said the Frenchman—winking, Augustine thought.

'This is a very spirited representative of the French nation,' said Augustine to his friend.

'He speaks with great *sans-souci*,' answered Hartnell. 'Let us move on. I am proud of my Frenchman—*le professeur* Salendroit.'

They left the delightful Frenchman, and went downstairs. The first room they went into contained six students and one teacher. The teacher went from table to table, sitting down when he got there, and giving his fullest attention to what was offered him; then, in a longer or shorter time, he moved on. His movement was circular, so every student got to know about how long he would be before he came round again. In some cases the student was not ready for him, and then he passed on.

Hartnell and his friend moved around to the various rooms, in all of which the same method was observed. Hartnell's idea was that anyone who wanted to study almost any subject could find a teacher who would coach him in this way. They then returned to the office upstairs, where the secretary was waiting with a number of things to consult Hartnell about.

When he had dealt with them, he turned to Augustine and they went together into the inner office. They had another whisky and soda each, and Augustine complimented his friend on the Institution which he controlled. '*Vous avez une jolie boîte*, to put it in French,' Augustine said. '*Le professeur* Salendroit pleases me very much.'

'And how about Soames, my literary man? the one we first visited?' asked Hartnell. 'I wish you could make the acquaintance of some of my colleagues. I have not got at all a bad pick. Next, how about you, Augustine? Would you come along and give us a talk?'

'Certainly,' was the answer to that. 'In its way, Harty, you have a show here not as far removed from my intention as you think. When you come over to see me I will explain what I mean. I wish to develop a Christianity which takes us nearer to the Soviet than to the orthodox end. The Russians whom I invite to my Church, I feel very near to. But let us talk about that later on. Meanwhile let us think how much I can say to these young men of yours.'

They then discussed, for a short time, the kind of talk that Hartnell would like him to give. When the visitor took his leave shortly after this, Hartnell told him of a bus which would take him practically to his door. It ran every quarter of an hour. It was in this conveyance, No. 1001, that Augustine found his way home.

13

The Miniature Recommended

Later that day Augustine wrote out the talk he had arranged to give at Hambledon College the next morning. It was roughly written, to enable him to talk it rather than to read it. This was what was there when he had finished.

'Gentlemen,' it ran, 'I am very afraid that there will be few of you who share my beliefs. It is a terrible thought, but the majority of young Englishmen are without a religion. I do not think that this is the case anywhere else in Europe. And what I shall be talking about is Religion, for there is nothing else that I can address you about.

'I cannot understand your not being interested (which is what it amounts to) in God. As a clergyman I should be more popular if I cracked jokes and talked about nothing in particular—really attempting to prove to you that I am a bad priest. I am not that. When I inherited my church I tried to make it a living church. Most churches are places which a small number of people go round and sleep in for a short period every Sunday morning. The Vicar is a man who gives them a pi-jaw, during which period, whatever happens during the rest of the service, they sleep, some of them falling asleep on one another's shoulders. The first time I mounted the pulpit I made a sound like a pistol shot. It startled them so much that they remained, in the main, awake. I then gave them a talk about what a church is. I explained what God is, and frightened one or two of them. For God is, of course, a terrifying reality. I had thought that I knew all about God, and had Him in a pigeon hole. But I met Him at the corner of a street—He entered my mind with a bang, and nearly burst my head open. I had to explain that kind of experience to them.

'I am a Catholic—what is called an Anglo-Catholic. There is no difference between the one and the other. The Roman Catholic would not allow this identity. But everyone was a Roman Catholic here until a blackguardly king cut himself away from Rome, for principally mercenary ends. For years afterwards there was little difference in the service in our churches. And even now, in the better ordinary Anglican churches, there is a memory of Rome. We Anglo-Catholics like to remember as much as possible of Rome, draw near to what must have been the service in an English church at the time that wicked Monarch I have spoken of cut out for himself a kind of miserable independence.

'The main advantage of the Roman connection is that, had you lived in Rome, in the first or second Christian century, you would have been so near to Christ that your following of that Teacher would have been the same as a man turning to Communism in the 'twenties of this century. By this I mean a European: in Europe you are as near to the source of the new creed as if you had been in Rome at the time of the crucifixion.

'I am not here preaching Communism, but merely quoting it in order to give you a sense of the nearness of the presence of Our Lord in the century or two immediately succeeding His crucifixion. These two events had this similarity, that both appealed to the majority of men—to the slaves of the

Roman Empire and to the working population of our Empire. Some hope was given, in both cases, to these miserable populations—the idea being that the fatherless had been given a father, the hopeless a hope, the scorned and neglected a great friend.

'How could a mere teacher, a little man like Jesus, arrogate to himself this position of mesmeric guidance? That could only be done, evidently, with a great deal of magnetic power—which spread itself outwards throughout the Roman world, and then, of course, it reached outwards to living men in the whole of our world. Jesus himself must have been like a mesmerist, or like a magnet to the human spirit, which was attracted to it, and adhered to it in mesmeric embrace.

'Rome and Alexandria, and I suppose Antioch as well, were the big centres receiving the magnetic influence of this wonderful Individual; Rome is still with us, and that is why I think that a symbolic attachment to this old centre, where Christians had congregated for so many centuries, is a good thing.

'Well, I have stated fairly clearly what my religion is, and why it is so nearly Roman. But I have not come here to convert you to my religion, but for some rather different purpose. I want to tell you how I became, to some extent, a holy man. For I am not, of course, in the fullest sense a holy man even yet. There would have to be some great blow to make me that. In a French church I went through the Roman liturgy, and felt how wonderful it was, the pressure, as it were, of all these bodies, instinct with belief, all pressed together, straining towards God in one close society, a thing I had never felt in an English church. I wanted to join this compact mass and to offer my adherence to this mighty religion, that we Europeans have had for so long. This will seem to some of you a *crowd* experience, and not a direct enough contact, as it were, with God. But this I cannot go into at present. I just want to say that the presence —the pressure together—of a number of emotionally sympathetic believers, as one still finds in a Catholic society, is a very good way of beginning to understand this Faith, which is so far left behind in our country, in England.

'There were, at one time, masses of slaves camped in the desert, waiting for the end of the world, which they believed was likely to come at any moment. Such excitement as this can never be repeated. But we can train individuals to abase themselves before a Power which is so overwhelmingly great that they learn to think of themselves as a fly, or some small insect. The great thing is to make war on self conceit, and teach people to feel small, to feel so small that they have never experienced anything like it before. To feel small is the essence of religion. The world is full of people who feel big. They go about, swollen in some idea of their own personal importance. To get rid of that is the first step towards God. As an experiment, try to see how small you can feel. It is impossible to feel too tiny. You want to feel the ultimate next thing to nothingness—to zero.

'That is the principal difficulty in running a church. You cannot take people to God, strutting and puffing themselves out. You have to say to them "Two months ago, when we first started working together, I told you to reduce, to lose weight, in the way a fat person should. It was agreed that you would grow quite small. But I do not believe you have lost an ounce in weight or an inch in height. You still are pleased with yourself. How do you dare to pray in so bumptious a mood? You must make an effort to *reduce* spiritually. If you do not, we cannot communicate with one another."

'I slapped one man for evidences of pride that I saw in him. He was very indignant, and said he would write to the

Bishop. I told him to do so at once, and the Bishop wrote back to say that the tone of his letter was so inflated and full of pride that he could quite understand my gesture. I heard this through another member of the congregation, who came to me, and told me how this strange man wished to appeal over the head of the Bishop, I think to the Archbishop of Canterbury. I told my informant to say to him that the best thing he could do would be to denounce me to God.

'I have instituted in my church a kind of confessional, similar to the Roman Church. Some people kneel down in the simplest way and divulge what they consider to be their sinfulness. There are occasionally women who think that it would be proper, in their case, to ask them to sit. I tell them that I cannot talk to people who are seated. And some confess, as they call it, boastfully. I say to them, "You do not come here to boast of your misdeeds, but to try and think of any evils you have been guilty of—things to be ashamed of, you know. When I had done something I was ashamed of I wished to confess it and to explain to someone or other what a worm I was. I always succeeded in finding someone willing to listen to me. But that is not the person one wants," I say to him whose confession I am taking. "One wants someone who objects to hearing all the sins one has to tell of, but is willing to do so because it is his duty."

'I believe that confession is a great discipline. One soon finds that one is holding back one's most disgraceful acts or thoughts. In nine cases out of ten the confession is no confession at all, but a sly way of boasting. Then I say to the person confessing, "Look here, that is nothing to be ashamed of, that is something to be proud of. That is not what I want to hear. Cannot you think of something really disgraceful and abhorrent? No? Well, you had better go away, and not come near me again until you have something to be ashamed of."

'If a man comes to me and tells me something abominable that he has done or thought of doing I tell him that already half of his sin is disposed of by the fact of his being so truthful about it. The other half is what I begin to talk to him about.

'I sometimes say, in a confessional, "That is a sin that I committed myself only yesterday. Let us confess to one another."

'When I mount into the pulpit I am always aware that I am about to warn this congregation of sins which I frequently commit myself. I know what I am talking about. But I think that every preacher, before preaching, should humble himself, and ask forgiveness, if any of the things he is about to say refer really to himself.

'The prayer you will see me make, kneeling, before I go up into the pulpit, will be merely a discarding of all the grosser sins about which I am going to speak to my congregation, or an attempt to do so by means of prayer.'

At this point, were the words, *a pause*. Then the manuscript continued.

'In coming to speak to a number of young men, all of you studying to prepare yourselves to occupy some place in life, there is, I learn, one type of instruction which you do not receive: namely, religious instruction. This is a great oversight by my friend Dr Hartnell, who is, himself, a Doctor of Divinity. Far more important than any of the things you are studying is the adult study of the Christian religion. You all know a great many things, in some you are experts. But few of you know anything more about the religion of Western Europe during the last two millennia than the Lord's Prayer and a hazy acquaintance with the Old and New Testaments.

'I used the word *adult* above, and there is something which, when you reach adult life, you should know about religion—something that has meaning for adults. The worst of it is that people regard religion as something they learn at school or get to know about from their parents; and there is the end of the matter. What is learnt in that way is usually incredibly little. When adult life is reached all men and women should have a fresh course of training in religion, which they can accept or reject, but at least they should have an adult understanding of it. That is why I do think, in a College of this kind, there should be some section of it devoted to this, and to nothing else.

'I do not mean that you should learn as much theology as is known to Dr Hartnell. I do not mean that—although it would be a good thing if you did. I mean that an abbreviated course of study should be obligatory for everyone, a course arranged by a practical man like myself—for I am not a learned theologian, like your principal, but a man who has already a considerable experience of day-to-day Christianity. Let us think, then, into what kind of compartments one would divide up the teaching of our religion to an adult. First of all, one could go through the various kinds of gods that humanity has had; describe the nature of our God, contrasting him with Brahma, with the God of Islam, and so forth. Next one might turn to the proof of the existence of God. Then one might deal with prayer.

'All these things would be regarded in a new light, as they would concern an adult, rather than a child. These, and a few more compartments, would form a short series which everyone in the College would be bound to attend. I can imagine myself visiting the College shortly after this course had begun, and going into a lecture-room, and finding all the students sitting on the floor to acquire humility. Perhaps on Sundays in the afternoon, one of the lecture rooms would be used as a chapel. I, perhaps, or some other clergyman, would officiate, and a high standard of religious consciousness would ensue. When Hambledon College was founded by a Mr Salisbury the idea was, it seems, to supply a type of instruction that can only be obtained at universities: since universities are very expensive many men are unable to go there. At Hambledon College, for a small annual fee, men could acquire some of the mental habits of a university like Oxford or Cambridge.

'Since Salisbury's time this idea has been modified, because it is impossibly ambitious, it was thought. At present it is a place of adult education, obtainable for a small fee, with a strong tutorial compartment which is of great use to many people and not easy to find elsewhere. The introduction of a short course of religious training would exactly suit this place. People might even be prepared for ordination. The Church of England is sorely in need of energetic young men, as circumstances make it difficult at times to find suitable incumbents in country parishes, because of the fact that the church is unable to devote proper emoluments for the upkeep of country vicarages. But we could raise a corps of men here for whom money is not the first consideration, who in fact, prefer to live themselves very near the poverty line, as a Christian ideal. People with a strong missionary spirit might quite well, in this way, paradoxical as it might seem, discover an outlet for themselves in their course of training at Hambledon College.

'I was educated at Eton and Oxford, and I have had every opportunity of studying the power of snobbery in the Church. But I can assure you that snobbery is losing ground every day, and people who are timid, as they feel themselves threatened by the ogre of snobbery, have many means today of sidestepping this abominable dragon.

'This College was originally intended to supply an

alternative road for those blocked by the twin dragons of money and of snobbery. Although not needed as much as formerly, it would be a mistake for anyone to feel that the world is free of those dragons.

'Hambledon College will be more complete for the introduction of religious instruction of some sort. I hope, from today, this matter will be considered seriously by the men responsible for the quality of this unorthodox school.'

Father Card handed this rough draft to Father Horridge and asked him to have a look at it, and talk to him about it after dinner. This the redoubtable Horrid did, and what he said was very complimentary. He admired every utterance of his chief, and he described parts of this address as 'beautifully expressed'.

'I recognise,' Horrid said, 'several members of our congregation in those passages about the impossibility of finding a discreetly modulated nature, prepared to present itself in prayer to the Almighty God. We are used,' Father Horridge added, 'to the towering personalities who condescend to their spiritual leaders. So enormous a man physically as you, Augustine, must always be in a dilemma, with some Tom Thumb strutting about in front of you. I think your address to the college will puzzle some of them there. People are so ingrainedly accustomed to one form or another of conceit, that they must always be shocked at a suggestion that they should train themselves to be unassuming and the reverse of pretentious.'

Augustine said, 'You must not think that I have members of our congregation always in mind. There is no satire, really, on our flock in that paper I have just written.'

To which Horrid answered, 'I indeed hope that that may be the case.' He said this with a slight wink.

Augustine, as arranged, went to Hambledon College the

next morning and delivered his address amidst some excitement. Noticing how favourable the reception had been, he said, at the end of his talk, that he hoped some of the young men listening would pay a visit to his church, and he asked them to write down the address, and means of reaching it. From Hartnell he received a fee, which he considered far too large for what he had done. And Hartnell and he agreed that they should in future mutually assist one another. For instance there was to be, quite soon, a special occasion at St Catherine and the Angels, and Hartnell promised to be present, and to play any small part required of him. For the rest, they very cordially shook hands, and agreed to see each other as promptly as might be.

Augustine began to feel that it was magic, for the No. 1001 bus seemed to be waiting for him at the corner of the next street. He was easily transported to within the stone's throw of an urchin of the Clergy House.

14

Mary Alerted

When Mary returned from a long week-end in the country, she found three or four communications from the Clergy House of St Catherine and the Angels, all invitations of one kind or another. The following Sunday was to be a rather exciting one.

On Saturday, at eleven o'clock, she rang the Clergy House. It was Horrid who answered. He ran to inform Father Card. 'The A.1 Bloom of Youth is on the line,' he announced.

'Tell Miss Chillingham to transport herself here in a taxi-cab. Say to her nothing must count with her but this absolute command.'

Horrid spoke in an earnest voice to Mary, imploring her to comply.

On arrival, Mary was brought *en grande vitesse* to the Vicar's cell, Horrid paying the taxi. She found herself in the presence of seven men. Father Card indicated, very gently, a comfortable visitor's chair, near the farther end of a long desk covered with papers. Like a small jury, five men, whose faces were unfamiliar to her, sat beyond the table, in a portentous cluster.

'I was about to read a part of the address which I propose to deliver tomorrow, Miss Chillingham. I say to the congregation:

'Imagine yourselves a revolutionary, in Moscow, the autumn of 1917. A friend has asked you, urgently, to go round to see him. You pay this visit with a certain misgiving, you cannot say exactly why. When you enter your friend's room there is a revolver on his table. He sits behind the table while he is speaking to you. He explains to you a programme—the programme of the Party to which he belongs. It sounds to you, from the first word he speaks, a terrible, merciless outline of action, so terrifying that it makes your flesh creep, and you eye the sidearm which lies upon his table with growing misgivings. As I have told you the date, and the place, and that you were a revolutionary, I do not have to tell you that the policy this man was advocating was probably that of the Bolsheviki, and that you were what is called a Menshevik.

'As you sat there, your horror would grow. Now, my friends, change the date; change the time. Supposing that your friend were Jesus Christ, and that you had been asked to go and see him—suppose that he had unfolded a programme as desperate as that of the Bolsheviks. Supposing you sat there and trembled, and did not know what you were going to do when your friend asked you if you would adhere to this programme of his.

'Now, to take a further step. Let me say that the real, unvarnished programme of our Saviour differs very little from that of the Bolsheviks; that, if heard for the first time, in its full implications, it would sound simply like that. To the ordinary man it would be terrifying. He would attempt to escape from the room as rapidly as possible. Yet, my friends, what I have to say to you is really as intensely frightening as a Bolshevik programme. Jesus, properly understood, has just as desperate a message as had the man we conjured up, in the first instance, with the revolver on the table. The "Gentle Jesus, meek and mild," known to us as children, was absolutely misleading. So, when a Russian churchman comes to this church, there is nothing menacing about him except in the way that a Christian bishop would have been in, say, the second century A.D. In those early years of the church a Christian would have been an alarming person, in a sense. The air would be full of the odour of Martyrdom.

'Now, fellow Christians, let us take ourselves seriously today, just as if we had lived in the early years of the Church. Also, it would be as well to understand that the basis of Communism is Christianity. Christianity is alarming, no more, no less. Members of the congregation, I have, in the main, devoted this morning's service to thinking along those lines. It will have seemed very sensational in places. I could have made it much more so.'

Father Card turned to Mary Chillingham. 'Tomorrow's service, as this quotation from my sermon will have suggested to you, will be notable for the presence of three Russian priests—two of them Vicars, like myself. The church will be decorated with posters from the Soviet, photographs of religious services in Moscow; we are placing these in position today. We are dining the three priests this evening. One of them speaks fairly good English.

'Now, Miss Chillingham, there are many members of our congregation who do not understand what I shall be saying about Bolshevism. There are some who are hostile. It is our business to win over these people. There is nothing very terrifying about our congregation. I should be very obliged if you would face this throng, at the end of my address, hold up your hand, and declare yourself, in something like these words; "ladies and gentlemen, I follow Father Card wherever he leads us in this live Christianity." '

'I will do anything that will help,' Mary replied. ' "I follow Father Card" shall be the watchword.'

The five strangers remained grim, though not un-friendly.

'You are the only lady we are able to ask,' said the Vicar.

'How about Lady Metcalf?' interrupted the smiling Horridge.

'A surgeon's lady? We are speaking a different language.'

Horrid, cowed, bent his head.

'After you, Miss Chillingham, have played your part—and for various reasons which might offend susceptibilities, so I will not mention them, no one but yourself could ade-quately play this rôle—this very fanatical-looking young gentleman here' (and Father Card indicated one of the five strangers) 'will spring up on the other side of the church, and proclaim his allegiance in rather the same way. What is to occur afterwards will be decided in detail this evening, but these five youthful supporters of mine will, in any case, take care of the situation, if there is any unpleasantness. There may be something in my sermon that is objected to.'

'If you will allow me to say so, Father,' Mary ventured, 'in dealing with the English it must be remembered that if you say something too intelligent to them they are apt to take it as an insult.'

'I think that warning is admirable,' said the Vicar. 'I will hold in check the Highland side of my nature—you are perfectly right when you warn me to play it down. However, I may be permitted to crack up God? I do not have to apologise for Him?'

'I should say, sir, in all humility, that it is precisely there that you have to be most cautious and circumspect,' said Horrid.

'I think he might be right there, too,' Mary nodded her head as she spoke.

A chorus of young men applauded the advice of the beautiful young woman.

'The English have no humility,' said Horrid. 'They prefer to think of God as of a man, rather like themselves. Perhaps an inch taller, but no more.'

Mary smiled at the curate, encouragingly, and said herself: 'The English would willingly let God die. You are proposing something against our natural, our national bent.' She spoke with her eyes down.

'Children, Children!' Father Card reproached them. 'Where are you going to stop? Am I wasting my time, then, as Vicar of this church?'

'Fundamentally,' was Horrid's horrid answer. 'But we believe in you . . . we will follow you. We believe that you are taking the only course, for the Vicar of a real church, Father.' The curate's face was suddenly coloured with an uninhibited fervour. 'The more one thinks about it, the more worthwhile it seems. What else was our Saviour doing? He also did not have a very understanding people.'

'Yes, Father,' said Mary, 'it was going the wrong way about it, to fill your ears with all the reasons, the exquisitely good reasons, for doing nothing at all.'

'There are no good reasons for doing nothing,' clamoured one of the five young men, and the rest of them growled their agreement.

'I think that's beautifully said,' the Vicar gave it as his opinion, indicating his approval of the most vocal of the five.

'What is happening here?' It was the voice of Father Wimbush which filled the cell with something like a leer in sound.

'We are discussing the events we have planned for tomorrow,' Horrid replied.

Wimbush entered, and placed himself in a corner.

'We are arranging a sort of salvationist outburst,' said Horrid. 'Miss Chillingham, it is proposed, will leap up and announce that she will follow anywhere that the Vicar leads.'

'Shall I leap up?' Father Wimbush began, jocosely.

'No,' said Father Card severely, 'no. You will endeavour to behave yourself.' He turned towards Mary. 'I am afraid, Miss Chillingham, that we must break up now, and plan out in private the further details of tomorrow's performance. Between now and six o'clock this evening, when our Russian friends are supposed to make their appearance, we will be working away, until we get everything ship-shape.'

'What will my rôle be? Can I not be of any use?' asked Mary.

'Well, yours is quite a major rôle tomorrow. Will you come to the vestry about half an hour before the service begins? Have your statement ready!'

Mary rose. 'Very well. I make myself scarce till the morning.'

Father Card accompanied her down the stairs, and warmly shook the hand of his charming adherent.

15

A Special Service with Three Russian Priests

When Mary entered the vestry the next morning, there were three Russian faces, and, associated with the bearded faces, a hieratic costume, and all around these strange visitants the body of the choir. Father Card, already gowned, was conversing with one of the Russian priests; as he saw her, he apologised to the Russian, and hurried towards her.

'Thank you so much, Miss Chillingham, for turning up so early,' he said, as he engulfed her hand in his immense paw. 'We are staging this morning something with a specially emotional appeal. My sermon, a piece of which you have heard, may result in some disturbance; my idea about your getting up and making a favourable demonstration would be intended, of course, to meet a possible protest. For a young and extremely attractive person like yourself to be ranging herself on the side of the Vicar, would be of great use, even if there is no open opposition. I am especially providing an answer to the "Red Priest" nonsense. I have chosen the moment when three Russian priests are here for my counter-attack. You see the idea?'

'I am very willing to make the statement you suggested,' said Mary. 'I am quite ready actively to discourage any hostile demonstration. I am glad you have got a group of young men to do some shouting on your side.'

'I do not know how to express my gratitude,' said Father Card enthusiastically. 'One of these Russians, Father Athanasius, is able to speak English; he would be most tremendously comforted if you would say something nice to him—something like this; that it is splendid of him to come over to England, where it is so necessary to prove visibly that religion has not been stamped out in Russia.'

Father Card and Mary Chillingham went up to one of the Russians, who smiled very cordially at the beautiful young Englishwoman being presented to him. He began speaking in fairly good English. 'I speak to the English here today. I bring to them the good-will of the Russian people who kneel as they do in prayer to the same God.' Mary said to the Russian priest what Father Card had outlined for her; and he responded very genially.

The members of the adult choir were the interested witnesses of these international exchanges. Mary told Father Athanasius that she hoped he would have a pleasant experience during his stay in England, and as she moved away from the Russian group her departure was accompanied by very cordial glances on the part of the three priests.

Shortly Father Horridge (the Horrid of the Clergy House) accompanied her to her pew; and she saw the five young men she had met in Father Card's cell taking their places in another part of the church. The normal congregation was beginning to arrive. Mary examined it as she had not done before, wondering what effect her words would have on it, and analysing the faces of this audience, which was going to be submitted to a new ordeal. What would it say to itself, what would its reaction be, when a Russian priest mounted into the pulpit, and began speaking to it with a strong

Russian accent? And then the Vicar's sermon near the end of the service? The passage she had heard in the cell in the Clergy House was anything but reassuring. A certain section of the congregation would be sure to show some kind of hostility. Ah well, she had agreed to serve the Red Priest. And if he was being more red than usual that morning, she had agreed to play the part of a red member of the congregation.

She had not long to wait before the door of the vestry opened and what was, on this occasion, quite a considerable procession began filing in to the church. The highest in rank did not appear at the end of the procession, as was customary, but Father Card was the first to make his appearance, with the three Russian priests. After the opening prayers the Vicar made his way to the lectern.

'My friends,' he intoned. 'I have here with me three Russians, priests like myself. One of them can make himself understood in English. He has been so kind as to offer to speak to you. Listen to this Russian, friends.'

As Father Card stopped speaking Father Athanasius began mounting into the pulpit. He fixed his eyes on Mary.

'I cannot speak good English. But I can say to you—Oh, Love one Another. If you will love one another you will find God. Only God loves. If you love you will find him doing that too. Christianity is all about that. Imagine that Christ lives in the next apartment. Learn to love that neighbour. I am a Russian. We have many faults, but Russians have the secret of love. Try not to think ill of us, for we have God. We most of us unexpectedly found ourselves loving somebody. We found it was God. People laugh at us for finding God. They think it funny to love so much. "How Russian that is!" they say. Forgive the Russian, God has made him mad.'

Mary watched the mild and bearded face. The eyes that

looked out of it, she saw, were mad. Athanasias bowed his head, his lips moved, he clasped his hands in prayer. A flood of beautiful Russian words came from between his lips. The congregation was quite silent.

As if she were dreaming, Mary saw the Russian coming down out of the pulpit. At the same time she heard the organ deep notes which she could not recognise. She saw Father Card advance quickly towards Father Athanasias; he bent towards him, made the sign of the Cross, and said some rapid words; then he led him back to where he had been sitting. The music changed, and they were back in the usual morning service again.

But Mary could not stop thinking of the Russian, who had made a great impression on her. She went on thinking about him until the time came for the Vicar to mount into the pulpit. She found that he was beginning his address with the words he had spoken in his cell. The image of the violent Christ seemed to rise into the air and dominate the congregation. He had the slow movement of wading forwards, as if against a tide, through his strange imagery. A sound came from the three Russian priests. The one who had addressed the congregation was speaking vehemently to the other two.

'If we can love our neighbour, as Father Athanasius told you that we should, and if that was successful in the way he indicated, it would be a very violent experience. Imagine yourself suddenly encountering God for the first time. It would be like colliding with a locomotive. It would blind you and deafen you. If you found you began to love in this encounter it would not be something agreeable. Such love as that would be like dying. The impact of the Russian love is terrible. Do not confuse the idea of love with anything soft and gentle.

'If I could make you understand what I am talking about,

it would be like a clap of thunder in the vault of this church, or like the bursting of a bomb.'

There was sound of protest in the centre of the church, and this was followed by a rush of feet. Mary looked around, and saw that the interrupter was being borne towards the door of the church. The five young men were in action, and it was but a minute or two for the disturber to make his violent exit.

The voice of the Vicar rose above the other sounds in the church. 'Do not allow yourselves, my friends, to be distracted by the interruptions of a foolish man, who has been put out of the church. There is always some likelihood of a disturbance when one is engaged in a great task, just as a noisy crowd would collect if you tried to speak of God in the street. I have been called the Red Priest, because I took the hand of a Russian priest. And even in this church one cannot speak too seriously of what our purposes are here, without meeting opposition and obstruction.'

Mary Chillingham felt something like the rising of a storm wind when she rose to her feet, turned towards the congregation, lifted her arm in the air, and loosed her voice in a ringing appeal. 'Fellow members of this congregation, I wish to say that I, for one, follow Father Card wherever he leads. His teaching is a live Christianity. I prefer Christianity alive rather than dead.'

A strident voice, which later Mary was told was that of Doctor Hartnell, rose on the other side of the church; 'I would like to second the appeal of that lady, for I am one who also is a follower of the Vicar of this church.'

Simultaneously a commotion occurred, which Mary recognised as the voices of the five young men. She could not hear what they said, except that they wished to follow too.

In full diapason the organ burst forth as if to lead the

tumult, and the greater part of the congregation rose, and appeared to be making for the doors. Most of them moved quickly out into the street, their faces disturbed with the liveliest alarm, though here and there were grimaces of mirth. The black-coated sidesmen hurried after them, appealing to them not to desert the church. A crowd collected in the approaches outside, and mingled with those stampeding, making it appear a very much larger exodus than in reality it was. It became an uproar; for any pair precipitately leaving the church could be heard saying 'the Red Priest has outdone himself' or 'I will write to the Bishop about this performance' or 'I believed at one moment that I was having a nightmare'. Or the crowd, as it joined itself to the fleeing congregation: 'I saw several Russians', and 'Oh, did you' came in reply. Or one would hear, 'I heard one of them say that they have telephoned Scotland Yard'. Or, a member of the congregation having trodden on the foot of a member of the crowd, there were shouts of abuse, and fisticuffs.

Within the church there was a residue, fifty or sixty strong, of the original congregation, who showed no signs of intending to desert. A procession, led by the choir, one of them carrying the Cross, the adult members in their rather elaborately laced surplices, the women with mortar boards, the well-drilled contingent of choir-boys looking very excited, and shrilly singing their part in the processional hymn, the three Russian priests chanting in Russian, the curates and the Vicar bringing up the rear, the residual congregation following these—all this body of people issued processionally from the church by the south door, and wound in and out the streets on that side till they reached the studio behind the Clergy House. When they had entered—a gathering of about a hundred people, all of them singing, but not all with the same musical inspiration

—there was a considerable din. They had been followed by the crowd, who filled the short street outside.

The cacophony of song gradually subsided. The crowd in the street heard the loud intoning of the Blessing, followed by the deep Amens, sounding like a muted roar. They drifted back to the neighbourhood of Victoria, discussing as they went the events of the morning, arguing about the Red Priest and his habits, about the appearance of the Russians, and the songs they had heard.

Inside the studio the gathering, with more orderliness, broke up and dispersed. The members of the choir disrobed, and stacked their surplices on a table. The church bodyguard of the five young men escorted the Russian priests to the Clergy House, where they were staying, hospitably entertained by the Fathers of St Catherine and the Angels. The residual congregation found its way back to its places of origin, and, finally, Father Card had personally bade goodbye to each and all of those who had formed part of this ceremony. And the last person whose hand he shook was Mary Chillingham, who stepped into a taxi-cab to take her home, by no means the least moved of all these various people who had assisted at this very unusual church service.

16

The Ghastly Girl

There were six women there, mostly Jane Greevey's age. One, who was much younger, was disliked by Matilda. 'What induced your guardians to choose Ghastly, Monica?' she asked.

Monica Blunt wrinkled up her forehead and scowled at Matilda. 'I have no guardians. But my father, who is a widower, is assisted in some of his decisions by two women, and one of these was a Ghastly girl. It must have been that.'

'Becoming the head of Ghastly, must have been rather wonderful,' Matilda barked.

'It had its advantages, you know,' Monica answered, with a look of hatred.

Casterleigh, or 'Ghastly', as it was familiarly called, was an extremely fashionable school, a few miles from Canterborn. Women who had been there were known as 'Ghastly Girls', The Hon. Monica Blunt was an almost absurdly typical Ghastly Girl. She was now thirty-nine years old, but she said forty, because otherwise, she said, people would suspect her of being forty, and she preferred being thought forty-one or two, and having the forty question settled once and for all.

She was an untidy, tweedy woman, the one-time head-girl written all over her. Deep lines scored her forehead as she mobilised herself to get to her feet, or to answer what was the ablative absolute. If it was the latter she would begin by scratching her head, and saying 'Let me see! What is it?' She smelled kind of musty too, when not repelling everything, as well as insects, by an indecent odour of camphor. And she was hated by most females, first because she was on the right side of forty, next because she was an Honourable. The disagreeableness of having the luck to have a father a lord was a feature of this Ghastly Girl that was not lost on Matilda, more especially as her own pretensions were social. But above all what she could not tolerate in Monica was a quite admirable defensive equipment. Usually the daughters of lords would be slapped down if it came to a fight; but not so Lord Starwood's daughter! This seemingly sleepy old Ghastly Girl had a darting mind, which Matilda loathed.

Jane supplied her guests on Tuesday evenings with plenty of gin. They were a great success as weekly parties. For such a dull woman, said Matilda, it was a shocking advertisement for gin. She did not like saying she'd been to one of Jane's many parties, personally, and if you met her on the way to one of them she would say, 'I feel you have as good as caught me pouring myself out a drink of gin.'

When Mary Chillingham turned up at this middle-aged weekly cocktail party she was somewhat relieved to see her sister's ex-Ghastly Girl friend, and sank down beside her on the settee occupied by Monica. That Youth and Beauty should associate itself with Rank displeased this middle-class gathering of Jane's.

'Was Henry Chillingham your father?' Matilda was heard to say before long, to which Mary replied, 'No, my Uncle. Do you know him?'

Matilda, of course, knew the famous hunting baronet of the northern county from which she came, and she had ridden to hounds often enough, thanks to the wonderful assistance provided by Chillingham Chase. So it was unlikely that she should not have been aware of a beautiful young woman issuing from the Chase in the way that the pack hounds did.

The ex-Ghastly Girl looked in deeper thought than usual, until these social misunderstandings had been adjusted.

Mary Chillingham and her sister's Ghastly friend became engrossed in what was practically a private conversation. They were in the midst of a crowd of middle-class women, and recognised that they were in the same sort of situation as two Chinamen surrounded by Europeans—or two Ghastly Girls in the presence of a lot of girls belonging to less exalted schools. They dealt with what were purely private subjects for a little, and then the newcomer looked over towards Jane Greevey, and her hostess gazed back chillily.

'I must apologise,' said Mary. 'Monica is practically my half-sister.'

'I do not see any reason for an apology,' Jane answered. 'What kind of cocktail do you like? A Martini?'

Mary Chillingham had not understood that this was to be a party. When the Ghastly Girl prepared to go Mary did likewise, and a room full of more or less silent women watched their departure. Matilda expressed the feelings of the group by saying, 'Exit the Quality'. Although she usually occupied the rôle of Quality herself, this was a case in which she preferred to be the voice of those who remained behind.

'I think it will be agreed that Jane's effort to improve the tone of her Tuesday gatherings has not been a success. It is as if I had brought round the Duchess of Somerset.'

'Except, Matilda, the Duchess would have shown better breeding,' said one of the middle-aged, middle-class, middle-everything ladies.

There was a growl of assent at this. A half-dozen pairs of eyes shone with mobilised Middleness.

Jane was distressed at this upheaval. She replenished the glasses, with a smile where that was necessary, but with a real cold silence for Matilda.

The pair described as the Quality strode away together, the ex-Ghastly Girl with a brow deeply wrinkled.

'I was rather alarmed to find *you* . . .' Mary said.

'I was rather surprised to find *you* . . .' retorted the other.

With an 'I'll come along with you, and see if Alice is at home', Monica Blunt, on learning that Mary was homeward bound, came to the above decision.

But as her sister had gone out to dinner and bridge, as usual, Mary thought she could do worse than spend the rest of the evening with Monica, so she invited this odd friend of Alice's up to her den. Mary mixed a cocktail for her visitor, and took one herself.

'You are comfortable here, Mary,' Monica said, looking round.

'It's poky, but I am free here,' Mary answered. ' "A room of one's own" is a great thing, as Virginia Wolfe said.'

'I do so agree with Virginia Wolfe,' Monica replied. 'There is a philosophy for women, isn't there? The "room of one's own" is a female dogma.'

'That is not a dogma very popular in this house,' Mary said.

'No?' The Ghastly Girl seemed to squint.

'Not really,' Mary told her. 'My sister has a special position here. She has her own money, left her by Douglas. So she is given a corner of the house all to herself. She automatically gets rooms of her own. I am different. I am the poor brat of the family. Hence this attic.'

Monica raised her eyebrows quizzically, and seemed to be

pinching in her nostrils. She was apparently digesting Mary's rather powerful cocktail. 'Hardly that of a brat' was what she thought.

'You probably know what the situation is regarding me,' Mary said. 'I mean that, in the ordinary course of things, Alice would tell you a bit about her young sister. You probably know how Mother badgers me to marry a young Grenadier, Arthur Wootton. But he is a mere baby. Her Majesty's Foot Guards are for me a dull subject.'

'I'd rather have a soldier than some sort of man I could mention,' said Monica; 'but I think I should prefer kilts to bearskins.'

'You prefer the sound of 'The Flowers of the Forest' to the 'British Grenadiers'? The distinction is illusory, and I come from the prosaic side of the Border.'

The Ghastly face was deeply furrowed, for Monica understood that momentous issues were being touched on by the sister of one of her greatest friends.

'It is very easy to see,' she stated, 'why your mother prefers a Grenadier to something you might like better. For, to begin with, your father, and two uncles, and innumerable ancestors, have had as their profession the military career.'

'I knew you would say that,' Mary replied.

'Your mother's reasoning would not stop there. In squaring up to her maternal problems, she would encourage her mind to stray over the alternatives to a career of Arms. She would pass in review a number of careers, none of which would be quite so respectable, if they were all more prosperous. She would see, first, a figure in a full-bottomed wig, with a mouth full of big words, vilifying and blackening a better man than himself for a substantial fee. Then she would see an equally verbose person, who might pick up a knighthood in the blood and thunder behind the footlights. She would weigh in the palm of her hand a peer of the Church; she would survey the medico, and fancy herself as the mother-in-law of a sea-captain, get a nautical whiff or two, stick a telescope to her glass eye; imagine the new member of her family thinking nothing of throwing a bridge over Niagara, or sticking a tunnel under the Volga . . .'

Mary's eyes grew bigger and bigger, and now she burst into an explosive laugh. 'Butcher, or baker, or candlestick maker,' she cried.

'Ah, no soldier's wife would think of those as an alternative. I have not failed to marry,' said Monica, 'because of my homely face or my thick ankles, but because of my mind. I have not a marrying mind. But in your case, Mary, your person is so terrifically marriageable that *in spite of your mind* you will go to bed with someone.' Monica gave the laugh of the Ghastly Girl.

'I envy you, I wish I had an unmarriageable mind. I am not like that; but I do not marry easily. My mind cannot marry with a boy of ten.'

Monica visibly pondered. 'You are twenty-seven, am I right?' Mary nodded. 'Most Englishmen are very immature. They grow up sometimes at sixty.'

'I can't marry an elder. I should frighten him.' Mary rolled about as she laughed, making her eyes large and 'frightening'.

'You need not make big eyes: the terror of the sexagenarian needs no demonstrating,' Monica told her. 'You might frighten me, if I were a man, at a much tenderer age than sixty.'

'Now you are being horrid,' Mary laughed. 'My problem will be, according to you, not to scare the wits out of my man!'

'I didn't say that,' Monica expostulated. 'It would be your

high percentage of sexuality that would cause the man to be afraid.'

The ex-Ghastly Girl looked at once mischievous and apologetic.

The apology had the effect of deepening the offence. The reaction was 'oh, that needed an apology? It must have been worse than it had seemed to me.' This technique Mary encountered for the first time. She also noticed that, had *she* been responsible for the remark, Monica would have been deeply offended, for the ex-Ghastly Girl was unlovely, to put it at the mildest. To say that a man who found himself in bed with Monica would be frightened would be strictly true; if the same remark were addressed to Mary, it would be so obviously untrue as not to make it offensive. Yet it would leave a strange aftertaste, especially if it came from someone positively ugly. What Mary reflected, immediately afterward, was that this rather distorted female (because of sedentary habits) was far more sensitive about her appearance than Mary would have supposed. All her subsequent experience of this close friend of her sister's confirmed this notion. She must, when young, have been pretty, or had pretensions. Mary memorised a question to her sister, clearing up this point.

But Mary had now become crouched and lined like her guest. At last she said something that startled the brooding Monica.

'I know you are considerably older than I am. I wonder if I might ask you . . . oh, it is rather a curious question. I am twenty-seven, which is not old, I know. At my age, did you feel yourself rapidly ageing? It is very morbid, isn't it?'

A Ghastly Girl, Monica realised, must be expected to have rather curious sensations. Without speaking, she surveyed the astonishingly beautiful young woman, crouched there before her. To possess all that desirableness like that might result, she reflected, in a dread of its leaving her. A young woman might develop a terrible fear: she might come to feel that time was slipping away unnaturally quickly.

'No, Mary,' said Monica. 'No sensations of that kind ever visited me. But then I never possessed such a wealth of beauty as you. If I had I can well imagine myself dreading the time coming when I should no longer have it. That sensation might develop into a morbid state of mind. I think you must blame your extraordinary good looks. You are unusually beautiful, if you do not object to my pointing that out. Such things only last for a very short time. This puts a woman in a very special position. It is like the possession of one of those wonderful voices, like Kathleen Ferrier's. I always pity a very beautiful woman, much more than I grieve for the opposite of that. A hag has no farther to drop, while, with beauty, one is conscious of the abyss.'

This seemed to Mary an unnecessarily severe snub. 'I was not discussing with you what you are so good as to term my *beauty*,' she said.

'I thought, Mary, you asked me whether, at your age, I had terrible sensations of time's flight?'

Hunched, with her hands clutching her right knee, with her forehead a bed of wrinkles, the scholar-girl watched her.

Mary threw up her beautiful face, and laughed. 'I did not mean by that question to call down on my head . . .'

'Of course not, Mary. But one thing leads to another.'

'Listen, I am exercised about the problem of my marriage. Alice must have spoken to you about it. My youth and my . . . beauty . . .'

'One thing,' Monica repeated, 'leads to another.'

'Okay!' Mary shouted. 'I wonder! It isn't true—but I give up.'

'These conversations don't mean anything,' said Monica. 'Do not let us argue bitterly.'

'Right,' Mary answered. 'Let us discuss my marriage, then.'

She went over to her piano. She announced 'Shas-ta-koi-vitch.' She then proceeded to play without great skill. Monica watched her approvingly. When Mary had finished playing the piece by the Soviet composer she paused, and gazed, enigmatically, Monica thought, at her visitor for a few moments. Then she turned to the piano again, and, to her surprise, Monica heard her playing 'Sheep may safely graze', Bach's famous choral prelude.

When Mary had left the piano and returned to her large chair, the two women smiled at one another.

'There was, I suppose, some symbolism in your playing,' Monica said. 'I shall understand in due course, I daresay.' And her screwed-up eyes accomplished a kind of wink.

'I proposed that we should discuss the question of my marriage, but I began, I fear, too enigmatically.'

'Well, Mary, you have left me with a Cupid in urgent flight between Moscow and Bethlehem.'

'Or put it the other way round! Then you have an aerial movement from Bethlehem to Moscow.'

17

To Hell with the Earl of Ames

The Sunday that followed was made memorable by the visit to an English church of a dignitary of the Greek Church. Actually this ecclesiastic was equivalent in rank to an Anglican dean, and he officiated in one of the few churches that are allowed to conduct services in Moscow.

Arthur had accompanied Mary to church that Sunday. He was in uniform, and Mary and this young Guards officer made a deep impression in a certain quarter, as the Russian visitor did on the congregation.

The organ filled the expectant worshippers with emotion as the music of the Russian liturgy assailed their ears. And from the vestry emerged the usual procession, moving to the rhythms of this exotic music, headed by the Russian cleric. A medium-sized, bearded figure passed before the irreverent eyes of the young officer and Mary Chillingham, and, at his side, Augustine Card. The Russian cleric seemed to glide along, nodding his head, as if accompanying the familiar music provided by the organ. The expression of his face was certainly not conventionally devout. His eyes were shining, as if the mind were beneath the stimulus of some queer experience.

'I believe the fellow may break into a dance at any moment,' whispered her companion to Mary.

Mary's feelings about the Russian priest had been very well expressed by Arthur, but she gave him a hoarsely whispered answer. 'If you ever get as far as Heaven, Arthur, you will be delivering yourself of schoolboy jests about the most eminent Angels.'

'Either that fellow's been drinking, or he has a screw loose,' Arthur persisted, in a voice no longer whispered.

The Russian did not dance, but as soon as he had found a seat his nods became more and more emphatic, and his geniality grew into an unmistakable smile. His lips moved incessantly, but no one would care to bet that unseemly sentences did not form part of his soliloquy.

'Our Russian friend has had a deplorably boisterous crossing from Helsinki,' Father Card announced. 'In spite of the fact that his asthma must have made this extraordinarily painful, he puts so brave a face on it that I would go so far as to say that he almost faces it with a smile.'

'Indeed he does, sir,' came from the young officer, in anything but a whisper. Mary rose and hurried out of the church, followed by her military cavalier.

When Arthur got level with her, both of them tearing along, 'I don't know if I shall have any breath left,' he said, 'when my apologies have got under way. . . .'

'What are you going to apologise for?' asked Mary.

'You left the church very abruptly, after my facetious exchange with the Vicar. . . .' Arthur suggested.

'I thought the Russian was going to prove too much for you; when I took you to church I did not foresee that your fifteen-year-old sense of fun would find so irresistible a stimulus.'

'My mirth was inexcusable,' Arthur said. 'I do hope you will overlook my misbehaviour, and walk a little less fast.'

'I did not ask you to walk in step with me,' said Mary, quickening her pace.

'No? I hope we don't run into a church parade of Her Majesty's Foot Guards.'

'If I alarm you by my speed, it would be all right if you dropped behind,' said Mary, if anything redoubling her speed.

'I can't be disposed of so easily,' said Arthur, his shoes clanging along beside her.

As she wheeled round into Ebury Square, Mary shouted, 'You force me to say that I have never been obliged to walk so quickly.'

Whizzing around to draw level with her, Arthur cried, 'nor have I!'

Facing the spacious pavements of Ebury Square, he said, 'Will you marry me, Mary?'

'Never,' answered Mary. 'I should never be able to escape from you, however quickly I walked.'

'Is that final?' he asked.

'Absolutely decisive,' she replied. 'You have worn me out.' Mary stopped. 'It is a strange question with which to finish a steeplechase. But I do insist that, at this point, we part.'

Mary and Arthur were standing facing one another. To propose marriage was usually a preliminary to an adieu, but it was not usually such hard work.

'I just want a few words, Mary, before I march out of your life for ever, if that is really what you want me to do.'

'Speak, Arthur, I will listen to your idle words,' Mary replied.

'Why do you treat me so rudely, Mary?'

'Because,' answered Mary, 'I have a contempt for you; when I pass an hour or two with you I am so deeply bored that I cannot see why you think it worth while to come smelling round this particular *jeune fille en fleur*.' Mary gazed sternly into the little round blue eyes in front of her.

'I don't mind you feeling a contempt for me, though I think you become rather coarse sometimes.' Arthur stood very erect, and gazed back bravely at his true-love. 'I am your slave, and all I have hoped was that in due course you might get tired of insulting me, and that you might in the long run consent to have me as a husband.'

'I am sure, Arthur, that you are a good soldier, and I approve of that. But what on earth has that got to do with getting into bed with a man for ever and ever?' Mary continued to gaze.

'Excuse my French accent, but *l'appétit vient en mangeant*,' said Arthur, reddening a little bit at his schoolboy French.

'No aphorism is so shallow and false,' Mary replied, tapping her foot. 'The appetite really does not do what you think.'

'It does not? I have been deceived. But let me pass on to something I am more sure about. The majority of marriages are not love-matches, are they? Are you quite sure you will always wish to be so unlike practically everyone else? I know that it sounds horribly vulgar, but with me you would probably be a Countess, before too long, otherwise I should never have had the impudence to approach you.' Arthur felt very dubious about the efficacy of this particular remark.

'Now, if you were sure of making me a Duchess,' Mary said, 'I might waver; but the other thing does not shift me the eighth of an inch. So we can get off that topic.'

Arthur had become very white. 'Well, I have no money to speak of . . .'

'I hope I have persuaded you,' said Mary, with a bright smile, 'that you had better pay your court to some little fool of a girl who can join you in your nursery, one who would be very thrilled at the idea of being a Countess, perhaps.'

Arthur drew himself up slightly, saluted, turned on his heel, and marched away. Mary watched him go for a minute or two. Then she clicked her heels slightly, turned about, and marched the length of Ebury Square.

As soon as she was in her own very private room, Mary wrote a humble missive to Augustine (as she now referred to the clergyman in her thinking): 'Dear Father Card. I was deeply angered by the misbehaviour in church this morning of the young man I was so unwise as to allow to accompany me. I most abjectly apologise, Father: and it will be the last time I shall run the risk of allowing this young boor to disgrace me.'

'The Red Priest at it Again' was the headline which, in one of the more aggressive of the daily papers, headed a censorious column the next morning.

'Cannot our Bishops restrain the Clergy in their dioceses from advertising themselves in this disgraceful way?' the protest began. And a large photograph, on the same page, showed Canon Card's son conversing with 'A Moscow priest who has sold out to Communism'. And then—'In St Catherine and the Angels this Red visitor sits grinning to himself. An officer in the congregation insults the vicar.'

All this, in Monday's newspapers, was alarming enough for Mary Chillingham. But she had to support little or no interference from the direction of her sister, and her father confined himself to ironical reference to her church, and the regular scandals that it could be depended on to 'keep us supplied with'. With his left eyebrow raised, he enquired 'what information Mary was prepared to furnish him with in regard to the latest "rumpus" at St Catherine and the Angels'. But Mary's mother, returning from a week-end in the country at about twelve o'clock on Tuesday morning, arrived with her mind inflamed from reading, in the course of the train journey, an article supplementing what the Monday edition had provided by way of information about the happenings in the church of the Red Priest.

This was an account, allegedly by 'One of the Congregation', of the real innards of Sunday's disturbance, arising out of the Red Priest's introducing a Russian cleric to his flock.

A beautiful young society girl was said to be the real storm centre. She had gone to church with a young Grenadier subaltern, by name Arthur Wootton, a nephew of the Earl of Ames. In response to an announcement from Father Card, who spoke in a complimentary way of this Russian guest, the young officer make a remark which was interpreted as offensive by many of those present. Immediately afterwards Miss Chillingham left the church. She was followed by the young Guards officer, who was seen to approach her in the street outside. But she apparently refused to accept his apology, or whatever it was, and the two rather violently separated.

'By all those going to this church with any regularity, as I have done for some years,' said the writer of this article, 'the reactions of the prominent members of the congregation to the eccentricities of Father Card have been closely followed. It was noticed that, as a consequence of the expulsion of a noble lord, for long associated with St Catherine and the Angels, by Father Card personally, General Chillingham and his family were no longer to be seen there, except for his daughter Mary. It was therefore to be assumed that this beautiful young lady differed from the rest of her family in continuing to support the young vicar, Father Card, popularly known as the Red Priest.

'All that an independent observer of these rather sensational events can deduce is that the young officer did not share the advanced views of Miss Chillingham whom he had accompanied to the church, and had expressed his disapproval. Farther than this it is impossible to go. One must await events.'

Mary read this article as well as her mother. Immediately afterwards she telephoned the Clergy House. She asked Father Card if he had seen the article. The Vicar had not seen it; with great affability he agreed to receive her in the course of the morning.

When she arrived at the Clergy House Mary was introduced at once into the 'cell' of Father Card. As on former occasions of her finding herself alone with him in his 'cell' she felt that Father Card had dispensed with his public mask. His still youthful face wore, in public, those deep furrows on the brow. Now they were totally absent.

He leant towards her, with an air of gentle intimacy, and in what he said he seemed quite unaffected. He read the article, and then looked up at her with a smile.

'Do you know who wrote this article?' he enquired.

Mary shook her head.

'If I knew who she was,' he said, 'I would send one of my curates round to have a talk with her. It is a woman, I imagine.'

'That is the impression it made on me,' she agreed.

'I would not call it *very* unfriendly,' he said.

'You mean as regards yourself,' Mary observed.

'Well, yes,' he said. 'And you, of course.'

'You do understand, Father Card, don't you, that the views on the Russian question of that young man who came with me to the church are not shared by me,' Mary seemed anxious to be reassured.

Father Card's laughter dispelled her anxiety.

'Lebedievitch is compromising sometimes,' he said. 'About his ridiculous jocosity your friend was quite correct.

144

He tipples; and that causes him to look quite merry at moments when people expect him to be decorous and properly solemn. He arrived here quite tipsy. He brought me complimentary messages from Marshal Voroshilov. If anyone overheard us at Victoria it will tend to confirm my reputation as a Red Priest!' The Father was exquisitely amused. 'Lebedievitch spent several years in Paris, and he speaks French very fluently. He can be quite funny sometimes.'

'Does he treat the Russian régime as a . . . ?'

Father Card waved his forefinger from side to side to express a negative. 'No, no,' he said. 'The only time that he is quite serious is when he is talking about Communism. *That* is a very serious subject. His life depends on it.' Card laughed.

'He is not a Communist?' Mary asked.

'I have no reason to believe that he is not one. He does genuinely succeed in combining Communism with Christianity. In fact he insists that they are one and the same thing. Lebedievitch, although he is embarrassingly indiscreet, is a religious man. He reminds me of one or two of those wonderful characters in Dostoievsky.'

'I know the men you mean.' Mary nodded.

'All the same,' Father Card said, 'I wish I could persuade him to play his part a little more carefully in church. With all the gems and silks he wears he cannot afford to smile so broadly at jokes that occur to him.'

Father Card was treating her as an intimate, although they had met so short a time ago. He had spoken, on the last occasion they were together, of her 'intelligence'. It was as if, without explaining this, he paid her the great compliment of speaking to her without any of the usual civilised dissimulations, because he recognised in her an intellectual equal. Mary was especially delighted. From this moment she began to look forward to these intimate conversations with

Father Card, conducted in the Father's cell with this divine levity.

When she felt she should return to cope with her mother she bade him goodbye, with an understanding that they would meet again before long. 'Come and see me again, soon, you will always be welcome,' he said, as he shook her hand, 'and let us consult. Tell me if you find out who wrote the article.'

When Mary reached her home her mother was waiting for her.

'Let us go to your den, Mary,' she said, a full-sized threat in her voice.

As soon as they were alone, Mrs Chillingham turned round and faced Mary, saying, 'What on earth have you been up to now, Mary!' She flourished a little the paper in which the article was to be found, regarding the part her daughter had played in the church scandal.

'Some obliging writer in that beastly paper has so fully informed you of my doings that what is the use in consulting me about it?' Mary flung herself down as usual on her small divan, and lighted a cigarette.

'May I take this as a fairly accurate outline of what has been happening during my absence?' asked her mother.

'How could that be *accurate*, Mother?' Mary enquired. 'But it is a caricatural account of certain events in which I played a part, though not quite so absurd a one as you see so impudently set forth in that article.'

'Have you broken your engagement with Arthur?'

'As that engagement was a figment of your imagination, Mother, how could I possibly terminate it?'

'As you know quite well, Arthur Wootton has regarded himself as engaged for a long time. Do you repudiate it —openly, I mean?' Mrs Chillingham actually glared at her daughter.

Mary laughed. 'We apparently live totally distinct lives, my dear Mother. In your private life Arthur Wootton and I have, it seems, been engaged to be married for quite a long time. Arthur has never seriously proposed marriage to me, or anything of that kind. Where do you get these notions from?'

'What the entire family accepted as a fact, then, had no reality?' Mary's mother demanded.

'Of course it had not. It amused you to believe it, my dear Mother.'

'Do you think to go about with a young man, like that . . .'

'I go about with Mister Bestens-Corbett.'

'That is like going about with your father,' the mother answered.

'Only because, if I say "Kierkegaard" to Hughie, he knows what I mean, whereas Arthur is not sure if it means a Tourist Agency or a brand of tea.'

'You have behaved very badly, haven't you, Mary?' Mrs Chillingham declared.

'I have done nothing of the kind,' was Mary's reply. 'But if you want me to pack up and go and live elsewhere I will be delighted.' Mary, at this, watched her mother's reactions.

'We are not the only people who will read this article.' Mary's mother tapped the paper, still in her hands. 'Arthur is the favourite nephew of the Earl of Ames. Some kind friend will show this article to the earl.'

'To hell with the Earl of Ames,' Mary exclaimed.

At this Mrs. Chillingham abruptly left the room.

18

A Stone-Age Man

B efore she left the Clergy House Mary had had handed to her a slender book. When she was alone in her den she pulled it out of her pocket. The title was *Living with a Man-eating Man.*

As Augustine had placed this in her hands, he had said, 'Did you know I am like this?'

She sat down, deciding to discover at once what he was talking about.

This was a small book, or pamphlet, of twenty or thirty pages. She stretched out and began perusing this document at once. Before she had finished, she answered, to herself, Augustine's question in handing it to her. The answer was 'Yes'.

'I lived for three years with a man-eating man—for what else is a "boxer"? This was a champion boxer, which makes the issue more clear-cut, more interesting. Boxing is hypocritically called "The Art of Self Defence". That is what the English call it. What it really is, is the art of killing with the gloves on. The fighting spirit in a man aims at something more drastic than "tapping the claret".

'The number of people who occupy themselves in public fighting is very limited. The number of true fighting men among these is fewer still. In fact, the trouble about the English boxer, of the Billy Wells type, in this century, has been that he has not been a really fighting man, but merely a boxer. The character of boxing in the United States has been quite different from this. The glass chins and soft hearts of the Englishmen were a constant source of amusement to the far tougher American critics.

'One has always wondered what it was persuaded these English heavy-weights ever to take up boxing professionally. They obviously misunderstood what boxing is, or what lies behind it. The negro never is mistaken about this question of what lies behind putting gloves on, and hammering away at another man's face. The gentleman's sword and pistol, used in duels to the death, have disappeared. All the instincts that once looked for an outlet in these weapons, in a cruder and rougher way are concealed behind the mask of the game of boxing. A man who devotes himself to this game is liable to be a killer in disguise. That is all that I am saying—a proletarian Killer.

'Angus Coin is the name of the man I shared rooms with during my university days at Oxford. I would not myself have chosen such a house-mate. It was a matter of convenience. I was there when he came up from Eton, with the most beautiful manners, and outwardly he did not suggest anything more serious than the sporting instincts of the gentleman. It was only a little later that I found that Coin had been, at school, a boxing champion, and that now that he had reached the University he had decided to make boxing his principal care. Within two months of the time we settled down in our rooms he had knocked out a couple of men, and was reported to be on the way to becoming a boxing Blue.

'He did not much like the company of other athletes with a taste for boxing; and from the start he seemed to approve of my society. So we saw a good deal of one another, more, I must say, than was agreeable to me.

'The man I am speaking to you about had the whitest skin I have ever seen on any man—when in the ring he was, with his shock of light hair, the living Blond Beast idolised by Nietzsche. When he fought, his blue eyes blazed, and his great arms whirled—as I have seen them do in a street fight —the perfect Goth, inspired by the Norse Gods.

'This Norse giant, this perfect type of a Stone-Age Cave Man was also a Dunce, he took to book learning with difficulty. I discovered him in our rooms at Oxford, struggling over the simplest mathematical problem. It was there that I felt, as I watched him crouched over his books agonised, that I had a man from one of the backward epochs of humanity in my rooms with me. I helped him with the simplest equations, took him, step by lubberly step, through the most childish Latin exercises.

'In his last months at Oxford he advanced fiercely into the realm of Divinity, uttering barbarous cries which horrified me. But for some mysterious reason, he felt at home there! He developed the most horrific theories. I had never felt afraid before, in his company. But when I became a Doctor of Divinity, I was frankly terrified. He locked me up in my room, on one occasion, and kept me locked up for a day until I agreed to praise the beauties of the most horrible heresy.

'This essay is the result of that three years' association with a man who was a boxer, and nothing but a boxer—an always victorious one. He led me to think a great deal about the meaning of this sport. And these are the conclusions I arrived at.

'Let me begin by comparing—

1. The Fighting Cock.
2. The Roman Gladiator.
3. The Fighting Man of Today.

'In essentials these three classes of fighting animal are

the same. At a boxing contest today you have the excited fans, howling encouragement at their favourites. "Kill him, Alf"—or whatever name the Champion goes by. The hero is implored to come as near to killing as he can get. And the true fighting man gets as near to killing as the law allows. On the Roman stage actors were killed. The knock-out of the boxing-ring is as near to death as one is allowed to go. But the nearer it is the better pleased is the audience, as were the Roman audience. And the boxing contest which is the nearest to a fight to the death is the most popular.

'My question is this. Does the real fighting man feel any different from the audience. I say the *real* fighting man, and it seems to me obvious that if he is real enough, as a good few are, his feelings are identical with those of the spectator.

'Now there was no question about Coin being a real fighting man. He was that in his bones. He assumed that I was as interested in boxing as he was. And I had to affect to share in the sensations of his victories, and his gladiatorial hopes for the future. He would discuss with me some champion whom he hoped to meet, and gossip about the weakness or merits of this famous young boxer. He would say, "I can last out twenty rounds, whereas he tires easily. After about five rounds I would watch, I would watch him, and then *Whop*, I would jump in and give him two quick upper cuts followed by a bang on the ear. I would get him down, I know I could. But whether he would agree to meet me . . ."

'Now Coin is a Stone-Age man. All the life of a fighter is lived in the Stone-Age, or some such epoch. No man of intellect or high intelligence can be a fighting man, simply because in order to be that he has to live a Stone-Age kind of life. To remain supremely an animal is essential for a successful fighter.

'But this is obvious, and one can go further and say that

in one of those fights he may get into, the man of intellect will probably not be very competent, simply because he will find it difficult to mobilise his fighting glands, which are Stone-Age glands.

'Let us trace the Fighter to his earliest appearance? That would be where he becomes the Cock of the walk at his school. To be that Cock (and remember that, at that age, he is almost purely animal), for him to be that Cock you would probably catch in his eye the sensation of the killer. He will threaten anyone who disputes his will, and blacken their eye if they try to do so, this terror of the playground. He becomes the fighting man from then onwards. The boy at school is a little animal, and with his animal psychology he is nearer to a killing in his games of aggression than is the man.

'It was a Stone-Age man, then, with whom I lived (of very limited intelligence), and it was scientifically very interesting. It may occur to you that it must be a little dangerous to cohabit with a Neolithic person, but it would only be that if you yourself had Stone-Age habits of mind.

'The fighting man is a person living out of his time. He sees all around him the mechanical inventions of a period different from his—for example the hydrogen bomb. An anachronistic individual is jealous about the backward Age to which he belongs. He may be said, figuratively, fiercely to gaze out of his cave at the motor-cars passing in such profusion.

'A creature of a very different age, like myself, is apt to be disliked by these Cromagnon or other men who crop up here and there. It would be amusing to imagine a creator showing us (in drama, for instance), a hero actor of a very highly developed age, the victim of the hatred of the creature of a backward age; on the principle of a Prospero being heartily disliked by a Caliban, who would be capable of interfering with the contrivances of his intellectual superior.

'It may surprise the reader that I am able to write so freely and frankly about a man with whom I have lived. But the reader would be very mistaken there. My friend regards anything written about him as publicity. He has a passion for publicity. He belongs to that class of man who could kill his grandmother, and willingly go to the gallows, gloating over the columns and photographs in the press, immediately preceding his necessary extinction. The history of Crime provides ample evidence of the lengths to which people will go in order to gaze at their photographs in the paper. My friend would forgive me for anything I said, if I published his photograph in the course of these pages. As it is, far from being annoyed, he chuckles over passages in which he is described as a moron. If we met in Piccadilly, far from knocking me down, he would ask me to go to his club and give me an excellent lunch. He would introduce me to all his friends as "the fellow who wrote that wonderful lampoon about me". "A clever man," he would say, "who, if he met the Prime Minister, would do a wonderful portrait of him." He thinks it is a great joke being called a Neanderthal Man—pronouncing it "Knee-under-tail". He will boast of the way in which he lived at Oxford with this "brainy feller" who did all his work for him. When he marries (it will probably be a Cromagnon woman) he will hand her this little study, as a proof of how worthy of study he is, and add what a clever devil I am.'

Her 'yes' had been very insulting, she realised that. This pamphlet must have been written some years ago, Mary thought. Could he see today Father Card, in his church, the author would form a very different opinion. What he said in the pulpit was anything but 'Stone-Age'. And he was no longer a fighting man, as explained in this pamphlet. He boxed a little, but that did not make him a fighting man.

As she mused, she wished she could show the author of this libellous piece of nonsense the splendid clergyman that Father Card had turned out to be. She would like to say to him, self-satisfied as he is, with a little D.D. after his name, 'Now what have you to say, clever guy? You took it for granted in your Oxford days that the brilliant young boxer would remain fixed in exactly the same mental attitude as then. And the dunce whom you saw struggling with his books you expected him to remain the same dull fellow all his life. Was it not very stupid of you not to be able to foresee, in the plunge into divinity of this saintly man, a promise of something far more extraordinary than yourself?'

She would give this fellow a good talking to if they ever met.

19

A Debate

Mary congratulated herself on having discovered a formula which had the compulsion of a spell. It disposed instantly of her mother. The words 'To hell with the Earl of Ames' did the trick. It also banished the Brigade of Guards from her life, and a new, and unquestionably an intellectual interest was there to fill the gap. Father Card was the magnetic centre of a fresh something, dramatic, and exhilarating, and possessing intelligence, which was a necessity. On Thursday morning, a letter reached her from this intellectual direction which gave her great pleasure.

'Dear Mary Chillingham: I think I spoke to you about talks we have in the evening, in the studio at the rear of the Clergy House. Next Monday evening, at five-thirty, we are having a little debate, and I should be most awfully pleased if you would come round and form one of us. Father Wimbush has agreed to lead off, and I am sure that he will be able to find several interesting things to say. Unless I hear to the contrary I shall take it that you will be present.

Yrs Augustine Card.'

She sat down at once to write a note thanking him for inviting her to take part in the debate, and saying that of course she would be there at the appointed time next Monday.

So, on Monday evening, she found herself once more standing at the small black door, on which was painted, in small letters, 'St Catherine and the Angels', above a white cross. She rang the bell. There was a quick, heavy step, and the frowning face of Father Card appeared, which immediately disposed of its frown upon seeing who it was.

'Ah, I am so glad you were able to come, Miss Chillingham! Come in!'

After he had closed the door he signalled to her, and she understood that he had something to communicate. They stood there together, and, in a low voice, the vicar said, 'You know Hartnell? I think I should say to you that he is the author of that booklet I gave you. I do not know if you have read it? . . . You have? Good. Well, we must at some time discuss that pamphlet. I just thought I should tell you that Hartnell is that biographer.'

Father Card then turned towards the table in the corner of the room, at which two men were seated. The room was unlighted, and the life of it was concentrated in that corner, with a map of Asia Minor pinned on the wall behind the two figures.

As they approached the table, Father Card announced; 'You all know each other—the more learned of my two curates, Father Wimbush: and my old friend Dr Hartnell. Will you sit here, Miss Chillingham?' he indicated a chair, and held it back for her to sit down. He himself took a place beside her. 'I must explain what is happening; and also say that we were expecting two more people, but as they are not here yet I think we will carry on. As you know, we have these little meetings once or twice a week. On this occasion, Father Wimbush is discussing the formation of our religion in the first years after the death of Jesus. That religion, as you probably know, is a complex affair, growing out of Judaism. The Jews only had one deity; whereas we have three. The paternity of our Jewish prophet, Jesus, is, according to us, mystical. His Father is the God of the Jews. So we worship three Deities instead of one, for we have endowed the Jewish Jahveh with a kind of Djinn in permanence, which we call the Holy Ghost.'

Father Card now turned to his curate, and said, 'Father Wimbush, will you please proceed.'

This priest was a medium-sized man of about forty; a sort of black cape, surrounding his heavy shoulders, terminated at his elbows. This, for some reason, in company with the bluish shade left by shaving upon his cheeks and chin, gave him a slightly rascally appearance. His fellow curate always asserted that he had all the marks of an unfrocked priest of the Roman Catholic Church.

Father Wimbush smiled, and bowed in the direction of Mary Chillingham.

'Miss Chillingham,' he began, 'we are engaged in studying the manufacture of our religion, in the early years of the Church. In the first three centuries there were a great number of bishops, so called, and a variety of other saints, clerics and busybodies, all over Africa, Asia Minor, Greece and Italy, and so on, who constantly called meetings, at various points in the Mediterranean lands, and usually succeeded in having some theory, some doctrinal suggestion, labelled a heresy.

'Now, displeasing as this may be to some of us, I am bound to state that every doctrine in our religion has, at one time or another, been a heresy, or, if not, a very shaky and controversial belief. This is not, as Miss Chillingham thinks, a rather outrageous statement. It is a matter of history. It is embarrassing to have to confess it—at least, for a man of my cloth—but all those doctrines which, to start with, were bitterly controversial, became indestructible dogmas of our Church. One of these is the doctrine of the Trinity, what it is that gives us three Gods instead of one. No doctrine is more solid than that one. Yet it may surprise you to learn that it was not "revealed", as we say; nor did it make itself known, very suddenly, one morning. It was, to start with, a theory invented by a Greek, Maxias, in the city of Rome, in the second century A.D. It was not, of course, immediately accepted by everybody. It was hotly disputed, and repudiated by Christians who disliked a plurality of deities. But a very influential man in Rome, named Tertullian, did, fairly soon, accept it. And, in the end, everyone, from the Pope in Rome downwards, bowed his knee to a Trinity of Gods instead of one. And it has never been questioned since.

'The Holy Ghost, or Paraclete, or simply the Pigeon, which we all bend the knee to as much as to Jesus Christ, is, to be frank, among ourselves, a vaporous oddity, again an imagination of somebody or other.'

'Father Wimbush!' It was the voice of Father Card.

'Are these remarks of mine impious? If Jesus had said, on several occasions, that he was the son of God, it would then be impious to deny that he was that. But nowhere did Jesus say that. That little bit of natural history, likewise, was not coeval with Jesus. It was manufactured a century or two later by some man concerned to make our religion as difficult of belief as possible, and the theory of revelation does not make things any easier, as it gives the whole thing a phoney sound.'

Mary Chillingham rose, and said to Father Card, 'I'm afraid I must go. I have a train to catch.'

The three men got to their feet, laughing.

'Miss Chillingham, do not catch that train. Father Wimbush has been deputed by me to say things to members of the congregation which are at once outrageous and true. I am afraid that he has, as usual, blundered into a sort of

statement to which no one in any church could subscribe—
put in the way he put it, that is, with his talent for the outrageous.' Father Card, as he was saying this, led Mary
aside, and in tones as low as possible, when they were some
distance from the other two, he said, 'I am terribly sorry,
I should not have allowed Father Wimbush to do this. He
is quite hopeless. I believe, because it was you, and because
he understood the value I attach to your associating yourself
with all our efforts, that he did it on purpose, in order to
drive you away—I really do think that was his object.
Come back, Miss Chillingham, and let us see what we can
do to smooth you down.'

They approached the table once more, and Mary noticed
how good-looking a man was the smiling Hartnell, this
bitter pamphleteerist who succeeded in sweetening the
atmosphere in the neighbourhood of the unfrocked priest's
face of Father Wimbush. Father Card now explained more
fully how the shock to Miss Chillingham had been produced.

'I cannot say too often how much I feel,' he said, 'as I am
conducting a service in the church, that amazingly few of the
congregation could give an accurate account of the religion
he or she professes. I am really conducting a service among
people quite ignorant of what it is all about.'

'I believe all the same, Father Card,' Hartnell insisted
with his friend the Vicar, 'that you do not know how
sublimely ignorant the average congregation is. So,'
turning to Mary, 'let us at least double anything that Father
Card says about the silliness of his flock.'

'Well, there you are! Hartnell has not piled it on a bit too
much.' Father Card looked approvingly at his old friend of
university days. 'I do not regard my function as Vicar of St
Catherine and the Angels as so profoundly undynamic as do
the other men who are appointed Vicar or Rector of a
London church. They usually leave their congregation as

they find it. Whereas what I aim at is to train it, as far as possible, into a receptive body.'

'Is not that proving to be a terribly ambitious project, Father Card?' Mary enquired.

'It must seem that to you,' Card replied. 'I regard it as my duty to make the congregation realise that they are in a church. I am convinced that the cause of the empty churches is that they do not understand what a church is, what religion is. They are unserious. It is vitally significant that they do not know what their very creed means. Such an expression as Communion of Saints—how many of them could explain it? Then there are a considerable number of elementary facts that every Christian should know. I will give you a few examples. What is meant by the Paraclete? Then—was God there when Christ was not? Any active Christian should have thought about that. What Father Wimbush was trying to do was to put any member of our congregation on the track of a lot of bold thinking, which, however difficult and riddled with paradoxes, it is necessary to indulge in. All this ignorance and indifference must be dispelled, even if it empties the church. We are contemplating some step to precipitate this show-down. *Think, or Don't Come Here* should be our slogan.'

'To think is the one thing that the English refuse to do,' said Hartnell, with a laugh. 'Your task is heroic indeed.'

'In the history of England,' said Father Card, 'this people has astonished Europe by the amount of thinking it is capable of doing, if led by the right man.'

'A magnetic personality!' almost sneered Father Wimbush. 'If only fate should hand them that!'

'Wimbush, how long have you spent in the vicinity of Father Card?' enquired Hartnell. 'You have been with him long enough I should have thought, to know that you are working with a person who is so magnetic as to supply all the people with whom he comes in contact with a galvanic shock.'

Father Wimbush's face was distorted with a blank refusal to take seriously the high estimate that Hartnell proposed for those who worked in the shadow of Father Card. His eyes darted about, refusing to meet anybody's for more than a moment, because he had a sneer hidden in them, and would not reveal it to his chief, nor to his follower, Thomas Hartnell. It was this suppressed sneer which was diabolically contorting Wimbush's face. Mary watched this emotional play with a little discomfort.

'I have been considering,' Father Card announced, 'some step of this kind: to have a one page pamphlet printed, containing all the kind of questions that every active Christian should be able to answer. I do not propose to burden any member of the congregation with a task of any kind whatever. But I would ask him to oblige me by indicating those questions in my pamphlet which puzzle him; to leave a message upon the ledge in his pew, asking for enlightenment. These would be collected before the following Sunday, and shortly either I myself, or one of my staff, would attend to what he wants to know.'

Father Card fastened Mary with his gaze, and then said, 'You see, Miss Chillingham, how I am preparing to build up a solid, a real congregation, as I call it, which will be the first of its kind in London. I must get together a small band of helpers—I hope that you will become one of them. For such a church as I am imagining does not merely need sidesmen to collect the cash, and charwomen to keep the place clean, and all such obvious things. Then, I am very conscious of the cultural vacuum in an Anglican church, and in an Anglican community or communion. We have not got what Rome automatically provides. Then my personal experience contributes to my contemporary pedagogy. I confess that in my first few weeks, learning my theology, I was unable to answer the simplest questions. I said to myself, in my third week, "What *is* this extraordinary religion I have set out to study?" ' Pausing, Father Card pointed at his friend, Hartnell. 'He is a Doctor of Divinity. I shared rooms with him at Oxford. While he was after his D.D. I was headed for nothing more holy than Greats. He knows what sort of fellow I was then. In the matter of religion—the religion I am now immersed in— I knew no more about that than a child of five. Is that an exaggeration?'

Hartnell smiled a half-smile of the sheepish variety. 'I'm afraid, Augustine, that is woefully true. You knocked people senseless, became a Blue whose feats are still remembered. But you could hardly say the ten commandments.'

'You see?' said Father Card. 'I was an ignoramus though I came of a great clerical family. And I hope, Miss Chillingham, you are beginning to understand the meaning of our extraordinary behaviour. Like a good Christian you sprang to your feet, and declined to remain with us, when we apparently were collected here to disprove the religion in which you believe: but I am sure you will make no difficulty about admitting that you could not have successfully answered Father Wimbush, and his contention that the expression "revealed religion" is just nonsense.'

Mary laughed. 'When I was up at Cambridge,' she said, 'I kept my nose to the grindstone more than you would give me credit for. I believe I have thought of an answer; but the point was . . .'

'That you thought we were a gang of Antichrists,' Father Card spoke for her.

'Well, no,' she said, 'not that. But I was astonished . . .'

'Thank you for that astonishment.' Father Card squeezed her hand.

Mary flushed and laughed. 'It was not only you who were responsible for my astonishment,' she protested.

Mary saw the dark-haired and dark-skinned, blue-shaven face of the leering priest turn sharply in her direction. Where, she wondered, had she seen that face before? She had felt this before about Wimbush. Now she realised what he looked like. It was a hot afternoon in an Andalusian sun when a procession of priests had passed her in the street; a face like that had leered at her, out of a Goyaesque group. She had experienced at the time extreme disrelish, which accounted, in part, for what she felt about Father Card's curate.

The leer had not escaped Father Card. He leaned towards Wimbush, and, with a dangerous hiss in his voice, gave him an order. 'If you allow that punk-face of yours to defile this table, I will throw you out of the door, and there you will remain!'

The priest shrank from him, his face full of a green pallor. Mary was given no more glimpses of the offending leer, nor of the Vicar's capacity for violence. She wondered, with a sickening feeling, what all this might be about.

Father Card's voice, when he next spoke, had an unnatural sound, which caused Mary to fix her eyes on him. 'Let us examine,' he said, 'the term "revealed religion" a little more. The real essence of the question is that the word *revealed* does not involve a simultaneous revelation. Some of the deepest of our impressions take a long time to leave their mark on us. The revealing process, far from being instantaneous, might require a millennium, might it not, to be fully effective. In any case, no time is specified.'

'I perfectly understand what you mean,' Mary said, looking a little as if she did not.

'It was a casuistic sleight-of-hand of Father Wimbush,' Father Card continued, 'to introduce this question of *revelation.* It is true that we have made use of this rather complicated question before; but that was only in the case of a difficult customer, whom it was necessary to stump at all costs. It was most inappropriate in the case of Miss Chillingham.'

Dr Hartnell intervened, and said, in a voice of convincing quietness, 'I feel, if Father Wimbush will forgive me, that this correction of Father Card's is very just. For the rest, it does seem to me that his analysis of the problem of revelation is most convincing.'

'I would like to echo that,' said Father Wimbush, 'regarding the brilliant analysis of the problem of revelation that we have heard from Father Card.'

Mary felt that there was no sincerity in the utterance of the curate, so recently accused of casuistry. At that moment Hartnell, with an ingratiating smile, turned to her, and said, 'I think you must see now, Miss Chillingham, that anyone who had been misled by what you have heard described as the casuistry of our brilliant curate would find himself put right by the recent analysis of the Vicar.'

'It seemed to me just now,' Mary objected, 'that if Father Wimbush can be said to have been engaged in a line of casuistic argument, then unquestionably Father Card displayed a superior casuistry.'

Everyone seemed delighted with this observation of Miss Chillingham's, from Father Wimbush to Father Card. Indeed the latter seemed particularly pleased.

'That remark was very witty and very true,' he said. 'By the way, Miss Chillingham, we propose to found a debating society, in the winter. We very much hope that you will be a frequent participant at our debates.'

Mary expressed herself as very curious about this project of Father Card and his associates. She would, of course, be delighted to be present at the debates.

'But I hope that you will speak,' emphasised Father Card.

She was now leaving, and, after saying goodbye to the others, went to the door with the Vicar. In his leave-taking there was a definite affectionate coloration.

'I cannot tell you, Miss Chillingham,' the Father said, 'how much I have enjoyed your being present at this little bit of mismanaged debate. But do come again very soon, won't you. We will think of something less controversial to discuss.'

Waving her hand Mary walked briskly across the street towards the bus terminal. On the way she was thinking over, with some rather contradictory impulses, the events of the evening. But it took her some time to sort them out; and all she could say to herself at once was that friendship with Father Card had a very problematical side to it.

Spots of rain began to strike her. She put up her umbrella. She joined the queue at the bus terminal; and, since the rain was not very bad, she put down her umbrella. Going along Ebury Square in the bus she thought of this set of priests who seemed determined to tear their religion to pieces. She agreed, however, that she could not understand the advantage gained by having a triune God. She could get on herself as well with the single God of the Jews. This did not help her Christianity. And the sum total of her presence at the debate was to make her less attached to the Trinity— if she ever had been attached, she thought.

20

Kenya

When Mary went down to breakfast the next morning it was a dark day, so that all the lights were on. But she saw at once that something was seriously the matter with her family.

'There is bad news, Mary,' said General Chillingham. 'Your aunt . . .' he stopped for a moment.

Her mother's sister had for a considerable time lived in Kenya. Since the beginning of the Mau Mau trouble they had felt that, at any moment, news of the most dreadful kind might arrive. In imagination Mary was now confronted with a hideous vignette of her Aunt Blanche chopped up in pieces, her maid, Estelle, standing over her, her eyes protruding as she gazed down at the characteristic Mau Mau atrocity.

'Not the Mau Mau?' she said.

'No,' her mother answered. 'But your aunt's car has been in a head-on collision—her injuries are very grave—the hospital has sent a most alarming message. I have just cabled them, but there is nothing we can do, I am afraid.'

'Dr Penning can help you, Mother.'

'Help me? In what way?' Irritably her mother fixed Mary with her eye.

Mary whirled around, picked up the telephone, and quickly dialled a number.

'What are you doing, Mary?'

Mary began speaking. 'My mother is prostrated with

grief, Dr Penning. This is Mary Chillingham. Now, my aunt has had a very serious accident in Nairobi—Kenya, you know. I thought that your advice would be invaluable . . .' (a pause . . . the doctor was speaking) 'yes, doctor, I will find out.'

Mary turned to her mother. 'What is the name of the hospital?' she enquired. Her mother answered, gruffly. Mary turned to the telephone, and said, 'the Lister Clinic'. Hanging up the receiver, she said to her mother, 'Dr Penning is coming here right away.'

'Will you kindly tell me,' the General asked, 'what we are going to do with Penning when he arrives?'

'He will tell you what steps to take,' was Mary's answer. 'He has a friend on the staff of that hospital.' She received a cup of tea from her father.

Mrs Chillingham, on the other side of the table, began to cry, then put away her handkerchief. 'Blanche has very few friends there. Really no friend near enough to be of any use.' She was speaking to her husband. Mary was completely ignored.

'So Penning's friend might come in rather handy,' the General pointed out.

'It is conceivable,' admitted Mrs Chillingham.

A servant announced the doctor's arrival. Mrs Chillingham left the table to go into another room where he was waiting. A servant placed in front of Mary a plate of bacon and eggs.

'As soon as I have finished eating this, I suppose I had better arrange for air-travel to Kenya,' Mary said to her father.

'I suppose so,' replied the General.

'Two of us will be making this journey?' Mary enquired.

'Well, do you want to go? I am sure that Alice doesn't. You had better wait a little,' said the General.

Father and daughter were concerned purely with the problems of their breakfast for upwards of twenty minutes, when Mrs Chillingham returned. She resumed her seat at the table, and said to her husband, 'Well, Dr Penning will communicate at once with his friend in the Lister Clinic. I think, dear, that the sooner I get down there to Nairobi, the better.'

'Yes, my dear. I was thinking that.' The General turned towards his daughter. 'It had occurred to Mary, too,' he said. 'You won't be proposing to take Penning with you, will you?' . . . (Mary left the room). 'Mary has gone to telephone the air lines.'

'Good. I am in most capable hands,' Mrs Chillingham told her husband. 'Mary obviously wishes to be at her aunt's side.'

'And at yours, dear,' said the General.

The subsequent happenings were more or less automatic and rapid. Before they had left the house to go to the tourist office, a second cable arrived, informing them that it would be necessary to remove the patient's leg. Mrs Chillingham decided to hasten her departure in any way possible, and Mary said she would come with her. The General, with some difficulty, was prevented from flying also; at length it was agreed that mother and daughter should fly; in the event of Blanche's death the General would follow.

Thus it was that Miss Mary Chillingham was, with great rapidity, removed from the possibility of attending debates at St Catherine and the Angels, and, herself, given a quite new residence for the time being.

As soon as she and her mother arrived at Nairobi, they were to learn that Blanche's condition had critically worsened, and during the following week they were kept in constant suspense. Actually the operation had had that usual character of successfulness, which merely means that a leg has been separated from a body, and that the patient is still there. But Blanche was constitutionally in no way prepared for so major a shock. However, as she had watched the surgeon preparing to remove something which, at any moment, for a long time, might have been removed in a less ceremonious way by African butchers, her feelings had known a philosophic tinge. But a week later she showed signs of succumbing to the continual strain; and then, quite suddenly, died.

The production of her will revealed that Blanche had appreciated, more than was realised, the independent good sense of her niece Mary. So it was that, to her mother's astonishment, a considerable sum of money had been left to Mary, a far more desirable legacy than property in Kenya, masses of which fell to the lot of Mrs Chillingham.

Blanche had acquired a good deal of property in Kenya. She was a widow, who had become excessively rich upon the death of her husband. When she had found her money was going to be taken away from her in order to make a bloodless revolution in England, but that she might remove it, and herself with it of course, to a nice, gentlemanly territory called Kenya, well, she had transferred her wealth to this seemingly nice and quiet country, England's best-governed Colony! A considerable section of it she invested in farmland, and house-property in Nairobi.

Then the Soviet got busy. It sent a few able disturbers of the peace to this ideally quiet, safe spot, and soon quite a lot of nice peaceful Negroes were dancing around with long knives, cutting up the peace-loving English ladies and gentlemen, and rapidly converting Kenya into about the least desirable spot on earth for a peace-loving Briton to settle down in.

Inheriting these mistakes of her sister's, Mrs Chillingham

was now presented with a problem of immense difficulty. Was she to leave all this property to appreciate in value, and then attempt to sell it? Or was there not a considerable likelihood that things might grow worse instead of better? She had no one to consult, and so eventually decided to return at once to England.

Mary had realised very soon how ill-advised it was for her mother to think of stopping in Kenya to dispose single-handed of the property she had inherited. When, after an interval of indecision, her mother decided to return to London, where she could obtain expert legal advice, Mary was delighted.

As to her own inheritance, there had been a most fortunate clause in the will enjoining that the money marked down for her was to have priority over all other legacies, and to be handed over at the earliest possible moment. This imme-diate transference of the monies which she inherited was a provision which greatly annoyed every one except Mary. Approximately fifty thousand pounds was the sum involved —partly in cash, and partly in investments outside Kenya. The radical change produced by the possession of this money in Mary's position in the family circle, to start with, reacted with such expedition as to open her eyes as to what her condition had been before, and as to what it would be henceforth. It gave her, with a flash of a wand, as it were, an independence of the most palpable kind. She had been, up to that time, in her mother's hands. It was to her, and not her father, that she was compelled to turn if she wanted anything from a sixpenny piece upwards. It was from her father that the family wealth derived, not from her mother. But the handling of it was left, in great part, to that lady. Mary could not go over her mother's head, and appeal to the General. She had learned greatly to resent these maternal powers; and her mother had not troubled to conceal the fact that Mary was not her favourite daughter, and was, for whatever reason, discriminated against.

Mary had, from the start, been given a very inconsiderable allowance, and had, as a consequence of this, felt deeply aggrieved. She therefore felt herself, upon hearing of her Aunt Blanche's legacy, as saved from her mother's oppression. She now realised that her mother's willingness for her to go to Cambridge had been because that would get her out of the way for the years involved. She experienced, at the same time, a powerful movement of gratitude towards the dead woman. She had always had a friend in Aunt Blanche, had travelled with her in Italy as a schoolgirl, and gone with her to Scandinavia four years before. On this last occasion the older woman had realised how little help Mary had received from her mother in the way of money, and how little sympathy her sister felt for this extremely attractive young woman. She began to make her niece occasional presents, and kept in touch with her, showing a sustained interest.

Mary's hotel life in Kenya had been deeply boring. She had, however, got a letter written to Father Card, in which she had said, among other things, the following:

'To be entirely frank, I believe I should find Father Wimbush a man who would succeed in making my visits to the Clergy House less delightful than they otherwise would be. Do you ever find that you come up against a person who has the capacity of influencing the temperature, even for you? But, speaking of temperatures! We complain of the absence of heat in England: and gleefully the English have settled in some of the hottest places on the earth. Our black brothers here come after us with a long knife. Give me good, cold, draughty old England, and the Briton whose blood is not always boiling inside him, and whose knives are not so long.'

Father Card's reply explained how it came about that a man like Wimbush was employed by him as a curate. 'To find a curate who would fit in with all my special requirements is not an easy matter. As a result of having a father highly placed in the Church, and, in a more intimate way, having one of my best friends established as a vicar in the country, I learn a great deal about the difficulty of securing enough new clergy to go round. To persuade men to adopt a calling which provides them with a salary inferior to that of a labourer, is not easy. The most extraordinary type of fellow is being ordained today. It is nothing for a hairdresser to become an Anglican clergyman—there is an instance of this in the country diocese of which I am speaking. Under such circumstances, to find an efficient, respectable curate in London is not as easy as you would think. Wimbush knows his onions, he knows all there is to know about a church; and, although we disagree violently all the time, I have thought it best to put up with him until a nicer type of man presents himself. His behaviour on the night you came to talk with us was very tiresome, however, and I am now taking certain steps—among other things an appeal to my father—so that, by the time you get back, Wimbush will, I hope, be replaced. Come back to this cold disagreeable country as soon as you conveniently can. Some of our hearts are warm, if that is geographically uncharacteristic. Surely someone will be idiotic enough to acquire your property in Kenya. Surely the prospect of being sliced up never has been known to daunt the Briton.'

21

Messrs Dodds, Smithers and Yorke

One of Mary's first actions, on waking up and finding herself in England, was to pick up the telephone and get in touch with Messrs Dodds, Smithers and Yorke, who had always been Aunt Blanche's lawyers, and who were now the executors of her will. Mr Smithers was the member of the firm to whom she was referred, and it was with him that she at once made an appointment, and that afternoon went to see him. She was received with great deference by this gentleman, who obviously entertained the hope that Mary Chillingham also might become a client of theirs.

The first matter which the lawyer took up was the question of her immediate entering into possession of the sums bequeathed her, and of how that should be realised. Mr Smithers made it clear to her that his firm would be very ready to advance, up to the sum of, say two thousand pounds, any monies that she might immediately need. He explained to her that ready money found in her aunt's account at the bank would have to be put aside in case it were needed for the payment of death-duties. It would be her mother, as the residuary legatee, who would have, in the first instance, to cope with these taxes on her late aunt's estate.

Mr Smithers, who was acquainted, in the minutest detail,

with what this young woman had inherited, now enlightened her as fully as possible as to what she had to expect in the way of capital, and the income that that would probably represent. He hid nothing from her of the rapacity of the State, and what kind of proportion of her future income would be claimed by the Inland Revenue. When she left the lawyer's office, she carried away, in her bag, a cheque for a thousand pounds. She walked on air, but she had not only the sensation which caused her to do that, but the other sensation, which accompanied it, of rage at the thought of the tax-collector who would open his campaign almost immediately. The sensations experienced by her Aunt Blanche, which had driven that lady out of England, and settled her in Kenya, were now known to her niece. She felt at once an unexpectedly rich young woman, and one whose heritage would begin to be whittled away as soon as she began to avail herself of this sudden wealth. So she became, at one step, the bitter enemy of the State, and a girl who knew, with great suddenness, that she was, from a worldly point of view, important.

She had done her best to charm Mr Smithers, and make him an ally. And she had attempted to show him what a highly practical young woman it was within her competence to be. When she returned home after these great events she went up to her den, or, as it now was, cell, and attempted to adjust herself to these new circumstances. She found at once that she was in no way able to do this. She had not the necessary ballast to steady herself down, and proceed on her course in command of this vessel, but knowing nothing of navigation; or at all events, for a short while this is how she felt. She was a young woman who had always been very independent, and not, in any way, inclined to share her life with others. Yet this was a moment when she would have liked to ring up a friend, to take her out to dinner, to narrate her recent adventures, and to invite her to share the excitement with her.

As she really knew no human being whom she could burden with all this stuff, she could think of no one better than the Ghastly Girl to get hold of, and to come down on, not for sympathy, but for simple humanity, as one might begin talking to a sensible-looking person on a railway journey, and tell them one's life-story, since it had to be told to somebody.

But as there was no Monica Blunt available—she learned from a housekeeper at Monica's flat that she was away for the week-end—Mary went to a cinema instead, where she enjoyed the story of a young American girl who inherited a vast fortune. The scenes of this melodrama made her feel a very insignificant capitalist. After that she had supper at a place where she was quite unknown and, after that, took a taxi home.

As she was ascending the stairs, proposing to go to her den before turning in for the night, she was greeted by the familiar voice of Alice, who said, 'Hello there. Come and talk to me, Mary.'

She followed Alice into the kind of flatlet that she occupied in the parents' house. They went into a sort of den, for Alice, like herself, had decided to have a small bohemian closet.

'It is not often, Alice, that I find you at a loose end. Is your life completely furnished with Monica Blunts?' Mary enquired.

'Only one Monica,' Alice laughed. 'I prize her particularly.'

'One really has to have a little money in one's pocket to have a lot of friends. With the money jingling about in my pocket this evening I should have very much enjoyed chattering to some friend about my wealth, and so on.'

'Has your wealth materialised?' enquired her sister.

'The lawyer has advanced me a thousand pounds,' smiled Mary.

'That is the sort of lawyer to have,' her sister said.

'Don't all lawyers do that?' asked Mary.

'Not quite all,' Alice told her.

'You old capitalist, Alice, you must be laughing at me!' Mary said: 'but I shall soon get used to the feel of money, and soon lose it, I expect. I am already terrified about it, you know. I suppose that is because I have never had any. I wish I had twice as much, then I should really be able to enjoy it. The moneyed woman today lives with the tax-collector, who is licensed to rob her.'

'Don't I know it,' said Alice.

'But you have twice as much as I have, you lucky girl!' Mary said. 'When one has as much money as you have one does not think about it, I expect.'

'I wish that Douglas had lived,' Alice confided, 'and that we had had children. That would have been worth a great deal of money.'

'Yes, you had very bad luck,' Mary reflected; 'and Douglas was such a fine fellow, wasn't he! I remember being deeply impressed by his kilts. Marriage is a very big subject with me—very urgent. You know that Mother was always trying to make me marry that child, Arthur Wootton. I have not a young enough mind to marry just anybody. But I am probably too old to marry. You got all that done when you were nineteen. And I do not feel that my legacy is going to help in any way.'

'Oh, I don't know. It might make a great difference,' her sister answered. 'You will be able now to move around a bit more. A nice intelligent Frenchman might meet your requirements, Mary.'

'Perhaps my money dispenses with the necessity of a

husband,' was Mary's next thought on the married state. 'Why should one have another being who would perhaps complicate one's life so much? Considering Arthur Wootton as a husband has given me a view of marriage which is anything but idyllic. Perhaps I shall go off and live somewhere on my little capital. The *rive-gauche* perhaps, or say the Channel Islands; and in a very few years one would be too old for that nasty problem to worry one.' Mary looked over at her sister, who, in her view, had reached that safe remoteness.

'I think you look upon marriage from a very individual standpoint. You do not seem to allow for sex. Marriage, for you, has little to do with sex.' Alice was quite spirited.

Mary did not answer. Then, in a minute or two, she said. 'Sex involves so much indecency. Call it marriage, and it is all right.'

'What a puritanic statement,' said Alice.

'Well, I feel puritan just at present. However, whether I approach a double life from the point of view of sex, or of marriage, it is time that it happened, and I am most alarmed at not seeing any husband in sight. I am so constituted that sex would fly out of the window if a man said something too stupid. Can you suggest anything?'

'The most sexual thing that there is,' said Alice, 'is having a child. The steps you take in order to achieve that are physically extremely pleasant. But so is eating an ice-cream. So you must think of sex as the production of a child—the ice-cream is not important enough to rivet your attention. So, in your present state, eliminate everything from your mind except having a child. Therefore, think of nothing but a fine physique, well-shaped feet, a straight nose, et cetera. Then you know what to look for—speed up the finding of the man.'

'Right, that is simple,' said Mary. 'We ignore the social business, do we?'

'Of course,' said Alice. 'Bring him home, and tell Ma and Pa to mind their own business.'

'Although I have no railway porter in mind, nevertheless,' said Mary, 'I *might* find one, and I'm glad you feel that way about it.'

Mary rose. 'It was nice having a sisterly talk,' she said. 'Let us see each other more often, Alice.'

'That would give me great pleasure,' her sister replied, with a squeeze of the hand. Then, with a brief kiss, she said, 'Good luck with your thousand pounds.'

Mary went to bed feeling she had made a friend. In spite of her rather fevered state she slept well, and rose at the usual hour the next morning.

At breakfast Mary selected a copy of the *Financial Times*. As she flung it open, beneath the amused glances of her parents, she delivered herself of a speech at once aggressive and explanatory.

'As I am now a capitalist I must turn my attention, at breakfast time, to the weighty news of the day, which it was my habit, in the days of my beggary, to leave to my elders and betters.'

'The first thing to learn about capital is that it melts away like snow in the sun,' said Mrs Chillingham.

'You think that next year I shall look with loathing at the *Financial Times*?' enquired her daughter.

'You will perhaps find that you are a financial wizard,' suggested Mrs Chillingham. 'My sister wished you at the earliest moment to be in possession of what she was handing on to you. Have you been to Dodds, Smithers and Yorke?'

'Even so,' the daughter assented.

'Did Mr Smithers acquaint you with a few ugly facts?' Mrs Chillingham asked.

'At the moment I am in possession of a large sum of money,' Mary replied. 'That may be an ugly fact for you, Mother. For me it is the reverse. That is a matter of taste.'

'For your parents,' said the General, 'it is a fact which dispenses us from giving you a dress allowance, to go no farther.'

'Ah, mon Général,' cried Mary, 'the birthday present I shall give you will not come out of your pocket, now, will it?'

'I was not aware that you had realised where it came from,' Mrs Chillingham said.

'Oh yes,' Mary assured her. 'I did not dare to give such handsome presents as I should have wished. It was always very painful to me to give my father a silly little pipe, or something even more picayune.'

'You are in a position to give him a new car, aren't you? I do hope that it will be a Cadillac.'

'I have too little money to be so bountiful,' Mary replied. 'But when the day comes round we will consult together; and similarly for your birthday, Mother, we will have a nice little talk.'

Mrs Chillingham raised her eyebrows.

'Do you and Father ever go to the theatre?' Mary enquired.

'You are familiar with our lives,' answered her mother.

'Well, don't you think it is rather barbarous to go to the theatre so seldom?' the daughter asked. 'I was too poor formerly ever to say things like this. But now it is different. There is a play in which Wolfit is performing. He is a splendid actor, and you should at once buy a box or stalls.'

'All the plays he acts in are too terribly serious,' said Mrs Chillingham. 'Why should I go and be depressed by some high-brow play?'

'I will tell you,' said Mary aggressively. 'To be serious for once in a way would do you good. You ought to be ashamed of always patronising stupid plays.'

'We cannot allow you to act as censor, Mary,' said the General.

'The London theatre is controlled by money-bugs. The foreigner despises us for having such a theatre. Dublin is better than London. Edinburgh, Stratford, or Glyndebourne are more enterprising than London ever is. You ought to be more patriotic, my Mother and Father. You get my meaning?' Mary looked at her parents.

'Has your lately inherited wealth affected you in any way,' asked Mrs Chillingham.

'No, except, as I explained, I had to remain silent before that acquisition of wealth, or rather I avoided disagreeable subjects . . .'

'Oh, oh, oh,' called Mrs Chillingham.

'You forget that if I wanted a tooth brush, or if my shoes hurt, or if I wanted to contribute some small sum to the church, I had to ask you. My allowance was inadequate in such cases. Perhaps I had spent it on a cinema.'

'It amuses you to exaggerate,' said her mother. 'Looking back, you can pretend that you lived in a sort of Dotheboys Hall. I don't care, if it gives you any pleasure.'

'What I suggest is that you mention the clothes that I have been provided with by expensive dressmakers. But those were merely liveries which I had to wear, as otherwise I should have disgraced your doorstep, where I was incessantly entering and leaving. My hats were like the cockaded hats formerly worn by grooms. And, in general, my apparel was necessitated by my relationship to you. Need I go farther?' Mary asked, looking around the table. 'I lived extremely well, for I shared your food.'

'What is your grievance, Mary?' her father asked.

'None, except that now I shall have to help you pay the cook's salary, and the rest.'

'Nonsense, my dear,' said the General. 'This is not an establishment for paying guests.'

'You can easily find, Mary, between here and Gloucester Road, a good clean boarding house where you can pay for your food and lodging if you have a fancy to do that,' said Mrs Chillingham.

'If you can tolerate us, Mary,' said her father, 'you know quite well that we love to have you here.'

'We hope she can manage to be civil,' said her mother, 'heiress or poor penniless outcast, as she prefers to think of herself as being, before Blanche's legacy changed her situation.'

'You ask me what my grievance is, Father. I only have one central complaint; it is that my mother has always had her knife into me, for some reason, and I have suffered a great deal in consequence of that. You must have been aware of her hostility to me, although of course you could do nothing, as she is a very strong-minded woman. I am able now to speak freely . . .'

'You are not free to make a lot of fantastic statements,' Mrs Chillingham intervened. 'It makes no difference at all your Aunt Blanche having left you money.'

'You will soon find out whether it makes a difference or not,' said Mary. 'I am not at your mercy now, my dear Mother. I am able to express myself freely and am not silent because of fear of reprisals from you.'

'You have said that already,' said Mrs Chillingham. 'Repeating it does not make it any more true. I do not know what has happened to you. I am not sure that you should not see an alienist.'

Mary sprang up. 'If you think you can intimidate me by saying that I am demented . . .'

'Please, Mary, and you, darling' (turning to his wife), 'what is this extraordinary scene?' said the General. 'Mary, please sit down, and calm yourself. There is no justification for your accusing your mother of hostility towards you. I do hope you will apologise to her for all this disturbance.'

Mary resumed her seat. 'I quite realise the difficulty you are in, Father. All my life I have been in the same difficulty, therefore I sympathise with you. . . .'

'Mary, I do not recognise your voice,' said her mother, leaning towards her.'

'It is money speaking,' said Mary, with a smile.

'It is something or other—I think the devil has got into you. Until you have come to your senses,' said Mrs Chillingham, 'I do not propose to go on talking to you.'

Mrs Chillingham rose, and left the room.

When they were alone together, the General turned to his daughter, and said, in a quiet voice, 'Mary, my dear, do please go and pacify your mother. Ask her forgiveness. You have been very rude to her.'

'Father, I'm afraid I have upset your breakfast. It would do no good for me to go after Mother and try and soothe her down. I do not propose to kowtow to her. I will, if she prefers, take my meals in my den. But Mother is a very vicious woman. Now she has accused me of being mad, and I am not going to stand for that. I am awfully sorry, Father, that this should upset you. But I believe that matters will straighten themselves out, especially if you show a little firmness on my behalf.'

'If you make violent scenes, Mary, it is no use asking me to perform miracles of pacification. I will naturally attempt to make things all right between you. But you have been very aggressive, and it is up to you to say you regret, and so on.'

'Well, Father, this is a new situation. I have got some

money. Mother knows now what she can do and what she can't do.'

Mary rose, nodded amiably to her father, and walked out of the room. She went straight upstairs, and telephoned the Clergy House.

Father Card, who was not aware that she was a rich young woman, seemed, in spite of this, tremendously glad to hear her voice. His voice glowed. If she was free, would she come round at once?

'Is the invitation for the cell?'

'No. Come rather to the studio,' was Father Card's reply. 'There is not much privacy anywhere. But there is no privacy in my cell.'

22

A Proposal

Mary started off across Ebury Square to go to the studio, and as she walked she turned over in her mind a few problems connected with the Church of St Catherine and the Angels, and its notorious Vicar. Her circumstances were entirely different now from what they were when she departed for Kenya. The friendship she had formed before her departure must now be looked at in a different light. She realised, as she strode along, that her mother's bad treatment had been answerable, to some extent, for her anxiety as the years passed, and she imagined her good looks disappearing, and the passage into the thirties making her chances of marriage decrease. The man she was now going to see, eccentric as he was, had undoubtedly figured for her in the distance as a marriageable possibility, ridiculous as that might sound to some people. But that was before she went to Kenya. That was the result of a set of circumstances which no longer existed. Everything, now, was different.

Or was it so different? She could not answer that without a good deal of pondering—for if it *seemed* to be so different, that might be illusory. To readjust the world, the scenes in which she found herself, would take time. And she found that the word *time* drifted her back into the mood which had played so prominent a part in that period when she began toying in her mind with the idea of a very intellectual clergyman.

She crossed the head of the Mews where Jane Greevey lived, and a step farther she was passing the house in the basement of which was Hughie's abode. How astonished they would be if they could know what had happened to her. She must go and look up old Jane. And then, before realising how quickly she was walking, she saw the Clergy House at the bottom of the next street, and, before she reached it, the door of the studio was there on her right. She pressed the bell, and quietly the door opened, and there was Father Card smiling down at her. She followed the smile into the studio, and he reached a comfortable chair for her to sit down on, and himself sat, herculean and smiling, in front of her. But though he rocked about, the chair did not collapse. And his voice was softer than usual.

'Mary—may I call you that?—let me lose no time. You may be flying away again before long. I am well aware. Will you marry me?' This was as if a figure in Madame Tussaud's had come to life. Some weeks before Kenya, this figure had occupied the central position in her mind, as a possible, if not a likely. This figure had loomed there for so long now, yet what it had just said startled her a great deal.

First of all, the sensation was as pleasant as it was startling. Fate was speaking to her very suddenly—but how enormous it was! It had a soft voice for so large a figure. She heard it saying, 'You must think I am not much of a fellow to get spliced to. I am a clergyman, of all things to be, as poor as a church-mouse. I know I am too rough and big, and if I were unclergymanlike and squeezed you, I should probably crush you until you hardly had any breath left in your body.'

She thought—this trained fighting-machine could crush

most men—it was a redoubtable object to have so near to one, as if a locomotive had suddenly whispered to her a sweet nothing. It said it was poor—had she been proposing would she have had to say that she was rich?

She signalled with her hand to stop him. 'Augustine—may I be fresh and call you that?—these things are not impediments to marriage. But give me time to think if I want to marry. Yes?'

She rose, and the Father put his arm around her waist. He was so much taller than she was that he had to push his head down to seem to belong to the same universe as she did.

'You are a kind of giant,' she said. 'I have just received a proposition of marriage from a giant. Give me time to find a little breath. I have to find words to speak, but it is not easy.'

He still was holding her around the waist, when suddenly he gave her an alarming squeeze. This was a delicious sensation, but it made one's heart jump, of course. It was so superhuman a squeeze she shivered imperceptibly. She remembered that wonderful scene in the church, when he had the Russian priests to explain to his congregation, and both he and the priests terrified the majority of people. She had now to adjust herself to something the size of a dream.

As she poised before she plunged she tried to steady herself and consider what lay between herself and the mesmerist of some time ago. She knew that she had what was necessary for that purpose. It was something of considerable dimension. It was her sudden wealth which she could use almost to stun this mesmerist.

She was under no illusion about the sordidness of what it was that matched itself with this heroic figure, but she felt it straining her away a little, and she was ashamed as she realised she was reacting against something which she could not dislodge—whose weight she felt all the time, all around her—with warmth better than comfort.

Was she never to marry, was that what it meant? As to her past, her sexual experience lacked nothing. At Cambridge, out of wedlock, she had spent a week-end with Harry Ritchie. But that was not the sort of man she could marry. Now something from that past, that bohemian experience, held her back. Yet in entering the studio she had had no idea that the first thing Augustine would do would be to propose marriage. He had jumped her into a position in which she found herself carrying on as if she had never gone to Kenya and had her life revolutionised by the terms of her aunt's will. To walk around and renew her acquaintance with this Anglo-Catholic priest should not have been the *first* thing to do on her return to London. She had let herself in for all this—though, naturally not expecting the fellow to pitchfork her into something she was not ready for. Now here she was, having to think out all the most difficult problems of life, encircled by these enormous arms, and asked for a yes or a no—although there had been nothing of this sort in their relationship up to that moment. But although she might be unable to allow Augustine to retain his position as a *possible* in the foreground of her life, all the same she permitted herself to be elated at his proposal. It was really rather satisfactory that this brilliant, young —yes, still he might be called young—clergyman should wish to marry her, although, for all he knew, she was not a young woman of fortune, or so very eligible as she had recently become. She allowed herself to remain in a comfortable hollow of this vast body, hoping that he would not push her along any farther, down the emotional road in which she had so rashly ventured. But she could not resist the hot instinctive desire that the impending face would come a little nearer; and so, when his mouth reached down and seized on hers in a burning embrace, she responded, without any show of hesitation; with a warm hand she clung to one of his rather alarmingly large shoulders, tiptoeing ever so slightly.

When the door bell unexpectedly rang she was given, with the greatest gentleness, temporary adieux, as the big shape almost stealthily moved away towards the door; Mary slid into a chair, arranging her hair thoughtfully.

It was Wimbush. From Father Card's greeting, it was evident that this intrusion was not welcome. Mary noticed the curate's eye dart over at her. But Wimbush came no farther than the doorstep. He was dismissed in a hoarse mutter and she could hear him walking quickly away.

'That tiresome fellow!' Augustine said as he returned. 'He has no reason to come here. He must have guessed that I would particularly loathe to see him. If my cell is too public, and as busy as a railway terminus, as it is, I will build another cell, where two friends can sit and be with one another without impertinent interruptions.'

'I will help you build such a cell,' Mary heroically proclaimed.

Father Card took this opportunity to renew his embraces, her building impulse theoretically drawing them very close together. They gossiped and played in this way for about a half an hour more.

'We are getting along like smoke,' thought Mary, and when at last Father Card got up, and the moment came for her to depart, they kissed one another with a cordiality which was just as it should be.

'Are you saying "yes", darling?' Augustine pressed her to answer.

'No, no, please wait, Augustine,' Mary said, returning his embrace. 'Give me time. I cannot say "Yes" in an instant. Marriage is too great a thing for that.'

Augustine put his arm around her shoulders, and pressed her tightly against him. After a deep embrace he said: 'Very well, darling Mary, it is understood. We will wait a day or two. But do not let us wait too long.'

So it was in a new and glowing frame of mind that she made her way home. Hers was the full-blooded feminine response to the masculine attack. The full experience of her body had been given to Father Card's great offer.

On returning home, finding that both her parents were out, Mary lunched alone and afterwards retired to her den to collect her thoughts. She was glad to be left alone, and get her good reflective machinery to work upon the great event of the morning. In looking back at what had happened at the studio, the first thing that occurred to her was that she ought never to have gone there. She ought to go nowhere at this stage of the proceedings. She had not been ready for a proposal of marriage; and that was not surprising, because nothing which had gone before had prepared her for that. At all events, let there be no more mistakes. She would never go within ten miles of Augustine Card until she was prepared for anything that might happen.

First, she decided to fasten her mind upon the proposal, and think a little more about that—in fact, to think it out of the way. The economic factor was the major question. And, to begin with, they were not economic equals. Card did not know that, but, actually, he was her economic inferior; and that radical inequality was the principal stumbling block to marriage. Had he known that she was a sugar-baby he would not have proposed in quite that way.

On the other hand of course he was not exactly a beggar. She assumed that the incumbent of a church in a fashionable neighbourhood would be placed, from a worldly point of view, not quite unfavourably in the marriage market. Nevertheless, his stipend would have to be used up on the church, or so it seemed to her. Taking into account her bringing-up, and social habits, she really ought to marry someone with a considerable private income.

Now, what were her opportunities? There was nothing concrete within sight, except Arthur, and one more young man of that kind, whom she had rejected for the same reason; and then Harry Ritchie—who had been disposed of in Norwich—that purely ephemeral relationship, in whose case marriage had always been practically unthinkable. There was nothing concrete except these shapes; but certainly there were a half-dozen hazy figures of possible men, within her reach—but only in the way that, at any large dance, there were several young men with whom she would quite likely have a dance, and they *might* get terribly fond of her while they were so near to one another as the dance involved.

Then, with one's eye still on this large dance, if all the young men present were informed the day before that this beautiful girl had just inherited the equivalent of, say, fifteen hundred a year; what then? Would not that alter everything? Would it not be wiser to publish this fact, and then allow herself to float around for, say, one year? Would not that be the wisest course, from any point of view?

But there was one thing to consider, would any of those young men at the large dance be as interesting a man as Father Card? Would they not tend to be Arthurs, more or less? If she were to float around in 'society' for a twelve-month, was not 'society' a dull place? And had not her trouble with Arthur been just that—the trouble which took her to St Catherine and the Angels?

Well, where did all that lead her? Back to Card? Not

necessarily. Had she not a short time ago suggested to her mother that she should be given the chance of moving about the world a little, where she could meet men of all kinds—from Paris to California? Mary settled down at this point in a dream of great displacement. She saw herself in Washington or New York, introduced by the Embassy as a young English aristocrat, looked over by all the young men floating around, like herself, in rich circles. Would it not be worth giving that a trial?

After thinking deeply about this, and whisking herself all over the habitable globe, she was no farther advanced towards a decision. It meant spending a great deal of money, living in expensive hotels in order to impress, and so on. Then there was the established fact that if you went to look for something, the probability was that you did not find it; whereas, if you just sat down where you were, it was quite apt to roll up to your feet. This was all very depressing. With her cold-blooded approach, and her good intelligence, there was the danger that her experimentation might take her far afield, wasting her substance. There were, in these unemotional excogitations, two principal factors. The first one that she had passed in review was the economic, which was related entirely to her recent legacy. Under the heading 'sex' may be mentioned something of equal importance. The way she put this to herself was as follows: am I putting my money on the right man? She really knew very little about Father Card in that connection. They had not been properly alone at all. And before a woman could decide to get married to a man she should have passed some period in his company, and so have been able to come to an intimate conclusion as to what degree they were physically compatible with one another.

To put this brutally, what kind of a bedfellow would this boxing Blue turned parson make? It might be a terrible mistake to marry a clergyman. If the physical side of the business was wrong she knew just how intolerable that could be. Making guesses about this was so much less satisfactory than a testing would be. But she could not suggest a night or two in bed with a holy man. She regarded all this as horribly hard-boiled. But how was the question to be avoided? She would have to spy out the situation during two or three months; provide incidents which would disclose certain facts; invite rehearsals of conjugal bliss of one kind or another. At the end of such a trial period she would know better what to think about marriage. She was sure it would be all right with this hot-blooded elephant, but he was, after all, elephantine. She must go elephant-hunting, sexually speaking.

When she came to the end of a great deal of hard-boiled thinking Mary did a curious thing; she tossed up. She took a shilling out of her purse, and promised herself to toss three times to get rid of Card or to do the opposite. If tails were uppermost more than once, that would be in favour of Father Card. She threw the coin in the air, and down came a head. Up it went into the air again, and down came a tail. She felt she was in danger now. With her heart beating a little she flung it high, and it was again tails that presented itself to her.

As she had chosen this method, it was no use arguing with fate. You had to take it or leave it. It was Card who had won the toss—simply because she had arranged it that way; that, if the tails came down twice, it was to be Card. She decided that, the next morning, she would go again to the cell or the studio, whichever Augustine preferred.

The six weeks that followed were spent by Mary in what might be regarded as a very objective investigation of what was, from any point of view, a formidable customer to marry, of all things. She was bound to confess in the first week or so that the answer was not easy to come by. This very strong-minded elephant of a man insisted on his personal methods of going about his love-making, and, since that was restrained, she was not, confined to the limits of the proprieties, much wiser at the end of the six weeks than she was at the beginning. 'I think what I shall have to do is to take this mammoth on trust,' she told herself at length.

As almost every time they met he asked her to marry him, she could decide almost at any time she liked to convert them into an affianced pair. And at last, one day, she replied to his usual question, 'Augustine, I do not think that the mere passage of time makes us any better acquainted. But I have admired you for quite a little time now: it may be said that we love one another, mayn't it? So what am I hesitating about? *Yes* is what I will say, without more ado.'

Augustine fell into so long a kiss of burning thankfulness that, in the end, she had to rescue herself. She discovered that he was crying.

'I was so afraid you might say something else, Mary!' he told her, as he wiped away the giant-sized tears, smiling. 'How wonderful this is! My next question is *when* will you marry me?'

They arranged to marry as soon as was technically possible. Mary and Lady Imogen met the next day for the first time. The mother welcomed such a daughter-in-law as Mary; for of course she had been prepared for practically any eccentricity in the way of a woman. The niece of Sir Henry Chillingham, whom she and her husband knew very well, was so infinitely better than what she could have expected from the Red Priest, that she was quite cheerful when she broke the news to Canon Card. He had remained in their country cottage to complete an important sermon, and he arrived back in London in time to hear the great news before he went to bed.

'She might have been the sister of a groom, or she might have been a low caste Chinese,' Lady Imogen pointed out; 'but she is a very beautiful girl of a famous Border family.' The Canon agreed. 'Yes,' he asserted. 'I shall go to Chillingham Chase as a relative. That is, as you say, better than being fawned over familiarly by a coolie.'

Lady Imogen's rather mongolian eyes shone a little as she embraced her husband, as if he were himself the great eccentric, who, for once in his life, had acted sensibly.

Mary's encounter with Mrs Chillingham was not so epic as she had expected. A note handed to that lady by a servant summoned her to her daughter's den. She did not appear with much rapidity, for something told her that this request to go to the den meant a more weighty matter than usual. She swept in at length, bristling with negatives, in preparation for the worst. Mary rose from some pretended activity among the books in the interior of the den. She faced her mother, as if recalling herself to attend to something which had escaped her memory.

'Oh, Mother,' she said, 'I am going to marry Father Card.'

'How awfully peculiar,' said Mrs Chillingham. 'May I sit down?'

Mary sat down in front of her, and said, 'What is peculiar about it, Mother?'

'Mary, can you truthfully say that what you had to tell me, when I came into this room a few minutes ago, did not seem to you a little odd? Do you assert that my reaction was not expected?'

'There is no reaction of yours, Mother, which would surprise me. You regard what I told you as "peculiar". I could not have foreseen that you would receive the news I had to tell you in that way.'

'Anyhow, tell me what you have been doing. I understand that you have got engaged to be married to Father Card?'

'That is the idea,' said Mary.

'You understand, Mary, don't you, how your father will receive this glorious news; how enchanted your sister Alice will be; and I shall hold my head high for the next week or two, pointed at as the future mother-in-law of Father Card.'

'Alice is away.'

'Yes, Mary, but she will come back to find the family behaving in the usual imbecile fashion.'

Mary stood up. 'I have escaped the Earl of Ames,' she said.

'And you expected me now to throw a fit, didn't you?' was Mrs Chillingham's answer. 'It is just the sort of idiotic bridegroom I should have expected you to lead to the altar. He will have a nice little dot, won't he? And there is nothing so spendthrift as a parson. How Blanche will turn in her grave! In any case, you will not be naïve enough to expect *us* to help you to pay for your marriage, will you?'

'My legacy did elate me, Mother, in Nairobi,' Mary said. 'But I did not expect others to rejoice.'

'There was always a childish streak in my sister,' answered Mrs Chillingham.

'Thank goodness she sweetened your intrusion into the Chillingham family,' was the daughter's comment.

Mrs Chillingham made a rapid exit. Before passing through the door she threw over her shoulder, 'May your squalid and clownish match teach you a lesson I never could!'

23

Marriage

There was no question whatever but that Mary had become more particular since she had inherited money. She had made up her mind to marry Card, for whom she had a real affection, but she never felt quite sure that she had not taken a false step. Still, having committed herself, she would go firmly forward without allowing these uncertainties to influence her in any way.

Among other things, she went to see Hughie. He was not in his flat, and so she walked round to the garage. This was unquestionably locked. As she turned away, she thought she saw Jane Greevey's face through the curtain. She went up to her door, and rang the bell. Jane was soon there.

'I do not confuse your identity with that of your neighbour, Miss Greevey. Please believe that it was my intention to come and see you after I had finished with Hughie.'

'You would not offend me if you paid a call on him,' said Jane Greevey. 'But please come in.'

Mary passed into Jane's living-room; she glanced around, and said 'Nothing changed! How comfortable your room is! I shall be a sort of neighbour of yours. I am marrying Father Card.'

This information appeared to be a shock for Miss Greevey. Mary perceived that Jane was attached to Augustine, and was sorry that she had given her this piece of news quite so quickly.

'Marrying so spectacular a man as Augustine Card is rather venturesome, don't you think?' Jane sat down.

'Is it all right if I sit down?'

'Of course, do please,' said Jane, giving permission although the visitor had not waited for it.

Matthew Arnold was on a table at her side. Mary picked it up.

'Oh, I remember seeing this the first time I came. I thought you underestimated him, I remember.'

'That is quite correct. I have learned better now. "Apollo comes leading his choir the Nine . . ." You see, I know him quite well now. Also "Dover Beach".'

'Bravo,' said Mary. 'I am so glad you like him. I must bring Arnold and Father Card together. His taste in verse is very imperfect. I will send him a copy.'

'I say, Miss Chillingham, I must congratulate you on what you tell me—that you are going to marry Father Card —you know I admire our Vicar. The "red priest", they call him. Do you believe,' Jane asked, 'that he is really "red"?'

'I do not believe he is "red" at all,' Mary answered. 'I should not marry him if he were "red". I should not be equal to that; I am rather a nervous woman.'

'I don't believe you are,' said Jane. 'You seem to me very brave.'

'Thank you,' said Mary. 'But I am not brave enough to marry a Bolshevist, and I am sure that Augustine is not that. If he were, I'm sure he would talk about it. And he has never breathed a word about Communism to me. He is quite a fearless person. He would not hide it up if he were really a "red".'

Jane got up and went across the room. She picked up a magazine, and returned, handing it to her visitor.

'This is a silly magazine,' said Jane—and its title, *The Womanly Woman*, did suggest that she was not exaggerating.

'But there is an interesting article in it about Father Card. I thought perhaps that you would like to read it. Take it away with you—I have finished with it.'

Mary opened the magazine, and, turning a few of the pages, there was a large photograph of Augustine. She burst out laughing.

'The villain!' Mary cried. 'It is an excellent photograph.' She read, underneath, the title of the article 'A fearless churchman'.

'Thank you, Miss Greevey, I will put this in my bag. I am very obliged.'

'Perhaps Father Card would like to see it,' Jane suggested.

'Like to see it!' Mary cried. 'I expect he has seen it. Probably his curate has brought it in to him. Or—is it not an interview? He is interviewed nearly every day.'

'No,' Jane said. 'It is not a straight interview, but I think the woman who wrote the article had seen Father Card. It is a sort of interview.'

'Anyway, he will be glad to see that his photograph is moving around in the parish, for I shall tell him that I was given the magazine by you.'

'Father Card is certainly something of an idol,' said Jane Greevey. 'But surely it must bore him terribly—all these magazines wanting to interview him.'

'I ought not to disillusion you,' said Mary. 'But Augustine is not so averse to a little advertisement as you would think. I think all famous men are rather "hams", don't you?'

'I am not so cynical as you are, Miss Chillingham. I suppose I must be what is called an idealist. I could not be made to believe that great preachers are great "hams".'

'I should hate it if you regarded me as hard-boiled,' said Mary. 'I'm afraid I shall soon, if I am not careful, be creating the impression that I am not in love with my future husband. I am, in fact, madly in love with him. Head over ears. I should become quite silly if I confessed to you how much in love I am.'

'I understand perfectly,' said Jane Greevey. 'You did not deceive me when you were laughing about the photograph of the man you are to marry.'

'Splendid,' laughed Mary. 'I am so glad I was not able to deceive you. . . .' She looked round towards the window. 'By the way,' she said, 'how is old Hughie getting on. Is he away? I have not seen him since my return from Kenya.'

'No, he's not away,' said Jane, 'he is in great form. I will tell him, when I next see him, that you were enquiring after him, and I will tell him too the news you have given me about your engagement to the Vicar.'

Mary thanked her hostess. A little surprised that no drink had been forthcoming, before long she took her departure. As soon as she had left, Jane mixed herself a cocktail, feeling really the need of a little stimulant. It was a stiff one, for she had, so to speak, all the stuffing knocked out of her by Mary's news.

Mary's impending marriage had a different effect according to the quarter that the news penetrated. The society columns in the newspapers and magazines for instance were inclined to be facetious about the coming marriage of this unusually beautiful young woman and the handsome Red Priest. Their visits to fashionable night-clubs elicited comments on 'dancing parsons', which was the kind of limelight that Augustine, who was a born client of Durrant's Clipping Agency, appreciated.

His huge form wove in and out of the scented throng, and fairly often they would meet either a friend of his or one of Mary's. 'Here is my latest trout,' Mary would say. 'He is a whopper, isn't he?'

If an old Etonian put in an appearance, Augustine's eyes

lighted up. Here was the past, and, unless he had some particular reason for shunning him, he would move aside and say, 'Army or Navy, Parliament, or field sports?' The man would say what he did and what a lousy time he had. Or Augustine would start with a 'You know what my racket is by my dog-collar.' If they had been friends at school or university they came together for a longer period. He enjoyed planting his biceps on the table and saying, 'I put on weight in the right place'. This public life in fashionable spots pleased both Mary and Augustine. The champagne bill was heavy, but he seemed determined to forget that he was dancing on an overdraft. Half the dance floor at any of the places they went to was Eton or Oxford, but Mary had no feminine equivalent to look out for. In the taxi-cabs they hugged one another, and once or twice Augustine was as immodest as was necessary to inspire Mary with a bride's appropriate satisfaction.

A furnished flat at the eastward end of Ebury Square was available at once, and they took it. As the day of their marriage approached, Augustine became increasingly nervous. His anxiety turned out to be economic.

'Augustine, I have a little dough. How much I do not know, but this is better than nothing, is it not?' Mary told him. And thereupon produced, beneath his astonished eyes, a weighty cheque. It was for five hundred pounds, and with this amount she was able promptly to reduce the bridegroom's fever. He at once supplied her with adequate presents, met the bills of Moyses Stevens' floral contributions, any car hire needed, and so on and so forth. Indeed, Mary rapidly discovered that, with no support coming from her parents, if it had not been for Aunt Blanche's bequest no proper 'society wedding' could have been staged.

Father Card had presumed that Mary, although her

parents were obviously rich, had no independent means of her own, and Mary, on her side, had revealed nothing relating to Aunt Blanche's legacy. That could wait, she thought. They could somehow or other get through the costly business of marriage, and then, later on, she could reveal herself as a fairy princess—but, of course, a somewhat thrifty one. He had, so far, not, quite obviously, been welcomed by his future-in-laws, which, he had concluded, was a result of his manners as a vicar. That they had held themselves aloof from the marriage activities he attributed also to that.

The weather was auspicious, and it was a fine May day when Mary and Augustine, finally, were united at St Bernard's, Knightsbridge, with a bishop officiating. It was a very glittering sacrament, as well as a social event of some magnitude. Augustine's best man was Lord Pastonbury, who had been his closest friend at Eton and Oxford. Mary was given away by General Chillingham, who did not share the feelings of his wife about this alliance. Her sister Alice was present, but did not succeed in looking very enthusiastic. Mrs Chillingham could not be persuaded to come. The reception afterwards was held at the Munster, a first-class hotel of the second order, with as good food as Claridges, but which could not ask as much for its reception rooms. The presents made quite a gratifying display, Augustine's contingent the most impressive (owing to Aunt Blanche's munificence).

The honeymoon was spent in Canon Card's exquisite cottage. As to the amorous showing of Augustine, his exertions nearly made an end of the Canon's antique four-poster. Otherwise, he proved himself no exception to the rule regarding the giant's tendency to laziness. After the excitements of the day, he was soon asleep. On the other hand, as to his fecundity, before the end of their honeymoon

Mary discovered that she must expect a child. Augustine dug for two hours every day in the garden. It was surrounded by a massive yew-hedge. He found a local man to box with. Once or twice Mary came into the garden, where the boxing took place, in the privacy produced by the yew hedge, and afterwards, when they were alone, she said to her husband, 'Are you sure, Augustine, that you won't hurt that young man? If he was injured anywhere it might cost an awful lot of money.'

Augustine pooh-poohed his wife. 'He is a "tough boy". It is most unlikely that in our very quiet little bouts anything would happen to him.' This conversation occurred after the first time that Mary went out to have a look. The second time she was even more alarmed, especially when he knocked down the young man. She said afterwards, 'Teeny, are you sure . . . ? He went down with a big thump. It can only have been an accident if he was not hurt.' To which Augustine replied, 'I know it must look like that. But really it isn't, it doesn't hurt a bit.'

Mary fancied that Augustine grew bigger and stronger every day. On the whole, she thought that her own love grew daily, although he took his lover's task in too leisurely a way.

24

The Beginnings of Married Life

And now their married life in London began, they both started collecting items of furniture towards a home of their own. Mary was averse from spending any more of her capital. As she was going to have a family she felt that she might need to have all her little fortune and more, for Augustine had not exaggerated when he had said that he was as poor as a church-mouse. He had a considerable stipend, but nothing more. Mary developed an attitude towards money which she undoubtedly inherited from her mother. She suffered at the spectacle of money which had been hers disappearing, not to say running away. Augustine, quite soon, concluded that it was a stingy woman (however beautiful) he had married.

It was not long after their return from the honeymoon that Father Card found himself alone with Mrs Chillingham. Actually they had met in Piccadilly, and walked towards Hyde Park Corner. For some reason the Munster Hotel was mentioned, and Mrs Chillingham remarked, 'I never think much of the Munster, do you? I suppose . . .'

'It was not the hotel I should have chosen,' said Father Card. 'But, as you may have guessed, I was compelled to depend a good deal on Mary's generosity. She lent a hand, you know, with all those expenses. . . .'

'You are no doubt aware, Father, that Mary is in a position

easily to meet such expenses. My sister left her the considerable sum of £50,000. You see, we are not as rich as all that; and, since Mary was so well provided with money, I did not feel that it would be fair for her parents to overtax their limited reserves on the occasion of her wedding.'

Father Card had looked very grave. 'Your daughter has not made these facts known to me. Under those circumstances, I think we might have been a little more lavish in selecting our hotel. But still, lavishness is not a good Christian characteristic.'

'I am very surprised, Father, to hear of Mary's reticence. I took it for granted that she would have informed you of the extent of her fortune.'

Father Card realised that he had been given this information from some spiteful motive, and, not for the first time, he understood that his wife's mother harboured anything but sensations of love where her daughter was concerned. He was very glad to be in possession of these facts, and decided, on the first opportunity, to let Mary know that he was no longer in ignorance of the extent of her fortune. And it was about money that Augustine and Mary fell into a quarrel, out of which they found it impossible to drag themselves.

Mary was determined not to be impoverished by the man she had married; and Augustine, on his side, would regard his marriage as a failure, if his wife steadfastly refused to place any of her wealth at his disposal. All their conversations, having money as a central factor, were embittered, as a consequence of what Mrs Chillingham had told Augustine; and at the end of a great number of disputes, having the availability of their common wealth as the essential subject—and Augustine insisted on regarding any money possessed by either as a collective fund—each of them began to regard the other with enmity.

But this is how the struggle had begun. Horrid, who kept the church accounts, had informed Augustine on his return from the honeymoon, that a sum of a hundred pounds was immediately necessary for the payment of certain bills whose settlement had become due. This sum was not available from the sources on which the church economy depended; and when Augustine and his wife were next alone together, after his conversation with Mrs Chillingham, he explained the situation to her.

'Teeny darling, in this case I cannot help. The fact is that the expenses connected with our marriage and stabilising ourselves domestically make it necessary for me to pull up. Otherwise I shall begin spending my capital, which I do not wish to do. I must keep my spending within the limits of my income; the hundred pounds you need would take me outside that, and we have the rest of the year to consider.'

Augustine's brow was deeply wrinkled. After a heavy pause, he spoke. 'I am insanely bad about money. You know what I get as vicar; a thousand a year is good for a parson. What you have, you have never told me. I should not have dreamt of asking you, Mary; but, when I met your mother the other day, she informed me, off her own bat, of the extremely large legacy which you have received from your Aunt Blanche.'

Mary looked very angry. 'Augustine,' she said, 'that you and my mother should put your heads together is not very nice, is it? Surely you can see . . .'

'Darling Mary,' he cried, 'you must believe me when I say that that information came from your mother without any prompting from me. She obviously wanted to tell me. I cannot explain that, and I do not wish to make bad blood between you and your mother. Of course, I am sure that her intentions were of the best. But . . .'

'I hope you will believe it, also,' Mary broke in, 'when I

tell you that I was about to speak of the amount of my capital, and what the income from it represents when taxation has been considered. It is all rather complicated, and it is because I am not clear myself as to how much I have to dispose of that I have hesitated in going into all that with you. But do believe me that I was hiding nothing from you, but merely delaying to talk to you about it. My mother is no well-wisher of mine. You probably understand that her *revelations* the other day were, in intention, excessively spiteful. But please do not allow her little plan to succeed. Teeny, my darling, you do not surely believe that I would try and hide from you a fact of such importance as that—information which you are entitled to have as my husband, and which it was extremely silly of me not to make you acquainted with long before this.'

Augustine took her hands in his, and moved them up and down, in a sort of vertical see-saw movement.

'Of course, most implicitly I believe every syllable of what you have told me,' he said, in a voice deeply sincere. 'Do not let us allow filthy lucre to contaminate our love. It was very naughty of your mother to place in my hands, before you had time to do so, an information which, as you say, would be a necessary part of our life together. It was obviously her intention to steal a march on you. It would be physically impossible, as you have pointed out, for you to dream of hiding such a circumstance as the amount of your wealth. But you must forgive your mother for what you regard as her treachery. She has been rather ill-advised than wicked—do remember that.'

'Of course you say that,' Mary retorted. 'I know my mother's feelings about me only too well, as a result of endless dirty tricks which she has played me. . . .'

Augustine raised his shoulders in an immense shrug. 'Forget all that in this instance, my dear. We must not go back too far in any human relationships, must we? A beautiful young woman and her mother must be expected to collide all along the course of their grown-up associations. You are too good and too generous, Mary, to understand the problem, no doubt. But be gentle with the poor woman.'

This first dispute ended gently, in one sense. But the hundred pounds required for the church was not forthcoming. And that evening Augustine suffered from a tiresome headache, which necessitated Veganin, and an early night.

The non-appearance of the cheque festered for a week or so. Then Augustine opened the subject again in a rather firm way, which came to a head-on collision with Mary's obstinate refusal to depart from her principle—that money *might* be forthcoming from her income, when not overstrained, but never from her capital.

They had formed the habit of breakfasting about eight-thirty. After that they went round to the Clergy House, went up to Augustine's cell, which was used as an office, and the business of the day began. Letters were opened by Horridge, half of which were usually bills. Analysed into its components parts, the hundred pounds in dispute was always turning up. 'Pew repairs,' Augustine would say— 'No means of paying—Distressed clergyman. Must wait.'

Horridge smiled gently, and consigned the papers to a little drawer reserved for anything to do with the hundred pounds that was wanting. Mary would participate in the mirth.

But this was how things proceeded for about a week, at the end of which time Mary preferred to remain at home, and Augustine went round to the office by himself.

The first time this occurred he said to his curate: 'Madame Teeny thought she would examine the *Daily Mirror* this morning.'

Horrid noticed that everything was not quite as it should be. His Vicar had picked too lovely a creature, it seemed to him. Beauty was giving trouble, as was to be expected of a glamour girl. Now, instead of shadow-boxing, the Vicar left the Clergy House, going wifewards, no doubt. Augustine began going to Lords or to Hurlingham; once he and Mary went over to Eton; another time they went up to Oxford. On both these occasions memories of youth were poisoned by the consciousness of debts accumulating.

It was now about three months after their marriage; and one day, at breakfast, Augustine brought things to a head. He announced that he was going to the Jews for the urgently needed money, which was growing in size week by week.

'Don't do that,' said Mary. 'I will give it to you. But you must adjust your church expenditure to your means. You have not married a banking account, but merely a woman. The next time you threaten to go to a moneylender, I shall pack my bags, and leave a man whose love for me is dependent on my handing out money.'

Augustine sat staring at her, his face becoming quite colourless.

'You had better keep your money,' he said at length. 'I find I have married a stingy bitch. No one would believe it to look at you.'

He abruptly left the room, and Mary heard the front door bang a minute or two later.

Mary's first action was to telephone her mother. Mrs Chillingham was breakfasting, but she said she would expect Mary in what was still regarded as her 'den'.

When Mary found herself alone with her mother, she informed her, briefly and coldly, of the situation which brought her to her mother's—she did not know quite why. Her mother accepted this offensive thrust, and asked her kindly if there was any step she could take. 'Shall I have a chat with the Red Priest?' she enquired.

It was at length agreed that she should do just that, being the bearer of a cheque for twice one hundred pounds.

'This has resolved itself into a question of money,' Mary remarked.

'Everything does in the end,' answered her mother.

'Why did Aunt Blanche ruin my marriage?' cried Mary. 'Anyhow I will buy a period of tranquillity, and think things over.'

Later that morning, Mrs Chillingham's chat with Father Card was helpful. It had a matter of fact, not to say cynical tone. She agreed with the priest that, if a woman possessed a considerable sum of money, she could not hope to keep it intact, once marriage had complicated her life. She would do her best to make Mary understand. Meanwhile, they could consult together—son-in-law and mother-bird, as high contracting parties; she produced Mary's cheque for two hundred pounds, and Augustine gratefully took it.

'I hope Mary will return about tea-time,' he said, as they parted.

Mary and Augustine reached their flat at about the same time that afternoon. Tea was ready, and they went into the living-room together. Up till then they had said nothing except for a 'hello' from Augustine. When they were seated at the tea-table, Mary began the conversation with an uncompromising suddenness.

'Am I a bitch?' she led off.

'What an abomination, that word!' exclaimed Teeny. 'Who was the beast who used it?'

And so, in a spirit of mutually agreed humour, the hard facts of the situation were dissolved away. Both knew that a breathing-space, nothing more, had been purchased by two hundred pounds.

25

The Ghastly Girl Again

At the Clergy House a change had occurred about this time. Father Horridge, the senior curate, surrendered his curacy at St Catherine and the Angels, in order to take a post of some consequence in the Colonies. In his place came a young man of great promise, a Father Harold Makepeace. He had distinguished himself at Oxford, and had just been ordained. This tall, very self-possessed-looking young priest did not merely replace 'Horrid'; he seemed to demand more authority than that. He was not a 'secretary', and had to be handled quite differently. He wore his hair *en brosse*. With his height and good looks, as he became a little more experienced he would be the natural figure to replace Father Card in the church, during an absence of the Vicar.

From the first it seemed to Mary that this prepossessing young man was not greatly liked by Augustine. The next thing that became apparent to her was that she appeared desirable to Father Makepeace. Following this, she noticed that it was not agreeable to Augustine that his new curate should experience these sensations. Also, in their debates in the studio, Makepeace did not adapt himself to Augustine's views. He had views of his own, and did not hesitate to voice them. In brief, this young man was above himself, and actually in competition with the Vicar. Mary would see the Vicar's blood rise into his face in a dangerous way. This amused her at times; and she was fond of quoting Father

Makepeace, as though his opinions were authoritative, and worthy of quotation. Teeny never failed to respond angrily.

Since things were rather prickly and apt to degenerate into an ugly argument at the cell in the morning, Mary avoided it. She would go shopping, or visit the former head-girl of Ghastly. At her wedding Monica Blunt had come in a very smart outfit, and Mary surprised herself by the cordiality she felt for this friend of her sister's. She had gone to see her, in her delightful little flat in Chelsea, almost at once after their return from the honeymoon.

'Now I understand what you meant by the Cupid flying from Canterbury to Moscow,' Monica had said. 'I wish I had understood at the time.'

'Would you have intervened?' Mary enquired.

'Perhaps,' Monica said, with a wink.

The friendship with Monica Blunt developed quickly, until at last Monica became the woman she was most disposed to see. Mary immediately confided to her the money conflict, and asked Monica what she advised her to do.

'Do what you are doing,' Monica replied, in a hardboiled voice. 'If you reduce your capital you will regret it. A man who begins digging your money out of you will be selfish in other ways too. Or so it seems to me.'

This encouragement of her 'stinginess' influenced Mary. 'I love my Teeny,' she said. 'But, as your discerning eyes must have seen, not quite so much as I had expected. This great big man is a darling, but he is a lazy devil—you see what I mean?'

Monica saw what she meant, and sat smiling to herself, hunched up, and lines of fun scoring her forehead.

'How much love does a girl need?'

'Lord Byron says that love is woman's whole existence. For me, he exaggerates. But I want a good deal from time to time, don't you know.'

'I should be inclined to administer a little Spanish fly to your sluggard,' Monica suggested roguishly.

'If you desert the celibate state, pick a little man!' said Mary. 'My considered opinion! But I love my old lazy-bones, and I'm glad I married him.'

This last was not the kind of remark that pleased the Ghastly Girl. Mary took her out to lunch. They went to a small restaurant off the Kings Road, Chelsea, called 'On Bouffe'. It was run by a Frenchwoman, and the waiters were real Frenchmen—a rare combination. Presumably the cook was French, for the food was extremely good. Mary went on talking about herself, which seemed to interest the Ghastly one.

'Have I told you that we have a new curate?' asked Mary.

Monica shook her head.

'He is a good looker, and a clever young man.'

'How old?' asked Monica.

'About my age,' said Mary, 'perhaps a shade more. He is down from Oxford, not so very long, and he really did things there. He knows a lot. Everyone hates him.'

'It could not be otherwise,' was the opinion of Monica.

'That is just what I think,' said Mary, nodding heavily, 'but I am trying to convert my Teeny—Augustine, you know—trying to make him keep his rage in check. It is awfully bad for a man like Augustine to bottle himself up, I know. But I can't have them persecuting Mr Makepeace.'

'Why?' asked Monica.

'Have you read Chesterfield's *Letters*?' Mary enquired. 'You remember, then, "The Graces, always the Graces".'

'The most difficult injunction it is possible to imagine. Your Teeny will go berserk if you push him too hard.'

'I am determined to civilise my Teeny,' Mary said. 'He has this frightful body, and, naturally, what goes with that is something I cannot allow. When we go out to dinner together, if a man at a neighbouring table is rude, because he is a clergyman, and he thinks it safe to have a bit of fun, Teeny's eyes have a most unpleasant glint. Before he married me he used to box incessantly with his former curate, for instance. I think he worked off his feelings in that way. Mr Makepeace refuses to help him do this. He won't box.'

'To be married to a boxing Blue is a little disquieting,' observed Monica.

'Yes,' Mary agreed. 'But he drinks practically nothing. I can never be thankful enough for that. So many of the women I have known had drunkards as husbands. I sometimes feel that my Teeny has some of the elements of a Saint. It may sound ridiculous, but he has the makings of a holy man. To see him stretched out in the morning on his chaise-longue, talking to his former secretary, was an impressive sight. He reminded me of those holy men of the East.'

'I thought the fakir was always a thin man, who usually stood on one leg,' suggested Monica.

'In the middle of the morning he and Horridge used to go off and box. He never hit his curate, because he was so unathletic a man. He just tapped him, and exercised himself by jumping about. They liked one another. I used to admire his gentleness.'

'You lost your heart to a gentle giant,' said Monica, smiling her gentlest smile.

'Put it that way. The combination of great strength and great gentleness,' Mary said.

Monica screwed her face up, and said, 'Are there any women in the Clergy House?'

'Only Emma, the housekeeper-cook. She is neither a beautiful nor a dynamic character. She is just Emma.'

'I see.' Monica nodded. 'You are most fortunate in having no women.'

Mary laughed, but Monica continued. 'I have known some very enticing cooks,' she observed.

'Emma may be enticing to Father Wimbush, but to no one else, I think.' Mary called the waiter, and they ordered their coffee. 'He,' said Mary, 'Father Wimbush, lusts after all of the other sex. So *even* Emma . . .'

'Who is this lustful Father?' enquired the ex-Ghastly Girl.

'He is the second curate,' Mary said. 'Have I never spoken of him?'

'No,' said Monica. 'So all the illegitimate children issue from him? What a grand, what a classical figure is a lascivious curé!'

'We believe he is an unfrocked priest. I'm sure that that was his trouble.'

'I must hear more of him,' Monica said, smacking her lips.

Mary asked her friend if she would have a Benedictine or anything, and got the answer 'Benedictine', and after that the conversation shifted to the theatre, and Mary suggested that they should have an evening out. Monica offered her two or three plays and she chose an American comedy, which had just come on. 'I will get for us a box,' Mary said.

After she had left Monica, she had an appointment with Mr Smithers. During an hour or so with the lawyer she went more fully into everything connected with her finances. She took a great interest in the problems concerning her money. She found that the income she would receive would amount to nearly two thousand a year, and of that she would lose to the Inland Revenue nearly a third. That would leave her approximately fourteen hundred.

When they were together that evening, she said to Augustine, 'I saw my lawyer this afternoon, and went more fully into the matter of my probable income. It turns out to be about fourteen hundred pounds a year, after my supertax has been dealt with.'

Augustine listened gravely, but said nothing.

Mary, after a pause, continued: 'I have been thinking about this, Teeny, and I have come to the following conclusion. Although no money will be forthcoming at once, Mr Smithers is perfectly ready to advance me another thousand pounds, until I get straight. He has advanced me one thousand already, you know. Now, it would be convenient for you, would it not, just as it would for me, to have money in advance. As soon as I receive Mr Smithers' cheque, I will pay you five hundred pounds.'

As she had said this, Mary was watching her husband, and she could not fail to notice that there was no joy in his eye as he listened to this proposal. No, she thought; the devil wants to have a slap at my capital.

'That would be very generous of you, Mary,' was what he said. And he continued: 'I am a mug about money. Bills keep rolling in, and I find it frightfully difficult to keep straight, as you know. But it certainly would be a relief, to say the least, if I had five hundred pounds in advance, to face my creditors with.'

'Well, I realise that in the Clergy House you paid no rent and, as a bachelor, lived quite cheaply. Now you have an expensive house-rent, in this flat, and there is heating and lighting and servant's wages and you have to feed *me*. As I am able to pay, I think that is very unfair,' said Mary with emphasis.

Augustine shook his head.

'I greatly appreciate your kindness, Mary. Most men, when they marry, automatically undertake the upkeep of a wife. That is legal. And that is what I undertook to do when I asked you to marry me. I did not suppose that you had any money to speak of, and I would have gladly fed you, heated you, and kept a roof over your head. Oh, and Mary, I would have paid all the dressmaking bills.'

'Well, these conventional expenses were not necessary,"
said Mary. 'I offer you exactly half my income.'

Augustine did not meet this with a proper enthusiasm;
in fact, he seemed disappointed. Here was Mary, advertising
her favourite proposal, again a stern refusal to look in the
direction of her capital, but a perfect willingness to share
her income. So, instead of a Teeny full of gratitude, here
he was quite the reverse; looking sourly at her handsome
offer, and still intending, it was obvious, to reserve the right
to make a raid upon her main fortune.

So Mary, in fact, was worse off than before. For it was
quite clear that this man, being married to her, would insist
on not allowing her to keep him at a distance where her
heritage was concerned. If Augustine Card had a fancy for a
beautiful little house in the country, like that of his father,
would there be no means of persuading Mary to give him
a few thousand pounds to help him to buy it? No, she
would tell him that she would pay the gas bill or buy him a
pair of shoes, but that she would not part with so huge a
sum. All that he actually wanted at the moment was a car
—not too small a car for so large a man, but still, relatively
cheap. And he needed all his spare money for things
connected with the church. But it was no use talking to the
woman in whose keeping he had placed himself about a car
which he was unable to afford. She would pay the telephone
bill, but not run to such an expense as a car. She would tell
him that it did not merely mean the cost of the machine
itself, but also a garage in which to house it, and very
expensive petrol to be able to run it.

He scowled at her, and was very disagreeable for the rest
of the evening. It was not as if she had offered him a half of
her income, but as if she had refused to give him a cent.
They went to bed in a bad humour.

26

Meeting of Mothers-in-Law

When Lady Imogen Card mounted the steps at the thin end of Ebury Square, Mrs Chillingham was waiting for her in the drawing-room. As she entered, Mrs Chillingham sprang up, and greeted her with a special politeness. 'It is unfortunate,' she said, 'that we meet so seldom. I suppose we must have a different set of friends.'

Lady Imogen answered, 'You are younger than I am, and probably are in a different generational stream. To indicate where we are to be found, we frequent the Duchess of Bridport and Fulham Palace, or we see the dear Archbishop, when he is London.'

'The Archbishop is of great wit, isn't he,' said Mrs Chillingham.

'And he is a most saintly person too,' Lady Imogen murmured. 'But, as you see, we have a rather shoppy visiting-list.'

'Shall we go up to my personal retreat, Lady Imogen?' said Mrs Chillingham. 'A drawing-room is rather a frigid place for two people to sit in'—and she led the way to the boudoir attached to her bedroom.

'What a charming room,' said Lady Imogen, as they entered. 'You have a most attractive house. You are encompassed by very smart railings, with a deliciously military appearance.'

'Yes, our military friends greatly appreciate the parade of railings,' said Mrs Chillingham. 'I wonder your by now clerical eye notices our sergeant's guard.'

Lady Imogen sank into one of the two large chairs with which this room was provided. 'I have wanted to have a talk with you for some time,' she said, 'but was rather shy about taking up your time.'

'I am delighted that you came, Lady Imogen, for I too have been looking forward to a little talk, we hardly have met since the marriage of our children.'

'That is it,' said the other, 'that is it. There are our children, and it never seems to occur to *them* to pay us a visit, so the least we can do is to pay a visit for them.'

Mrs Chillingham nodded her head, and said, 'That is a delightful idea,' and they smiled at one another. 'Now what can I give you? Will you have a cup of coffee? or would you rather have a glass of sherry?'

'If it is not too terribly inconvenient at this time of the day, might I have a small cup of coffee?'

Mrs Chillingham pressed a bell, and in a couple of minutes an immaculate, a very smart and pretty servant made her appearance. Mrs Chillingham conveyed to this young woman the nature of their requirements, adding something to the coffee.

'Do you often see Mary, your daughter?' asked Lady Imogen.

'The answer to that, Lady Imogen, is—absolutely never!'

'Oh,' said Augustine's mother, taken aback. 'I should have thought that she would often come round and see you. Augustine seldom seems to find time to come and see us, but we live farther away; but a young woman . . .'

'My daughter and I are on the worst of terms, I am sorry to have to say.'

Lady Imogen showed signs of confusion, as if her

hostess's revelation of the lack of cordiality between her daughter and herself had displeased her. She behaved as if she were searching for a new approach, and said, in a few moments, 'Do you ever go round to see her—where she lives, I mean?' Lady Imogen asked this with some hesitation.

'I should not be very well received,' answered the mother of Mary.

'Good gracious! What an unnatural child your daughter appears to be!'

'A holy terror,' said her mother.

Lady Imogen in obvious desperation said: 'In spite of these appalling circumstances, I must all the same deliver myself of a little matter that I had in mind to talk to you about. My son, Augustine, is almost mad with anxiety, and every time he does come to see us he relieves his mind by confiding to us what is troubling him. He is in the state of penury that afflicts most men of his cloth—he has huge bills which he cannot settle, and he is sorely tempted to borrow sufficient money, in order to settle the worst of these. We cannot help him, for the simple reason that my husband, who is a most generous man, has impoverished himself beyond belief. Augustine tells us that his wife, Mary, inherited a considerable fortune just before her marriage, but that she steadily refuses to help him out of his difficulties. She always confronts him with the same cry—"My income, but never a penny of my capital." She does not very faithfully act according to this dictum of hers certainly. But, he feels the least she could do would be to lend him a thousand pounds, which she could well afford.'

'But Lady Imogen, what would have happened if your son had not married? Would he have disintegrated and become the victim of the Jews? Was it providential that he married Mary, and does he think that she should put at his disposal her entire fortune, in which case she would have no money left in the event of a family of any size—supposing she continues to have children, which is probable, seeing that both parents are young and healthy . . .'

The door opened and the coffee with some excellent biscuits arrived.

'I have not asked *you*, Mrs Chillingham . . .' said Lady Imogen.

'I am quite aware of that, but you came here to ask me . . .'

'I have asked you for nothing . . .' Lady Imogen protested.

'Here, let me give you a cup of what is really very excellent coffee,' said Mrs Chillingham. 'And these biscuits, also, are the best I can find in the neighbourhood.'

Lady Imogen took the coffee and the biscuit, her face contorted with a natural combativeness, which had had no opportunity of relief. 'I am sure this is a first-rate biscuit, but if you will excuse me I will put it aside on this plate, as I never eat at this time of the day,' she said.

'Perhaps I should not have offered you the coffee?' said Mrs Chillingham.

Lady Imogen looked at her stonily.

'As I have told you, my daughter, Mary, is on the worst of terms with me, and if I asked her to give a thousand pounds of her capital to Augustine she would explode. I should really get no result, except that she would say (I hope you will excuse my daughter's language) "Why the hell don't *you* give it him, Mother?"'

'My conversation with you, Mrs Chillingham, the air becoming quite blue, enables me to say what a horrible life Augustine is having with your daughter.'

'I am glad I have been able to convey a little of the horror inevitable in living with my daughter. There is really no way of avoiding it, and I am sincerely sorry for what Augustine has to support. Perhaps we might put our heads together and attempt to contrive a substitute for the thousand pounds which Mary refuses to produce. My husband and I alone would be quite unable to meet the flood of debts incurred by your son, but perhaps *together* —the General and the Canon might be able to do a little something.' Mrs Chillingham sat with her eye upon Lady Imogen, ready for anything that lady might say.

'I do not think it would be very much use, or that it would be quite fair,' said Lady Imogen, 'to ask a poor parson like my husband to step into the place occupied by your daughter—who quite recently inherited fifty thousand pounds, according to the papers—and somehow find one thousand pounds for poor Augustine, when she, Augustine's wife, could easily spare that sum. I am not surprised, Mrs Chillingham, that you do not get on very well with Mary. But in spite of this I think you could approach her—for her steady refusal to help my son is really disgraceful, and leaves us all in a very awkward position.'

'I have a certain sympathy which a mother-in-law must feel for Augustine,' said Mrs Chillingham, 'although I do not like so much the Red Priest side of him. But I do not think I could persuade my husband to contribute very much towards the thousand pounds he needs so badly.'

Lady Imogen was very red in the face, and she looked at her hostess, from her mongolian eyes, with something remarkably like hatred. 'I came here with the intention of urging you to intervene, to use all your influence with Mary to persuade her to come to the help of my son. You seem to suggest that I came here to ask *you* for money. Nothing was farther from my thoughts. But I can see that you are determined to twist my appeal in the manner in which I have shown you to have done.'

'You will allow me to say that it is quite untrue to describe me as engaged in a twisting operation. Let us, Lady Imogen, rather talk sense than the reverse. I have a suggestion to make. Let us organise a Flag Day for Augustine, which, I'm sure would result in his accumulating a large sum of money from among his well-wishers. Another suggestion is that you should approach Mary yourself. You seem on excellent terms with my daughter. Could not *you* propose to her a raid into her private fortune to the extent of one thousand pounds? That, surely, is worthy trying. Thenceforth you might remain on the worst of terms with your daughter-in-law. But we would then be in exactly the same boat.'

Lady Imogen looked at her wrist watch. She had grown strangely stiff. She faced Mrs Chillingham with something not unlike a scowl.

'You are a very clever woman, Mrs Chillingham. . . .'

'Oh do not say that, Lady Imogen, for when people begin to call one another clever it is an ominous sign.'

'I will not call you clever,' said Lady Imogen, 'but I leave you with a feeling of having been what the Americans call out-smarted.'

She rose. She would have liked a glass of ice-water, but she would not ask Mrs Chillingham for that, or anything else. She strode stiffly out of the room, Mrs Chillingham a step or two behind her. 'I have not been able to help you,' she said. 'I regret that.'

Lady Imogen received this dumbly, and went on a little unsteadily down the stairs.

'Do let them call you a taxi,' came from Mrs Chillingham on the landing above, as a man-servant appeared in the hall.

Lady Imogen proceeded on her way without any sign of having heard these amiabilities. She was assisted out by the butler.

When the door closed, Mrs Chillingham turned back to her boudoir, where she sat down and took up the telephone. She dialled Mary's number, and in a moment or two heard her daughter's voice. 'Ah, Mary,' she said amiably, 'I have just had a severe struggle in defence of your capital. It is safe—I thought you'd like to know.' Then she hung up, a fragment of a hoarse laugh reaching her before the telephone clicked off. She smiled very drily, and went straight down to lunch.

27

Address on the Indian Religion

The not very large table in the studio had been re-placed by a long refectory table. At this about thirty people could be accommodated and the form taken by the debate was a gathering along both sides of this. Also lectures, or religious harangues, were arranged by the audience establishing themselves on either side of the table, and the lecturer sitting on a high chair at one end.

Mary took part in these debates, and was always present at the lectures. Father Makepeace was advertised as giving an address on Indian Religion, on one of these occasions, and she made her appearance in the studio five minutes before the talk was due to begin. Augustine was already there, and she took her place at his side. In public he always showed the same deference to his wife, and when she sat down beside him he turned to her with a smile and said, 'So you were able to get here, Mary.' He said, behind his hand, in a voice which could only be heard a short distance away, 'I do not suppose that Father Makepeace knows very much about Indian Religion.' Father Wimbush took his place opposite to them, bowing to Mary. Augustine whispered to him, across the table, 'Get ready for Nirvana.'

'I'm always ready for that,' answered Father Wimbush, with a wink and a grin.

Father Makepeace entered the studio, holding a large

portfolio and a book; the tall, cassocked figure strode to the chair at the head of the table. The chair was arranged so as to elevate its occupant some inches above the level of the table, and a desk rose from it for him to place his papers on. Father Makepeace was an imposing figure, stern and self-confident, and Mary arranged herself to listen to him with none of the critical sourness displayed by her husband. A complete audience of about thirty people, members of the congregation and one or two others, was in place, their faces turned towards Father Makepeace. He looked at the clock, and he and Father Wimbush signalled to one another. Father Wimbush stood up, and said, 'Ladies and Gentlemen, Father Makepeace is now about to address you on the subject of Indian Religion.' He sat down, and Father Makepeace bowed towards his audience.

'Ladies and Gentlemen,' he said. 'Most people, perhaps, would think of Buddhism in connection with the Religions of India. But Buddha was not approved of by the religious in India because there was not very much religion in his teaching. In speaking of Indian religion we mean the Vedic tradition, in one of its many forms; or, not to disperse our attention into these various channels, we will confine ourselves to the Brahmanical central doctrine.

'It may be said that, in a general way, the Indians have one God, Brahma. No country could provide more of a plurality of gods and goddesses than India. But for our purposes we may confine ourselves to the Divine Principle in which the maximum of power is concentrated.

'When we, Christians, pray to our God it is to a mighty presence distinct from us—separate, and immensely different. The essential difference between the Indians and us is that they are always attempting to coalesce and become one with their deity. *Brahman—atman* represents this oneness of the worshipper with what he worships.

'Indian religion, in its essences, consists in identifying the Dynamism and the Permanence of the one Central Being. This may be described as the realisation of Brahman.

' "The chief motivation of Vedic philosophy . . . has been . . . the search for a basic unity underlying the manifold of the universe." It is impossible to find a better verbal statement than that. The mathematical expression is $1+1=1$. The well-known literary expression is to be found in Goethe, in his *Hexeneinmaleins* (witch's one time one).

'Now the God of the Indian is immanent. When the Indian is attempting to identify the Dynamism with the Permanence he is welding together the Human and the Divine. He is a unitary man, whereas the Christian is a triune man. The mathematical formula of the Christian is $3=1$; and one of his three Gods is, in fact, human.

'What is the difference between the man who is profoundly attracted to the One, and the man who finds himself attracted to the Three? I will attempt to answer this question, after I have said some more about the grand basis of the Vedic religion of the Indian.

'There is a Vedic hymn which is of central importance. It is ancient, and it derives from a period when food was regarded as the essential divine substance of human life. But let me quote. "This life-sap builds up and constitutes all the forms of life. Changing its forms it remains nevertheless indestructible. The creatures thrive by feeding on each other—feeding on each other, devouring, and begetting —but the divine substance itself lives on, without interruption, through the ceaseless interruptions of the lives of all the living beings. Thus we find verified . . . and experienced in the aspect of its holy mystery, the primary law of the terrible *Arthasastra*: the ruthless struggle for life that prevails in innocence in the realms of nature."

'I quote this from what I consider the best book on the

religions of India. We are here surveying Feeding as Divinity. It is a savage unitarianism—the eating of God. This is oneness most basically achieved by the devouring of divinity.

'Thus we get man as a drop in the Niagara of the wholly dynamic rush of the universe.

'Now we come back to *einmaleins*, and thence to the illogic of the universe. For $1+1=1$, when the ones marry. But if they have children, then $1+1$ may make 12.

'The *einmaleins*, the ideal oneness of the religious man, when that is most successfully achieved is when he is most alone. He is then identified with the Divinity. He would not be most successful in his devotions with his entire family of, say, ten offspring with him.

'However, ladies and gentlemen, it would be quite wrong to give the impression of the Indian as a solid unit, with a hard outline. He is anything but that. There is nothing so complicated as is the Indian, so unready to present himself as a simple, straightforward figure.

'When two Europeans think about one another—say myself and Father Wimbush—they think about the *gross* body (as the Indian would say). It is a simple, limited shape.

'But not so the Indian. An Indian has, not only his gross body, but also his subtle body. He has a mass of things, stretching out all around him. His *atman*: *brahman*—his true Self—is I suppose the most solid thing about him. But you cannot see it with your eyes, nor can you perceive it with any other sense. None of an Indian's personality belongs to the visible or visual world. The part of an Indian friend that you see is not the most important part of him. He is an intricate monster of wrappings, some subtle and some gross, some belonging to one order of substance, some to another.

'I do not mean to say that two Indians, say two Indian politicians, deal with one another in this complicated way.

They are both visual creatures, just as everyone in this room is. Yet, in philosophic thought, we know that they are monsters of a most intricate kind.'

'Excuse me, Father,' Father Wimbush began. 'Are not these complicated monsters you speak of built up by philosophical terminology? Is it not as if you said that the people walking along Piccadilly were visual creatures, consisting of a suit of clothes, beneath which were small leather receptacles for their feet, and, at the top, felt or cloth hats, and, in the case of women, with different kinds of suits, the legs surrounded by a skirt, and so forth? In other words, simply what the eyes can see, and nothing else, would reduce these people to what I have roughly indicated. Then that visual man, as we might call him, would be filled with, in the first place, all we know of him—we know he has a skeleton inside, and we know a good deal about the structure of his body and also of his mind, and so on and so forth; then, in addition to all that we know of him, there is *all that we think of him*; we may think that he possesses a soul, a psyche; and, if the observer happened to be a surgeon, his visual man would be a complex of what he *knew was there*, and what he saw, so that it would comprise a very intricate creature. All I am saying is, Father Makepeace, that you are talking about what the philosopher sees, and no one else.'

'What I meant, Father Wimbush, was that our European Man, even for the philosopher, is much more just the uncomplicated *visual man* of commonsense, with, perhaps, a small filmy thing which we call a soul added, whereas any Indian philosopher, of the least complicated kind, would have in *his* human being, a great mass of metaphysical parcellings, at the centre of which would be the *atman*, and it would be a most intricate set of bodies within bodies, and would stretch out far beyond his gross limits.'

'So long as you are not claiming that the butcher, the

baker, and the candlestick maker are such complex creatures as all that,' said Father Wimbush, 'then I am satisfied.'

Father Makepeace drank from a glass of water provided for the speaker. Then he faced the audience again.

'All I am saying is, that, in his general attitude, the Indian is a very different man from his Vedic ancestors. Brahman orthodoxy did finally accept the primitive pre-Aryan philosophy and cosmology (through the medium, mainly of Sankhya), but the distant, pre-Aryan beliefs were entirely unlike the Brahmanic ways of thinking characteristic of India.'

At this point an elderly man raised his voice a little, and thrust himself into the argument.

'Allow me to say, Father, that I have lived in India, and I disagree with one of your statements, and would like to say that in India the politician is not what you call a *visual man* any more than anybody else. In Mahatma Gandhi one was conscious of the same super-visual condition as I have frequently met with in philosophic teachers.'

'The Mahatma was a very unusual man.' Father Makepeace replied. 'I referred to ordinary politicos.'

'There are no ordinary politicos in India,' said the elderly interrupter. 'As to Gandhi, I never could see him properly, he was so un-visual.'

'This in no way affects my argument,' said the priest. 'And I should have thought that it would only be an Indian who found it impossible to see a man because of his enveloping subtleties.'

'May I suggest,' Father Card broke in, 'that our brilliant lecturer should come out from behind the veils of Indian philosophy, and tell us a little more about Indian religion.'

'Hear, hear. Hear, hear!' clamoured a lady parishioner, banging the table at the same time.

'May I say that I am in complete agreement with Father

Card, and hope that the speaker will in future be less obscure,' said another lady parishioner.

'I feel rather alarmed at the expression of displeasure on the part of the ladies in our audience,' said Father Makepeace. 'I cannot employ words which would be understood by a child of five, but I will endeavour to express myself at as unlearned a level as possible.'

'I shall be very grateful if you can manage to do that,' retorted the first of the lady interveners.

There was a stir and a muffled sound throughout the audience, and Father Card spoke. 'The Father who is addressing you has given you his assurance that he will abandon the learned mode of his address.'

'Hear, hear!' exclaimed one of the audience, and Father Makepeace flushed a deep red.

'If the Vicar feels,' the priest began, 'that my way of expressing myself is too involved . . .'

'No, no, Father, please proceed!' said the Vicar's wife.

'Thank you, Mrs Card,' said the priest, bowing.

The Vicar laughed a little, looking sideways at his wife.

'Ladies and Gentlemen,' said Father Makepeace. 'I do not think that I can go on with this address. I hope you will accept my apologies.' Father Makepeace rose, picked up his book and papers, and walked quickly out of the studio.

There was a general movement in the audience and everybody appeared to be talking. Father Card's voice rose above the noise. He stood up. 'I am sorry that our plan to provide you with a talk about Indian Religion has been a failure. Our curate whom I entrusted with the delivery of this address is, I fear, not in very good health. I could see at once, from the way that he began his outline of this great and difficult subject, that he was not master of himself. I regret that you have been brought here tonight to be present at this fiasco, but we will make up for it at our debate tomorrow night, which will take place as advertised.' This was the signal for the departure of the audience. Father Card walked round the table, and entered into conversation with one of his parishioners who was about to leave. They were joined by two other members of the disintegrating audience. They drifted towards the centre of the room, and eventually, seeing that the remainder of the guests were disappearing into the street, they went towards the door, and Father Card shook their hands before they left. When everyone had gone, he came back to the table where his wife and Father Wimbush were still seated.

'Phew!' he said, as he took his place beside Mary. 'The wretched Makepeace let us down badly.'

'That is not how I would put it,' Mary said. 'It seems to me that you let Father Makepeace down.'

'How was that? Do you mean me?' said Augustine.

'Everyone seemed inclined to find fault,' Mary protested. 'And you did not support him, Augustine. You laughed insultingly, you know.'

'Me? Did I do that, Wimbush?' asked Augustine.

'Well,' said Father Wimbush, 'you certainly laughed. If I had been in your place I should have laughed louder than you did.'

'I thought he had begun a very good address,' said Mary. 'But if you had adopted the same tone to me as you did to him, I should have left the room just as he did. He is a very brilliant man. How would you like to be treated like that, Augustine?' Mary looked reproachfully at her husband.

'Rot,' said Augustine, looking very cross. 'That fellow is abominably conceited. He does not ask my permission to discontinue his address—he just marches off, if you do not treat him with sufficient deference. I must see if I can get another curate.'

'Meanwhile, Teeny, he is, after all, a gentleman.'

'To hell with that! It is inexcusable for him to imagine himself the cat's pyjamas. He thinks he's so big that this place is not big enough for him. He holds his nose up in the air, and the trouble is to stop him playing the vicar. He is mightily offended if you tell him to pipe down. He was taking all his Indian religion out of a book, and was very displeased when Father Wimbush brought him out of the clouds, and a little bit nearer to earth.'

'Yes,' said Father Wimbush, 'anyone would have thought that any railway porter in India was a metaphysical diagram —a jig-saw puzzle composed of philosophical contraptions.'

'This is not fair!' exclaimed Mary. 'You are jealous of that learned, handsome colleague of yours.'

'That paragon makes me feel small, that is the fact of the matter,' said Father Card. 'I must send him back where he came from, and tell them that we are all people of a normal size here, he makes us feel as if we were in Lilliput. Ask if they haven't got any one smaller.'

He stood up. Addressing Father Wimbush he said, 'If you don't hurry he will be hustling Emma, and get all the food.'

With a hoarse laugh Father Wimbush sprang up, exclaiming, 'You are right at that! I shall go hungry to bed if I'm not smart.' And with a still harsher burst of hilarity he hurried through the studio door.

After switching off the electric light, Augustine Card and his wife followed Wimbush out of the door. In silence, they returned to their flat. As they reached it, Mary said, 'I must say, Teeny, that I think you treat your new curate unnecessarily badly. What has he done to deserve so much ill will? Is he too clever or too good-looking? You used not to treat Horridge in this way.'

'You don't have to spend your time with him in the Clergy House as I do, Mary,' said Augustine. 'If you did, you would feel very differently about him. He is unbearably conceited.'

'I know he refuses to box with you,' laughed Mary. 'But I don't blame him. I think it would be very unwise of him to put on the gloves with you, Teeny.'

28

A Stretch of Months

The next morning Mary accompanied Augustine to the cell in the Clergy House. Up to lunch-time the curates used this as an office or common room. Since his marriage Augustine was not to be found there every morning and so the curates had it more to themselves. Mary wanted to be present in case his colleagues were uncivil to Father Makepeace.

Makepeace was there already. Mary gave him a cordial good morning, and said, 'I was so disappointed when you broke off your address, Father Makepeace. I was extremely interested in what you had said so far. Your "*einmaleins*" theory was wonderfully interesting.'

'I am glad you were interested, Mrs Card. Books on Indian philosophy are either by Indians, and are very boring and unreadable, or else they are by Englishmen, and are almost equally bad.'

'That is what I have found,' said Mary.

As usual, Mary and the new curate got on very well; and, as usual, Augustine did not relish this at all. On this occasion he scowled, seeing his wife and curate agree so sweetly, and sank on to his chaise-longue. 'I am afraid that my wife's idea of your performance yesterday differs greatly from mine,' Augustine said.

'I gather that, sir,' Father Makepeace answered.

The curate established himself near one of the windows,

and began to write. Father Card opened a letter, and was at once absorbed in it; whereas Mary read a book.

'Here is a parishioner who is no great admirer of yours,' said Augustine to the curate. 'He is an officer who was stationed in India.'

'That of course makes him a great expert about the British Army in India,' said Mary.

Augustine began writing, and in about five minutes he handed to Father Makepeace a sheet of paper and a letter— the letter of which he had spoken, and his reply. The curate took them over to where he was writing by a window. Shortly after reading them, he tore up the sheet of paper he had been handed.

'This is the best thing to do with your letter to Major General Sir Frederick Blackwell,' said the curate.

Augustine continued to lie at full length on the chaise-longue, staring at Father Makepeace.

'How dare you do that, sir,' he said.

'If you write another document of that kind to General Blackwell I will dispatch a letter myself to that gentleman, informing him what I think of you, which is not very much,' said the curate.

'I would not recommend you to do that,' said Augustine.

'I would, however, do it,' retorted the curate, sitting up bellicosely. 'I have testimonials from Oxford, rather different from what they give to an expert bruiser, and I do not propose that you should attempt to degrade me while acting as curate at this church. I will communicate with the Bishop if you show yourself inclined to write letters of that sort about me.'

Augustine swung himself around, and sat up, facing Makepeace.

'Augustine,' commanded Mary, 'please forget that you are very strong. It is irrelevant. You know you cannot insult this young man, then give him a beating. So what is the use of sitting up, and looking threatening; you are making a fool of yourself.'

These words fell like large stones in a pond. Father Card transferred his gaze to a neutral point. Father Makepeace rose, saying, 'I had better go to my room.'

There was a minute or two's pause; and then the curate spoke again.

'I apologise for what I said just now. It was very priggish, I am sorry to say. The remarks of a derogatory kind about the Blue were ridiculous. A Doctorate is in no way superior to a sporting decoration.'

As Father Makepeace stood there apologising, Augustine said, 'I have a thing or two to apologise about also.' He held out his hand towards the curate, and the latter grasped it.

'That is as it should be,' said Mary. 'I do like to see people doing that, instead of squaring up to one another.'

'Well,' said Augustine, 'you've got your wish.' He flung himself back on the chaise-longue, and smiled at his curate, who nodded and smiled back, and left the room.

Mary had risen to her feet, but she now sat down again, and laughed.

'You are a baby. If I were not here, all kinds of horrible things would happen . . . quite unnecessary things.'

'You take too much credit to yourself,' said Augustine. 'Two men availed themselves of your speech, that is all. Of course I could not beat up Makepeace, after being very rude to him. I was delighted to get out of a little difficulty. You made it possible and easy to do so. Thank you . . but do not be so self-satisfied. You are a convenience, nothing more.'

'I like that. Another time I will leave you, and you will find yourself in a horrible mess of your own making.'

At this point Father Wimbush entered the cell, but, noticing that the Vicar and his wife were having not too cordial a conversation, he said, 'I beg your pardon,' and hurriedly left.

Mary laughed. 'You have a letter or two to write,' she said. 'When that's done, we will go out and have a walk in the Park, and I'll take you to lunch at the Ritz.'

This benign ending of a dangerous situation did not cause Augustine to love his curate any more, nor did it cause the curate to refrain from irritating Card. It was now the beginning of October, and the winter was soon with them. Russian prelates arrived to contribute to Father Card's Red reputation. There were no particular rows in the church; but the Vicar was always badgering the congregation about its imperfect Christianity, and staged one thing and another to give the newspapers something to write about. For instance, at Christmas time, superbly dressed men in oriental garb arrived at the church door with a camel. Obviously it was the birth of Christ being portrayed dramatically. People gathered all around the church, and watched the camel. Then men disguised as Asiatics of 1 B.C. went in and out of the church, and eventually the three kings, with enormous crowns, issued forth, and went away with the camel, photographed a number of times. A nativity play was performed in the church, and amid great excitement Christ was born. At the Feast of the Childermass the parents of Christ could be seen escaping on a donkey, Mary riding and Joseph on foot. Herod's soldiers appeared, and discovered that the birds had flown. The neighbourhood was in an uproar half the time with the excitements of Bible history. Herod's soldiers would meet the guards marching from Chelsea Barracks, and groups of fugitives with camels and carts would disorganise the traffic flowing into Victoria Station.

Father Card would incessantly beseech his wife to advance a little of her capital to finance these displays—to provide enough money to attract Gielgud in the part of John the Baptist, and to get a whole company of smaller actors properly dressed and accoutred. But there were many domestic disturbances, for Mary steadily refused to de-capitalise herself, even to the extent of one hundred pounds. Even, as the time approached for the birth of her child, she would roar about the flat, 'My income, but not a cent of my capital!' Augustine would tear his hair, and show her the photographs in the press of camels and kings and other marvellous sights; 'all unpaid!' he would exclaim. The neighbourhood of St Catherine and the Angels was des-cribed as 'Our London Oberammergau' in the press; and while many of the inhabitants of that particular district gave their services as Herod's soldiery, or something of the sort, for practically nothing, there were quite a few Equity members who demanded the full rate of pay of screen extras. Some of the money for this was derived from Canon Card, who, like his son, was not averse to press advertise-ment. There were many bitter talks between Canon Card and his son on the subject of the stinginess of Mary, which there was no way of overcoming.

Then, in the beginning of March of the following year, Mary had her child. The birth occurred in the London Clinic, and was an expensive affair, but this was not objected to by the father, who presided, and innumerable photographs were taken with Augustine dandling the child, who was a boy, offering him a glass of champagne, or putting a wafer saturated in it between the infant's lips. One of the Russian priests came in, in full regalia, and the Clinic had never seen such a performance. The press was enlivened with photographs of Chillingham Chase and Craigliven Castle, and with Father Card as a new-born baby.

Mary and Augustine were not drawn closer together by these festivities. The latter was glad to have a son, but regretted constantly that he had not chosen a richer wife, or one a little more free with her money.

General Chillingham and Lord Pastonbury were the two Godfathers of the child, and the Hon. Monica Blunt his Godmother, when the Christening came round of Basil Tertullian, as he had been named. Mary was overjoyed with him, and saw him expand and heighten with delight, even if it was only a fraction for some months. She saw, in this fat little baby, traces of the enormous muscles of his father, as also she recognised the facial lineaments. She was, at one time, tempted to bestow a lump of her capital upon her husband, but sternly refrained from doing so. Her childless sister Alice came round to the flat a little later on, with all kinds of indigestible things for Basil. These were devoured by Mary and Augustine, as it was too early yet for Basil to eat Bendick's lovely sweet-meats. But Alice brought him rattles, and little garments, too. The nurse he had acquired at the Clinic was a pleasant woman, and she remained with him for the first few months, until Mary and her husband's quarrels became so frequent that the nurse left, and another Swiss nurse came in her place, more impervious to domestic storms.

In June the weather was good, and Mary took her child and his nurse down to Canon Card's cottage. When they returned at the beginning of July, she went two or three times to the theatre with Monica, and it was after the theatre on one of these occasions that disaster overtook her.

When she entered their flat at about twenty minutes past

eleven Augustine was lying in wait for her, very white and agitated. She found him actually behind a door. His eyes were like those of an animal.

'What on earth is the matter, Augustine?' Mary asked. 'What has been happening?'

'Come with me—quick.'

'How do you mean—where are we going?' Mary was trembling. 'Do explain!'

'Come, my dear,' implored Augustine. 'Do not let us waste time.'

They hurried out into the night. Augustine did not speak, he urged her along in the direction of the Clergy House. Mary heard the voice of this silent man saying with apparent passion, 'The man of God and politics are deadly enemies'. Then she heard the hissing words repeated without any consciousness that they were overheard. As they approached he grew very nervous; he believed he saw a light in one of the rooms, where there was no explanation for a light at that hour. But he hurried her past the Clergy House and round the corner, until they reached the studio. Looking around as if he was afraid of being followed, he inserted his key in the lock, and went in ahead of her. She hung back. Something impelled her to shrink away from this building. Augustine reached down and practically pulled her up into the studio, saying, 'Come, Mary. Are you scared? Come quickly, or we shall have someone coming round from the Clergy House.'

Mary stood just inside the door, trembling from head to foot.

'What is the matter, Teeny?' she asked, her teeth chattering. 'What have you to show me, Teeny? Is it here? Have you got it here?'

Augustine took her by the forearm, and held her lightly. 'I have killed Makepeace,' he almost whispered. 'We had a fight. He struck me, and you know, Mary, that I couldn't be struck by anybody. I let him have it, and before I knew what was happening he lay on the floor without moving. I thought it was a knockout, but then I saw it wasn't that. I could not revive him. His heart must have been bad. Anyhow, he's behind that screen.'

He began pulling Mary towards the screen, and she resisted, trying to go in the opposite direction.

'Darling, why won't you come, Mary?'

'I don't want to go there. I don't want to see anything!' The screen was in a different place. She could see that, and began whimpering, 'I won't go near that screen, Teeny. Have you had a doctor to see what is behind the screen?'

'No doctor,' muttered Augustine. 'No one has seen this.' He took a quick step forward, and lifted the screen away from what was on the floor.

Mary's 'Oh' was more like a thick squeak than anything. She clasped her hands, which were quite cold, and stood gazing, as if transfixed, at the familiar face of the curate, who she knew was dead at once, and drew in her breath with a sort of hiss. This was the first time she had seen a dead body, though she had seen films of the dead after the War, and during it. She wanted to give him back his life; she could not bear this dead man, for as he lay there, obstinately dead, he was a witness against her husband, and he wanted to be a witness.

'How horrible!' she said, seizing Augustine's arm, and dragging it towards her, for she was afraid. There was a gash over the curate's right eye, from which blood had flowed, and a strange ugly mark on his left cheek.

Mary stepped towards a chair, sat down in it, and asked for a glass of water. She lay over one of the arms of the chair, and she began to vomit. Augustine crossed the room quietly, and brought her a glass of water.

'Here, take this. I wish I had something else for you, but drink this down.'

Mary was sick again, and said, 'Put the screen back, Teeny. I can't bear to look at that.'

Augustine replaced the screen in front of the body, and went and sat down near Mary. She said, in a weak voice, 'I do hate this. Ugh. What a brute you are! When I saw you knocking down that man in your father's garden, and you said that was all right, that *it did not hurt*, I should have squarely told you that I would not live with a wild animal. Now, here we are, a pretty thing to have to face. They will lock you up at once, I suppose. You have done this kind of thing as a sport for years, however, and you ought to manage to get yourself somehow out of this terrible mess.'

'I can prove I have knocked down a hundred men, like that one in the cottage garden that I used to practise with. They none of them died. I can prove that too.'

Mary had kept her eyes fastened upon his face, as Augustine had rehearsed his evidence for the defence. She had acquired a sort of strength as she watched him, and she spoke now with a stronger voice.

'What are those awful marks on his face, Teeny?' she asked him.

'Oh, at one point I thought he was shamming,' said Augustine. 'I prodded him with my foot to make him stand up and fight.'

'How ghastly,' she said. 'What do you feel like when you are doing these things?'

Augustine could find no answer, but stared miserably at her.

Mary seemed about to spring up, but instead she sank back, self-pityingly. 'For my sins I have joined my destiny to yours,' she said, 'and if you go killing people I have to do the best I can for you. As early as possible tomorrow morning I will get a first-rate lawyer to take care of you, and I will stand by you during the trial that must follow this.'

Augustine's face had lost all of its colour.

'Not necessarily a trial,' he said. 'Is not this called, in law, an accident?' He seemed appealing to Mary to settle that the charge would be the lightest one. But Mary was not prepared to do that. This man had dragged her into a big nasty trial, and it was contemptible of him to try and hide himself behind her.

'Look,' Mary said harshly, 'do you realise what you have to do? You have to telephone to the police. They will want to know when you killed Makepeace. They will want to know why you did not immediately send for a doctor. I do not know why you *did* not do that. But tomorrow I will get you a lawyer, behind whom you can place yourself, and he will deal with the police. If I were you I would keep your mouth closed as tightly as you can—you understand? Refuse to say anything until I get you a lawyer.'

'Mary, I will follow your advice.' Augustine looked at her for a minute or two. Then he said, 'Actually there is nothing to hide. I shall tell them what happened.'

'No, you won't,' almost shouted Mary. 'If you do that, I am not going to buy a first-rate lawyer to defend you. I should be wasting my money. You must get ready to remain silent until your lawyer arrives. You understand?'

Augustine looked timidly towards Mary. He began to practise silence at once. There was a hush in the studio. But Augustine was preparing to burst out of it. There was something he had half a mind to bring forward—a big something, with which this deadly hush could be disinfected.

'Something was going on about which you know nothing.' Augustine's voice was oddly confident. 'The rejuvenation of my church hid what I meant to be dynamite.

Jesus was a stick of dynamite. That man struck me in the face—*me*! He must have been mad. He did not know I held in my hand the bomb of Jesus!'

Augustine sprang up, his eyes glaring around the studio.

'What are you shouting about,' Mary demanded angrily. 'Augustine, did I hear you say that Father Makepeace struck you?'

'Yes, of course he struck me,' answered Augustine. 'If he had not done that he would not be lying there. But he must have been made of glass. Or he had a sick ticker.'

'Do you mean his heart was weak?' enquired Mary. 'If that was the case . . .'

'His heart,' growled Augustine. 'He can't have had much of a heart.'

'If that can be proved . . .' Mary told him. 'But look here for the moment you must only think of one thing, getting hold of the police. Go over there to the telephone, and dial . . . what is it? 999, isn't that it?' Mary pointed towards the telephone. 'When the police arrive do not behave like a fool. Tell them that you had a fight with this man, and that, when you thought you had knocked him out, you had, in fact killed him . . . or better, he had died. Now, confine yourself to that. If I see you letting your tongue wag, I shall walk out of the room, and you will get no lawyer from me in the morning. Go now and telephone the police. We can wait for them, sitting where we are.'

Augustine Card rose, and slowly went to the telephone. He picked up the receiver, and dialled 999. The response was prompt. He said, 'I am Father Card of the Church of St Catherine and the Angels—Victoria. I had a fight with the Reverend Harold Makepeace, and he died in the course of the fight. He now lies dead in the studio in the garden of the Clergy House. Number 15 Carol Road.'

The voice he was speaking to asked him, had he sent for

a doctor? He answered 'No', and was informed that a
police car would be there very quickly.

'I don't mind, if you think it would be any use,' began
Augustine, hanging up the receiver.

'What? . . . of what use?' Mary asked, a pencil in one
hand.

'He said of me, the man of God and politics . . .'

'Yes, I heard you repeating it just now,' she interrupted
him brusquely.

'If it would help any, I can, I could inform the inspector,
that it was my plan, with a dozen young men to march with
Jesus into Whitehall . . .'

'Augustine,' Mary exclaimed, 'if you do not undertake to
keep your mouth shut fast until a lawyer shows up . . .'

She was interrupted by a sharp knock on the front door.
Augustine moved over to the front door and two policemen
were admitted. The senior of these two men began asking
the usual questions, covering the identification of the body
and of Augustine and Mary; the time of the fight; the
causes for it; the time of the man's death; why Father Card
had taken so long in telephoning them; why no doctor had
been called in; home address of the Cards, etc. They were
interrupted by the arrival of the doctor, who immediately
began his examination of the dead man. Augustine was
surprised by the shortness of the interval before the doctor
asked his first question. Turning towards Augustine, he
said, 'What is this mark on this man's face?'

Augustine took a step towards the body, as if he were
short-sighted, or, in any case, had to find out what the
doctor was talking about.

'In the course of the fight,' he said, hesitating, 'I must
have done that, I do not know how.'

The questioning from the police sergeant continued, and
then the doctor finished his examination of the body, and

came over to where Augustine was standing. 'How long did this fight last?' the doctor asked.

'About ten minutes,' was Augustine's reply.

'Are you marked in any way?' was the doctor's next question: 'let me have a look at you.'

The moment he began a more intimate and detailed examination, the doctor recognised that this was the body of an athlete, and one of great physical strength.

'Your strength must be enormous,' he said. 'How did you get a body like this?'

'Oh, training you know,' said Augustine. 'I box.'

'Have you boxed a great deal?' the doctor, who was about six inches shorter than Augustine, screwed up his eyes as he watched the other's face.

'Yes, doctor. All my life,' answered Father Card.

'That man was like a plaything for you. Why did you pound him so brutally?' The doctor looked severe.

'We had a fight you know,' Father Card stood quite still, his cassock lay on a chair at his side. The sergeant and the doctor both looked with astonishment at this very large man. They looked towards the body on the ground, and the doctor jerked his head in to a nod. The sergeant said, 'A funny kind of fight—What do you say, doctor?'

'You will see from my report, sergeant, what I think,' said the doctor menacingly.

The sergeant nodded significantly. After these preliminaries were over, a constable was left to mount guard over the body, and Augustine and Mary got into the car with the police, and were taken to the nearest police station. There they were met by an inspector, and went into a room, with the sergeant and doctor, for another interrogation. As Mary said that she would like to have her solicitor, if any questions were to be asked, the police told her that she could go home. When she answered that she would wait for her husband and go home with him, the inspector told her that probably he would be stopping at the station. Upon this, Mary informed them that she would wait and see what happened.

The sergeant and doctor made a brief report; and then the interrogation of Augustine started. At the end of that time the inspector informed Augustine that he would be detained at the station. Mary protested very firmly at this, but the inspector did not modify his view of the matter, and, saying good night to Augustine, and promising that a lawyer would go into action in the morning, she left, and went home to their flat. It was evident to her that the line of the police would be that this had been an unequal battle, in which the smaller man had been practically murdered by her gigantic husband. What she must do, would be to secure the best possible counsel, and he would get to work, when it came to a trial, to reverse this view of the matter. She would think up everything she could, and move heaven and earth to get him released on bail to start with. It took her some time to get to sleep, but when the next morning she had woken up and had her breakfast, immediately she got in touch with Mr Smithers.

Augustine meanwhile made a brief appearance in the Magistrate's Court, and was remanded for a week in custody.

29

The Ghastly View of It

O n the evening following that of Augustine's arrest, Mary gave Monica dinner at her flat, a bottle of Montrachet going a long way towards enabling them to forget the improvised nature of the meal.

'I have something of private to unfold to you,' Mary said. 'That is why I invited you to share this homely meal with me. But the Montrachet will win your forgiveness.'

'You and the Montrachet together . . .' beamed Monica. 'But what was it that led us to desire this degree of retirement?'

'My husband's arrest for murder,' said Mary.

'I say! You have a good reason for observing a certain amount of privacy. But it is of course a mistake?' Monica grew interested.

'Well, he has been fighting all his life. At Eton he was laying out men even larger than himself. But this time he has knocked out somebody in private. And, what is worse, the wretched fellow died. A weak heart, I suppose.'

Monica was full of intelligent sympathy.

'But that is not murder, is it?' she asked.

'Of course it isn't,' said Mary. 'It is refreshing to be with someone who understands that. Apparently he is obliged at enormous expense to prove it.'

'I don't believe it,' said Monica, with great emphasis. 'Have you seen a proper lawyer?'

'Oh yes. That is all right. Augustine is locked up, and will go before a magistrate next week.'

There was an unpleasant silence. The two women sat looking at one another. Until not so very long ago these women's families had ruled the police. Monica felt sure that Mary was not using the right lawyer.

'Are you sure that the matter cannot be placed before that magistrate next week in the proper light . . . ?'

'You seem to think, Monica, that I have a poor woman's lawyer. But I haven't. My lawyer is a rich woman's lawyer. I assure you that everything is being done correctly. There is only one danger—that Augustine's tongue may wag. I have forbidden him to open his mouth except in the presence of a lawyer.'

'Has he anything to hide?'

Mary hesitated.

'Nothing,' she said. 'But there was something I had great difficulty in preventing him from blurting out to the police. It appears he was running some show . . . I had no clear idea what it was, but he said, as we sat waiting for the arrival of the police, that he and Jesus, with a dozen young men, had intended to march down to Whitehall . . . if this had not happened . . . !'

'I am not at all sure that murdering someone was not a lucky escape for you!' Monica looked into her friend's eyes, in so terribly well-informed a way that Mary answered abruptly, 'In what way do you mean?'

'My dear Mary, all I mean was that I have suspected Augustine for a long time of being up to something idiotic in that church of his. It was no business of mine, so I have remained silent. But it passed through my mind just now that you might have been in an even worse plight. Imagine if he and Christ had started painting the town red!' Monica sat looking at her friend with big baby eyes, fluttering her eyelashes a little.

'I really believe you have something there!' and Mary met her remarks with a nod.

'Merely a ghastly alternative,' said the ex-Queen of the Ghastly Girls. 'It would have been a real dilemma if he had brought to fruition what he was scheming in his studio, don't you think? We have in history dozens of instances of violent men associated with Jesus. Jesus is a dangerous man for that type of person. I do not know who such a creature as Augustine should choose as a friend, but I am sure it should not be Jesus. I wonder if you realise what he has been doing in that studio behind the Clergy House? Something much more serious than you imagine. And now all that is over.'

Monica did not stop long after dinner. As she left she kissed Mary, saying, 'My dear Mary, you will get through this all right. Obviously it is not a murder, but just a case of a man who was not in a fit condition to go and have a fight with Augustine Card. Only your husband will be twice as angry as you are. If I can be of any use, telephone me at once. Give me a call in any case as soon as you know what is going to happen. Let me repeat, this is perhaps for you a blessing in disguise.'

30

The Trial

Augustine only made one further appearance before the magistrate, when he was committed for trial at the Old Bailey. The attitude of the magistrate was that an enormously powerful, very large, trained boxer had a fight with a very much smaller, untrained man: the first of these two men battered to pieces the second, and in the course of this fight the smaller man was killed. The magistrate's conclusion was that there were grounds for a charge of murder, and Augustine was committed to the Central Criminal Court for trial. All that was said in the Magistrate's Court was of so severe a kind that the public, from the first moment that they became acquainted with this case, assumed a very adverse opinion of the prisoner—the fact that Father Card was a clergyman, known popularly as the Red Priest, and with all the dossier of this man that was held in every newspaper office—all of this coloured and weighted the mind of the public against Augustine.

From that moment onwards Mary, greatly shaken by the murder charge, did all in her power to prepare for the worst, in the case against her husband. Through Mr Smithers she was already in consultation with a famous criminal lawyer, who now secured a first-rate counsel. He was reputed to be the most brilliant young barrister in London. Mary succeeded in getting several articles written, to popularise a romantic and very intellectual picture of the Red Priest;

but although she tried very hard to get them published, she was astonished to find that no paper was prepared to take material concerning a case of that kind.

She herself helped the solicitor to build up a wonderful defence. The evidence of temperament that Father Wimbush was volunteering for the prosecution was so unfavourable to Father Card that the solicitor tore his hair, and assured Mary that this little priest would hang Augustine unless evidence of a contrary kind were forthcoming. Mary sent cables to Horridge, who was in South Africa, and eventually financed his passage home. Then Dr Hartnell mobilised other friends of Father Card of Oxford days; and Lord Pastonbury brought in an Etonian phalanx. In this way evidence of his good character—good heart—generosity—kindness, etc., was available.

As to Father Wimbush, with immense industry Mary had him traced back to his days in a Roman Catholic college, when he had been unfrocked for seducing a servant girl. She got other evidence against him, showing that he was untruthful, and that, under another name, he had been convicted of perjury fifteen years before. This wealth of evidence for the defence cost Mary a lot of money, for it was procured by a private detective agent, whose fees were fabulously high.

Another very useful thing procured by Mary, was a great deal of information concerning Father Makepeace. Doctors at Oxford and in his home-town, in whose care he had been, gave testimony to his weak heart, and one or two other pieces of valuable factual evidence, and, at his school, it was discovered he had been known as a bully. He had got into trouble for bullying boys smaller than himself.

As the time for the trial approached the press was full of articles about the question of responsibility, in hypothetical cases of death resulting from a pugilistic encounter. Opinion appeared to be about evenly divided, until a very popular lawyer came down on the side of such deaths never being murder.

Augustine was in Brixton Prison, and was frequently visited, all through the autumn, by Mary and various friends, such as Lord Pastonbury. His solicitor was an equally frequent visitor, and informed Augustine of the feats performed by his wife on his behalf. When she arrived at the prison, tears would roll down Teeny's cheeks, and she was so competent-looking that his spirits rose while she was there. They wavered between high and low. They rose after favourable news from his solicitors. He had warders to box with, and this delighted him. The Governor was a relative of Lord Pastonbury, and did what he could to make Augustine comfortable. There was a high-church Chaplain who often came and discussed this and that with Father Card, and became very sure of his innocence of murderous intent.

November was the month fixed for the trial, and day by day, as it drew nearer, Augustine felt increasingly nervous. Mary did all that she could to keep him cheerful; and he varied between elation, after a visit by Mary, and extreme despondency, on a day when he was not visited by anybody.

Sir Philip Sprigge, Q.C., was Augustine's principal defender; but on the first day of the trial it was, of course, the prosecution represented by the principal spokesman of the Crown, Sir Richard Peters, Q.C., who led off before a packed court, and made what is called a memorable speech.

'May it please your lordship.

'Members of the jury, we have to try a clergyman, which is a very painful thing to have to do. And what makes it far worse, is that the charge is the terrible one of murder. You will hear evidence showing that this Vicar had developed a hatred for his curate, contracted in the course of

their work together. This young man, Father Harold
Makepeace, had recently taken up his duties at the Church
of St Catherine and the Angels; and this very brilliant
young man had aroused the jealousy of the Vicar. It
appears that he had not submitted to the Vicar in the way
that gentleman preferred his curates to do. In debates he
had contradicted his senior, and, with what the Vicar considered arrogance, offered his own opinion on matters
under dispute, in a manner suggesting that he believed his
own authority equal to that of the Vicar, and suggesting that
his own knowledge was at least equal, if not superior, to
that of the older man. From the beginning the confident
attitude of this newcomer rankled in the mind of Father
Card, who had a very high opinion of his own leadership.
You will have, members of the jury, the most complete
evidence on all these issues. And you will come to believe,
as a result of this evidence, members of the jury, that this
very violent man was led, in the end, to find an outlet for
his resentment on the body of this too independent-
minded curate, and, once he had started, to vent his feelings
in the most terrible way on this young man. To understand, in all its horrible completeness, this tragedy, you will
have to know the unclerical backgrounds of the prisoner.
Father Card, as he calls himself, was, at both school and
university, famous as a pugilist. He was what is known as a
Blue at Oxford, defeating, in the boxing-ring, a gigantic
opponent, even larger than himself. Far be it from me to say
that a fondness for the art of pugilism connotes a brutal
temperament. But, that it may at times develop a brutal
disposition is quite certain. And I have evidence, which I
will give you, members of the jury, that this man had
become brutalised as a result of his pugilistic successes.
I will place in the witness box a police officer who was in
the habit of boxing with Father Card. And he will tell you

how, on one occasion, he was so badly injured by the clergyman—*in sport*, you understand—that he had to be sent home in a taxi-cab. All I am saying that this shows, is that, while indulging in this sport of his preference, he indulged in that sport with a brutal vigour beyond the limit of what we understand as sport. Augustine Card is two things. Firstly he is a very large and heavy, as well as a very tall man, of great physical development. Secondly he is an expert fighter. This is, obviously, a very dangerous combination. But he is, also—and this I propose to prove by means of witnesses—a very violent man. How dangerous the third of this trio is I need not stress. To have one of these qualities is quite dangerous enough; but, in conjunction, one shudders to think where they may land a man. You are all aware what the law is regarding a professional boxer. This trained pugilist, if, outside the ring, he should have a fight, as any of us might, the penalties are very severe if he should, because of his superior science, and ringcraft, do a man an injury. Because of these laws, which he is very well aware of, a boxer takes very great care not to use his skill too effectively in ordinary life, should he get into a fight. Now, in the present case, Harold Makepeace was a well-set up young man, but he was three inches shorter, and much slighter in build, than the prisoner; and further, he was not a trained boxer. Balancing all these facts, you will realise that, in engaging in a fight with Father Card, he was putting himself in a dangerous situation. But did he engage in a fight? That is one of the principal questions to be answered in this trial. Did he strike Father Card first, or was it the other way round? You may say that it would amount to the same thing; to be in a fight with this giant, both trained, and bellicose by nature, would be a dangerous thing to be—quite irrespective of whether you started it, or he started it. But, members of the jury, you, who are trying this case, wish to be satisfied on this point; it is, morally, of first-rate importance.

'Now, members of the jury, we have to turn to another issue. The medical evidence is very favourable to the prosecution. You will hear this evidence, and you will see that it shows how the prisoner, with the utmost brutality, after punching, in the most terrible way, this younger man, afterwards began to kick and trample on him. As a result of this, not only did the victim's face display the most shocking injuries, such as the loss of teeth, gashes on the forehead, and several deep bruises, but there were also a number of bruises throughout the area of the body. The doctor, whom I shall put in the box, will supply you with more specific, professional evidence.

'A very important witness in the case for the Crown is the other curate associated with the Church of St Catherine and the Angels, Frederick Wimbush, who will describe the proceedings leading up to this quarrel between vicar and curate. He will outline the debate which occurred, and the part played in it by the two men. Father Wimbush will also give you an idea of what had been the relations in the immediate past, between the prisoner and the dead curate. More important even than this, Father Wimbush will tell you what he heard outside the studio, while the fight was going on. It may well be that you will consider this our most valuable witness, for he too suffered from the bullying habits of the Vicar, and he can tell you how any attempt at independence on his part was resented. I do not remember any case of this sort, in which several men in Holy Orders are either in the dock or in the witness-box, or, for that matter, in the mortuary. It has been very painful for me to have to prosecute a man of Augustine Card's cloth, a man well-connected, and so closely related to that fine churchman, Canon Card of Jilliforde.

'And now, with the assistance of my learned friend, I will call the evidence before you.'

The activities of the Crown now took the form of a series of witnesses for the prosecution. The first called was one of the medical experts—Doctor Mason, the doctor who examined the corpse when the police were summoned to the studio behind the Clergy House where the body lay. Doctor Mason went in detail through the evidence already summarily outlined by Sir Richard Peters. He confirmed what the learned counsel had said, only in technical language. He was of the same opinion, that the attack, for it was thus that he described Father Card's side of the fight, was of the most brutal kind. The body of the victim was a mass of bruises and wounds. This could only have occurred as the result of very great violence. He invited the members of the jury to examine the photographs which had been taken of the body in the mortuary at the time when it was first placed there, and see for themselves what a terrible spectacle the corpse of this young curate unquestionably was. He did not remember ever having seen so pitiful a sight resulting from what is called a 'fight'—for a human body which receives such treatment as this had, demands some other name than 'fight' for the process by which it has come to claim a trial at the Old Bailey to discover what name to use for the man responsible for it.

The faces of the jurymen grew more and more horrified as they listened to the medical evidence. The next witness was P.C. Mast, who testified to the effect that he had frequently visited the Clergy House in order to put on the gloves with Father Card; and he described how, on one occasion, he felt so ill, resulting from the severe hammering he had received, that he had to be sent home in a taxi-cab, and was under the doctor's care for the better part of a week. P.C. Mast said that Father Card had such a terrible

257

punch that he did not know how hard he was hitting you. This statement was the result of a question from the defence lawyer.

The next witness was Father Wimbush. He turned out to be just as much a witness for the defence as he was for the prosecution. What Sir Richard Peters extracted from him was the bullying, in one form or another, that went on all the time, by means of which Father Card attempted to dominate completely the debates and lectures which took place in the studio, before a chosen audience, mainly consisting of parishioners. Father Card, he asserted, was a very vain man, and he was attempting all the time to impress people with his great personality, and to show himself in a position of rare authority among his clerical staff. When a new curate came to the church, Father Card would wish to dominate him at the outset, to make him do exactly what he told him to do; and he would bitterly resent any attempt to speak up for himself on the part of one of his subalterns.

How this applied to Father Makepeace was that Makepeace came from the university with a great reputation and many honours. He was a tall, handsome, self-opinionated man, who wished to cut a figure wherever he was; the result being that he and Father Card often collided at their meetings, and nothing was done by the curate to hide from the public, which was in the main the congregation, that he and his vicar violently disagreed on many points. He even did his best to take the Vicar down a peg or two; and this was deeply resented by Father Card. The Vicar, according to Father Wimbush, often spoke very intolerantly of what he had to put up with from his new curate, and of his intention to get rid of Makepeace and get a better man. Wimbush described how, time after time, at debates or lectures, there was so much bad feeling that he expected

Makepeace to resign his curacy, or Father Card to dismiss him outright. Now, coming down to the night of the tragedy, Father Makepeace and the Vicar had clashed incessantly; for the curate was displaying his superior learning, and attempting to make his Vicar look small; and Father Card was quite unable to get the better of him in argument, and could not disguise the fact that the curate was a more learned man than he was. It was about half past eight when the debate came to an end, and by a quarter to nine the studio was clear. Father Makepeace and Father Wimbush had gone to the Clergy House to have their dinner. At a quarter past nine Father Makepeace returned to the studio, which was used as an office by the curates, to do some work before retiring for the night. Father Wimbush, on the other hand, went for a walk, and returned about half past ten. He passed the studio, and was surprised to hear loud voices. One man exclaimed, 'not you, you unspeakable liar.' The voice of Augustine answered. 'Liar! you little tuppenny ha'penny pipsqueak of a man!'

Stopping to listen outside the studio door, he at once realised that Father Card and Father Makepeace were having a heated discussion. They were not near the door, but, almost as Wimbush slowed down to listen, there was the sound of a blow. Father Card's voice said, 'You cannot do that and get away with it.' Immediately afterwards there had been many more blows, several being exchanged before a tremendous crash against the wall of the studio announced that someone's head had made contact with it. In quick succession more crashes of the same kind occurred, and this was followed by a quick movement across the studio. Father Wimbush asserted that it was quite easy for him to identify the sounds of battle. Father Card had obviously pursued the curate, and on the other side of the studio the sounds of banging against the wall were repeated. It was the Vicar landing blow after blow upon Father Make-peace, who exclaimed 'Oh' at one point, and was responsible for other half-words, as it were, sounds of distress.

The sounds of a body being struck with great violence continued, until followed by a heavy fall, succeeded by sounds like kicking—a head being kicked, and then there was the duller sound of a body receiving the same treatment. This went on for a short while, Father Wimbush could not say for how long, then he inserted his key in the lock and opened the door. He had only opened it an inch or two, when it was slammed back in his face. He had time enough however, to see the face of Father Card, and, beyond that, a body on the floor. That was all he was able to register, except that the Vicar's face was different from what he had ever seen it before. Its expression was almost demented—he could describe it no other way. It was pale, the mouth open, with the teeth bared. That was all he could say about it. But he was so afraid, so he said, that he went away as quickly as possible, returning to the Clergy House. This was at about a quarter to eleven.

This evidence, as can be seen, could be used by the defence as much as it was of value to the prosecution. There seemed no question about that. It was so valuable for the defence that the prosecution might almost have suppressed it, if they could.

Sir Philip Sprigge at once rose to cross-examine this witness. It was established that the person responsible for commencing the fight was the victim Father Makepeace. Then the Counsel took in hand the questioning of Wimbush on the several points in his history which had been unearthed by the enquiry agency employed by Mary—namely (1) he was asked if he had been found guilty of rape while working as a teacher in the Roman Catholic monastery at Egham, as a consequence of which he was unfrocked;

(2) if, on another occasion, he had been convicted of perjury, and served a sentence of imprisonment. To both these questions Wimbush replied in the negative.

At this point Sir Philip closed his cross-examination, remarking, 'My Lord, I shall be calling further evidence on these points at a later stage of the case.'

'My Lord, that closes the case for the prosecution'— so spoke the Crown.

This ended the proceedings of the first day of the trial. Mary had been in court all day, with Monica Blunt, her 'Ghastly' friend. Augustine now looked over in her direction, and smiled, before the touch came on his shoulder and he was led away. Mary spoke to him in dumb show, waved her hand, and then she and Monica left the Court.

'Well,' she said, 'we shall have the defence tomorrow.'

Mary had been throughout closely in touch with Sir Philip Sprigge, the Counsel she had secured for her husband at so breathtaking a fee. He was well satisfied with the way the trial had gone so far, and assured her that she need have no fear that the judge might show an unintelligent severity. On the contrary, he was a good judge to have.

Horridge was waiting for them on the way out, and they went to dinner with him in a quiet restaurant not far from Victoria. As soon as they had installed themselves at the table, ordered their wine, their food and so forth, conversation began. Horrid was as sprightly as ever. He felt quite sure that the murder charge would be dropped—it could not be gone on with.

'I know it must,' said Mary.

'How absurd,' said Horridge, 'is the claim of impartiality of the prosecution. The counsel for the prosecution was so unfair about Augustine that I could have shouted at him sometimes.'

'You can imagine what I felt,' said Mary. 'But tomorrow

we will do our best to right the wrong done us by Richard Peters.'

'What I consider most unsatisfactory,' said Monica, 'is that the jury is allowed to sleep on the disgusting libels of the prosecution. It is such a pity that they do not arrange that the defence should be allowed to defend the prisoner on the spot . . . without any delay.'

'I think that is very unjust,' said Mary. 'If you give a slander of that sort time to sink in, it makes it all the harder to wipe it out, as we are going to do. But there it is, indelibly imprinted on the mind of the jury.'

'I can hardly bear, myself, to wait until tomorrow,' cried Horridge.

'Nor can I,' exclaimed Mary. 'What do you suppose I feel?'

After dinner they went round to Augustine's flat, where Horridge was sleeping, and continued talking until Mary sprang up and announced that she must go to bed, otherwise she would be a C.3 impresario in the morning. And heaven knows what all her witnesses would do if she were not there to keep them skipping. But she did not sleep. She went into the living-room and read a thriller, and in the morning had an incompetent boiled appearance. When the traffic acquired daylight sounds she slept, and it was difficult to wake her.

The second day began with the speech for the defence of Sir Philip Sprigge. After the usual preliminaries this brilliant Counsel opened his speech. 'Murder,' he roared. 'Murder, members of the jury, is a different charge from any other. It means that a man was so full of hatred for another that he wished to extinguish him, to blot him out

—to make him cease to live. Now this tremendous passion occurs, it seems to me, in a very different person from Father Card, who is mild and bland, a quite different type from the dark, intense individual who is prone to murder. And this, quite apart from the fact that he is a holy man, whose prayers rise daily to his Maker, and who is essentially unworldly. No, members of the jury, this should, if anything, be a charge of accidental slaying—at the very gravest it can only be viewed as a possible case of manslaughter; this must surely have been apparent to the magistrate who first committed the accused for trial. We now know—and you will shortly learn from the witnesses I shall in due course place in the witness-box—we now know from the doctors who attended Father Makepeace, the victim, that his heart was defective. Obviously his death was caused by a failure of the heart, which might have happened any time as a result of a much less severe ordeal than a fight with this massive and towering man. It may be that the justification for this charge lay in the rough handling that Makepeace had received. Now, any man would have a very rough time who ventured to fight this boxing Blue, this famous athlete. They could not do otherwise. But they would not *die*—not make a charge of murder possible—unless the heart happened to be weak. Many men have boxed with Augustine Card, and none of them has died. But, knowing that his heart was weak, Makepeace should not have dreamt of fighting so big a man—and the defence will show you that he was the aggressor. We have heard one witness, who is a police officer, P.C. Mast, who boxed continually with Father Card. You have seen this policeman, who is a large man. He had tough bouts with the clergyman, and once was sent home in a taxi, as a result of his distressed condition. But he did not die. His heart is sound—otherwise he would not have offered himself as a sparring partner to so fine a boxer. Now, members of the jury, it is absurd to charge this man with murder because a curate, treated by two doctors in succession, as you will shortly hear, for weakness of the heart, entered into a fight with an athlete of the stature of Augustine Card. Members of the jury, I think this charge should have been altered, before we began the trial, to what it should have been all along, manslaughter.'

This speech had a great effect, and its influence on the public, as reported in the evening papers, was decisive. Those who, up till then, had clamoured for a verdict of murder, and for the death sentence on this wicked priest, now changed their opinion. People returning from the City were heard to express themselves that evening convinced by Sir Philip Sprigge's eloquence.

There followed the witnesses for the defence. The first were the medical witnesses, one from Linden House School, the preparatory school that Father Makepeace attended, and then two doctors from Oxford, who saw Makepeace while he was an undergraduate.

Doctor William Middleton, of Lincoln, was sworn in. This doctor gave evidence that he had been the medical officer in attendance at Linden House School, Lincoln, during the period that Harold Makepeace was a pupil there. One afternoon, during a football match, Makepeace had a syncope. He fell forward upon his face in a faint, and shortly afterwards the doctor examined him in the school sanatorium, where he had been put to bed. 'I diagnosed him as suffering from a cardiac lesion. On account of this condition it was decided that he should play no more football, or take other violent exercise.'

The Judge asked Dr Middleton if he had considered his patient's condition of a chronic and permanent kind, to which the doctor answered that, for the rest of his period at the school, he was forbidden to engage in field sports of any kind, and he did consider that his heart was not strong enough to make it safe for him to do so at the time he left the school.

There was further evidence from a master at the school that Makepeace, who had been a big boy, although it had been proved that his heart was weak, had got into trouble on two occasions for bullying; that he had shown special unkindness to one boy much smaller than himself, and had been sent before the headmaster about this particular misdemeanour.

The next witness to be called was Dr Thomas Byng, who had attended Makepeace during his first year at the university. Dr Byng said Makepeace came to see him shortly after his arrival as an undergraduate. He told the doctor that he had not been allowed to play games at his preparatory school, because his heart was not very strong, and he asked for an examination to know if it would still be unwise for him to engage in any sports. 'After a careful examination I was of opinion that the wisest course would be for him to confine himself to a light daily exercise, walking or rowing, not to row competitively, but merely as a form of mild exercise.'

The next witness was Dr David McIntyre of Oxford. Dr McIntyre said that Makepeace had paid him a visit during his second year at the university. He complained of palpitations of the heart.

'I found nothing seriously wrong with him, but his heart was not very strong, and I told him that he should take care of himself. I prescribed for the palpitations, and I saw him a year later. He was working hard, and I prescribed a tonic. I diagnosed, at that time, his heart as "tired".'

The next witness called was the Rev. Andrew Horridge, known as Father Horridge while he was at the Church of

St Catherine and the Angels. Father Horridge gave evidence that Father Makepeace had succeeded him at the Church. Horridge had acted as secretary, however, to Father Card, and had every morning boxed with him for a short while. Father Makepeace had declined to act as secretary, and also had been unwilling to box with the Vicar. Horridge's experience in the matter of boxing was very slight. At first the Vicar had not regarded him as sufficiently robust to box seriously, and so they had, every morning, pretended to box; had tapped one another, and danced about. But a little later they had boxed more seriously, and the Vicar was a man, in his experience, incapable of brutality, a very gentle and considerate man. They got on well together, and the Vicar had never shown the slightest sign of irritability or of temper. Horridge had left him, most unwillingly, to occupy a post of some importance. In answer to an enquiry, Father Horridge said he had been astounded to hear of the charge of murder against his old chief. He had hurried back from Africa to do anything he could to help in establishing his innocence. Lastly, Father Wimbush had been there as curate with him, and Father Horridge had always felt suspicious of him. The Vicar had had trouble with him, Horridge said, had found him inclined to be tricky and underhand.

The next witnesses called were to discredit Father Wimbush's testimony in the box. They made it clear that he had started life as a Roman Catholic priest. He had been unfrocked, when quite young, his offence an assault upon a servant girl. He had been Father Patrick Collins. This Irish priest had changed his name, and been ordained in the Anglican Church. Prior to his unfrocking, he had been found very untrustworthy by other priests, one of whom gave evidence that Wimbush had been reprimanded by the Father Superior for his untruthfulness. Another witness attested that Father Wimbush had served a sentence in Wormwood Scrubs after his conviction for perjury.

The following witness was Lord Pastonbury, who had been an intimate friend of the prisoner ever since their Eton days. He had lived in close association with Card, and would vouch for his gentleness, and for his behaviour, at all times, as a Christian gentleman.

Next came Viscount Walte, who gave the same evidence as Lord Pastonbury as to Augustine Card's character at Eton and Oxford.

The final witness was Dr Hartnell, who had shared rooms at Oxford with Augustine Card, and who also had taken part in the debate which had culminated in the fight between the Vicar and his curate. As the counsel was taking this witness through the events which had been largely responsible for what had happened later, the atmosphere in the court was electric. Dr Hartnell especially emphasised the curate's rudeness to the Vicar, and Father Makepeace's obvious determination to advertise himself as a brilliant debater, his jealous disposition, and unfairness in debate.

After Dr Hartnell's evidence Sir Philip Sprigge made his closing speech. He pointed out to start with that the evidence of the doctors showed that Father Makepeace had always had a weak heart, and that altered the case entirely, namely that his death was the result of his defective health, and not of any brutality on the part of the prisoner. It made nonsense of the charge of murder. The death of Father Makepeace was quite clearly the result of a quarrel in which he struck the Vicar, and made it impossible that a fight should not occur—for Father Card was not a man to be hit with impunity. He was, at the time, admittedly very incensed against the cocky, disagreeable attitude of his curate, quite apart from being struck by him. In the ensuing fight, with a man of Augustine Card's great physical strength, it would be impossible that his opponent should not be badly hurt. 'It is quite fair to say, I think, that it would be impossible for Father Makepeace, if his heart had always been weak, to come through without something serious happening to him. Now, Father Makepeace's combativeness in argument, as a principal in the debate, is one and the same thing as the rash, ill-tempered blow, which precipitated the fight. And as we see him, all the way through his life, as a bully at school, where he was a big fellow in comparison with the small fry he then was in touch with, and his ambitious spirit at Oxford, in which he overworked and outstripped his powers, having to go to a doctor and secure a tonic to keep him going—in which we see a man taking risks with his health in his determination to shine at the University—in all of this we understand how this conceited weakling set himself up against this monstrously strong athlete, who really did not know how strong he was. You have heard in the evidence of Thomas Hartnell, that the subject of the debate on the fatal evening was 'Is Communism Christianity?'—that the Vicar and his curate had disagreed, as they always did. There was always the same misunderstanding. When the Vicar uses the word "Communism" he uses it idealistically. He says that the ideal has been lost in Russia.'

'Menshevist!' shouted a man in the rear of the court. The police hurried towards the disturber, he was seized and ejected.

'You have heard Father Card called a "Menshevist". That is what he is, in Communist language. He has been called "The Red Priest". But he is no communist, in the contemporary Russian sense. He praises an idealistic Communist doctrine—the one that the Bolsheviks overthrew. In the debate that preceded the quarrel which ended in Harold Makepeace's death, this was what was being

discussed. Let me summarise this evidence for you—
Augustine Card insisted that the root of Christianity is in a
kind of Communism, whose headquarters was in Alexandria. Makepeace disputed this. He asserted that that had
often been said on the Continent, but it was an idea advanced by people usually ignorant of Greek. Thereupon he
mentioned several treatises, quoting them in Greek, a
language with which Father Card is not acquainted, and the
Vicar regarded this introduction, by Father Makepeace, of
Greek, as a mere device to further the argument of those
who wished to prove that his belief was incorrect. This
was a device of which Harold Makepeace was very fond.
You have heard that Makepeace had begun to read out a
passage in Greek, from a book which is not translated,
which Dr Hartnell felt sure was understood by no one in the
audience except himself, and Card interrupted, saying that
Makepeace might just as well read something in Chinese.
An argument ensued, a very stupid one on the side of
Makepeace. This was a typical example of the kind of
bickering which went on all the time between these two
men. It was the Vicar's view that, owing to the interven-
tion of Harold Makepeace, many of his debates were ruined,
and this was merely another instance of his curate's be-
devilling of his work among his congregation in the séances
arranged by him in the studio. Members of the jury,
if, in the course of this speech for the defence, I began
to quote something in classical Greek, you would
quite rightly protest, for I daresay that very few of you
would understand what I was talking about. Well, that,
as Dr Hartnell has told us, was what Harold Makepeace
was doing at the debate at which he and Augustine Card
disagreed.'

Sir Philip Sprigge picked up a book, and began to read
from it. He continued to do this until interrupted by the

Judge. 'The reading of Homer, Sir Philip,' said the Judge, 'will not assist the defence.'

'I thought your Lordship would recognise what I was reading. But how many in the Court, I wonder, were able to do so? I began to quote the *Iliad* to give a practical illustration of what Dr Hartnell was describing.

'Turning to a very important witness, Father Wimbush, it must be said, to start with, that not very much trust can be placed in all the evidence of this unfrocked Catholic priest, more especially because of what we know of his reputation for untruthfulness. On the other hand, his account of what he heard from outside the studio seems, in the main, correct. It was his evidence that enabled us to know that the first blow was struck by the curate, whereas all that he says about Father Card must be under suspicion, seeing that his relations with the Vicar have been unfriendly throughout.

'It was Father Card's purpose to have what he called a 'live' church. With that in view, he encouraged the more intelligent members of his congregation to come in the evening to meetings in the studio attached to the Clergy House. He liked his staff to take part, with him, in the teaching which was the principal feature of these proceedings in the studio. He found, however, to his astonishment and disgust, that his conceited young curate was apt to contradict everything that he said, in lecture or debate. Outside of his religious life, and his work as a teacher, Augustine Card has been, also, very prominent in the athletic field, and has received many honours as a boxer. That this young man, who had come to his church as a curate, should quarrel with him, and eventually even strike him, has been a terrible thing for Augustine Card. For, of course, he could not guess that this man, who behaved in this way, had been under doctors' orders because

270

of heart trouble. And therefore, when struck, this athlete retaliated in the normal course of things as a human being, which Father Card naturally is, beneath his cassock. And then this bellicose curate died beneath his blows. This has been, for Father Card, as much as for Father Makepeace, a tremendous tragedy, for, when this case comes to be treated, as it undoubtedly will, as one of manslaughter, it spells ruin for this clergyman almost as much as if it were thought of as murder. So, you do understand, members of the jury, that even if your verdict modifies this charge, reducing it to manslaughter, it is still a fearful thing for this clergyman who is being tried. It is fantastic to think of what Lord Paston-bury has termed "this Christian gentleman" being guilty of a sordid homicide. I hope, members of the jury, that you will not only lift from Augustine Card this odious charge under which he has been weighed down for four long months of shame, but that the remaining charge, damaging as it is, will be in the end removed. It is a verdict of not guilty, members of the jury, that I am asking for.'

31

Hartnell and Horridge have a Deep Look

At the scene of the trial Horridge and Hartnell met and talked from time to time, and Hartnell asked Horridge to have dinner with him. It was the day during which both of these witnesses had given their evidence. At the dinner they began by discussing the technicalities of their evidence. Both had been engaged in white-washing, from the standpoint of character, in one way or another.

The Café Royal was the restaurant chosen by Hartnell. Neither of them was old enough to notice the great alteration, but they sat in the most recently built of the downstairs restaurants. It was very quiet, and after the noisy scenes at the Old Bailey this appeared to them a blessed oasis of peace.

'How do you interpret, now, the psychology of Card, in your *Living with a Man-eating Man*?'

'Oh, have you read that?' enquired Hartnell, surprised.

'Oh yes,' said Horridge. 'And I found it exceedingly interesting. I do not think that it would be a very good thing to have it read by people in the court at the present moment . . . by judge and by jury, for instance.'

Hartnell's eyes flashed and danced at the idea of his little book being perused by the learned judge and counsel, and also by the twelve not very inspired jurymen. 'Gracious no

—Heaven forbid!' he said. 'That, I am afraid, might put all sorts of ideas into their heads.'

'It certainly would,' said Horridge. 'It might turn the scales, I think. It might make it continue as a murder trial, don't you think?'

'I am afraid it might even do that.' Hartnell's face became grave.

'I have felt, the whole time,' said Horridge, 'that Augustine ought to be put on the witness stand. His personality would surely impress the jury, and it is as well that they should have personal contact with the prisoner.'

'If you got Augustine in the witness box,' said Hartnell, 'would not the danger be that he might become hysterical, and be moved to say that he felt guilty of this young man's death?'

'I had not thought of that,' said Horridge. 'But you are a real authority on Augustine Card; you know him much better than I do. I have wanted to talk to you about your opinion of the case—I mean in confidence of course.'

'Well, I have no occasion to hide what I think. I am not good at hiding my thoughts.'

Horridge could not help smiling at the idea of Hartnell showing a timidity about exposing his private thoughts. 'I was deeply interested to read your plain unvarnished account of your Oxford days,' he said.

'As a matter of fact, in such a heart-to-heart talk as we are having now,' said Hartnell, 'let me say that I find Augustine is not a very easy man to be quite sure about. I personally would not swear that he did not murder Makepeace.'

'No, Hartnell. The evidence of the weak heart makes an end of that. No charge of murder is possible once the fact is known that the dead man had always suffered from a weak heart.'

'I understand what you feel about Augustine, Horridge,

and I respect those feelings. But, actually, it is not true to say that a murder charge is not possible in the present case. A man with a weak heart can be murdered as much as anybody else; and, what is more, the weak heart cannot *guarantee* death, even in a very tough fight.'

'You want to get rid of Makepeace's weak heart. But even if a man went after Makepeace with murderous intent, there would be the weak heart, and long before the man had a chance to murder him, Makepeace would have died either of fright, or undue exertion, or of rage, or of cardiac failure.'

'You defend the victim's weak heart,' Hartnell said. 'Whereas I have in my mind the dark heart of this fighting man, and I feel if the will to kill were there it might reach its target quicker than the shaky heart. Perhaps I have a preference for will and intention rather than for the mechanical explanation.'

'I am not in agreement with your theory of the will-to-kill of the fighting man. I think that is an exaggerated idea, especially if you apply it to Card. In spite of his series of magnificent knockouts Card is, to my mind, a quite gentle man. He is not a dark murderer.'

'It does you great credit,' Hartnell said, 'but I should not like to be near Augustine Card with hatred for me growing and fostering inside him. I was in the lecture room on the night of the murder . . . you were not. I felt the poisonous atmosphere in that assembly. I saw Card listening with hatred to this little curate's coxcombry. When I heard that Makepeace was dead it seemed very natural to me that this dark deed should have happened—should have happened in the same room, after we had all left. I like Augustine as much as you do, and so I would back him up always in a court case—as I have in this trial. But that does not make me think any differently.'

The two men looked at one another, and the former,

'Horrid', felt himself convicted of sentimentality. Had he really underestimated Augustine Card?—had he been inclined not to see him very clearly, as he had looked at him through a veil of tenderness? But he was not ready to surrender his opinion, namely that this man had died solely because of his weak heart.

'That Augustine Card had murdered somebody agreed with my view of Augustine's nature,' Hartnell said, 'from observation of him during those early days at Oxford. He is a more violent man than you think. He would only be satisfied by the death of a person who was challenging him in a contest involving something so profound as that which was at issue between himself and the dead curate.

'Then, there is another thing. I do not know to what extent you have shared the beliefs of Augustine. His view of Christianity was very different from the orthodox. He would, in the end, have attempted to convert the congregation of St Catherine's and the Angels to his particular beliefs, as he has so many of my scholars. His mystique about poverty was aggressive. He had not had time to develop his theories, but he had chosen a strange spot to start his black evangel!'

The face of Horridge had undergone a sudden change. He had been shocked by what Hartnell had said. 'I had often thought,' he said, 'that Augustine was a socialist.'

Hartnell laughed. 'That was a mild way of looking at him. He is much more than that I do assure you. He has the extremism of the Asiatic.'

'Well, it is obvious that I never knew my Augustine.' Horridge was looking at the other's face, and decided that he too, with his black eyes, was a man of violence.

The dinner was over and the two men went out into Regent Street, where everything looked violent to Horridge also. The dark night seemed to be caught by the rushing taxis and was coming down lower than usual. They walked slowly along towards the Circus, talking as they went.

'I should like to come to Africa, and do something there,' said Hartnell.

'What do you think you could do?' asked Horridge, who hoped that he would not come.

'I suppose, a schoolmaster,' Hartnell said.

Hartnell seemed to have made the night blacker and more violent, and Horridge felt that Africa had not been a very dramatic place for him, but if Hartnell got there he felt that he would set it on fire.

'I don't advise you to come to Africa,' he said. 'It is a filthy climate for a European.'

Horridge began trying to discourage the other from an African visit. They parted at the Circus, taking separate taxi-cabs, although they lived in a rather similar direction. Horridge hoped that this man would not succeed in spreading all his ideas around the court. He gave him a disagreeable grin as they parted.

32

The Trial Continued

I n addition to Mary, Lady Imogen Card and the Canon
were seated in the well of the court reserved for such
close relatives, behind the counsels' table. Mary looked
haggard and anxious, quite unlike herself. Lady Imogen
was seen encouraging her, in this last life and death struggle
of the trial. Augustine, who gazed over at his wife and
mother, was very white, and even more unlike himself.
He looked very big between the two smallish warders, but
occasionally smiled wanly in the direction of Mary.

Now came the final speech for the prosecution. This
opened the proceedings on the third day. Sir Richard Peters
began by the remark that all the information brought
forward by the counsel for the defence made it seem that
they had to do with a question of manslaughter rather than
the fearful charge of murder, with which they began. It
was, of course, for the judge to decide, but, for his part,
Sir Richard would not press for more than a verdict of
manslaughter. He afterwards proceeded to say that he was
very shocked at much of the behaviour of the accused man.
'The spectacle of several ordained persons engaging in embittered arguments with one another is very unpleasant at
the least.' But, Sir Richard Peters pointed out, the necessity
to alter the original charge, owing to the evidence given,
did make it very difficult for him to say all he would like to
under the present circumstances.

The essence of this final speech for the Crown was, within obvious limits, favourable to the prisoner. Mary and Lady Imogen were intensely relieved in listening to it, and they clasped each other's hands and held them together until the end of his not very long speech.

Next came the judge's charge to the jury, or what is properly known as the judge's summing up. It was a very painful ordeal for Mary, and, of course, for Lady Imogen too. Augustine had been given a draught to enable him to sleep, and therefore had slept profoundly. But when he woke up it was as if he had received a blow, when he remembered what they were all waiting for—namely the verdict of the jury, and what the judge would give as his final advice to them. On the other hand, to Monica Blunt, it was quite obvious, after listening to the Crown's withdrawal of its maximum charge, that the judge would no doubt follow suit, and this she attempted to impress on Mary.

However, at last the moment came for the judge to begin. His first words were what Mary and Lady Imogen had been praying for; they made it evident that he would advise the jury to convert the charge of murder into one of manslaughter. That was all that mattered to Mary, at all events. But what he went on to say was of a less cheering nature. Having lifted the murder charge out of the way, he proceeded as follows: 'On the other hand, and what may seem in stark contrast with the cancellation of the murder charge, it does seem to me that, although there was no intention to murder, there must have been a great desire to hurt, otherwise Augustine Card would not have hammered this man so hard, and afterwards kicked him on the face as well as the body. This splendid athlete was exceeding what was necessary in order to defeat this man in the fight he was having with him. So there are two things to remember;

(1) if Makepeace had not had a weak heart he probably would not have died, in spite of the brutality of Card's attack; (2) if Card's intention had been to win his fight alone, then the battering of the body of Makepeace was far beyond what was necessary for that end—namely, the end of winning the fight.

'These two points, members of the jury, result in my calling your attention to the advisability of the murder charge being dropped, and a charge of manslaughter or, alternatively, of accidental slaying, being substituted. On the other hand in releasing this man from the maximum charge, it still leaves you with a very great deal of unnecessary brutality to include in what you have to consider in arriving at your verdict. The killing of Makepeace must remain a serious offence, since malice must still be alleged in the injuries he received, although death need not have resulted, and is adequately accounted for by the condition of Makepeace's heart.'

These, and other forms of words used by the judge, did lead the jury to realise that there had been, in the fullest sense, a punishable offence. The judge went, in great detail, into the circumstances leading up to what was being tried, and the result, in due course, was that the jury eventually gave its verdict 'guilty of manslaughter.' Upon this the judge pronounced a sentence of three years imprisonment.

And so the trial ended, to the horror of Mary. There had been a moment when she had believed that Augustine would be convicted and hanged. Then there was a moment when she felt, that, having escaped murder, there was a very good likelihood of his getting a big sentence for manslaughter—for she did not see how his horrible treatment of Makepeace could possibly be overcome. But she had spent a great deal of money, and Sir Philip Sprigge, although he cost a fortune, was a very good man, and he had dragged Augustine out of the mud and got him a light sentence for a man beginning at murder.

But now the three years seemed bigger than all the things he had escaped put together. Why could she not buy the judge? However, there was no opening that way. It did not matter how much more money she spent, nothing could be done now. Her Augustine was going to be abolished for three long years. And what were they going to do afterwards? Her capital had diminished, and, on top of that, Augustine was commercially kaput. He would be ostracised everywhere—as a clergyman, what sort of future was there for him? None. He could be a shoe-black, but that would be about as high as he could get. Then how about Basil Tertullian? She would have to drop Tertullian, and call him Basil. Her life was ended. All she could do would be to scrape together the capital that was left, but then there would not be enough money to keep an enormous man, a child, and herself. She saw all this with the clarity that had always been hers. To see everything so clearly was terrible. She would go down and speak to Augustine—they would probably let her do that. But what would be the use of it? There would be nothing she could say to him to cheer him up. He had a clear way of seeing things too, though, once the boxing Blue was on top, he was as blind as a bat. There is a tiresome little clerk-like man who annoys him. All his intelligence flies out of the window. Because this nonentity was annoying, he kills him. It was the limit in silliness to kill anybody, but the boxing Blue was on top. She hated those enormous muscles—she could have taken a knife and cut them off.

She was standing in a room with the counsel, with Sir Philip Sprigge. She could have slapped his face. There he stood, grand and self-satisfied, all wig and gown. She hated

Sprigge. He had so much of her capital—she could have taken him by the shoulders and shaken it out of him. If she went on thinking about this for a day or two she would go mad. She flew out of the room, determined to see Augustine at once—at once . . . or never. She must see Augustine now, or she would never want to see Augustine again. If she were prevented from seeing him for a month or two she literally could not face him then.

Pursued by Sir Philip Sprigge, she dashed along the corridors. She put her arm under the arm of a P.C. and flew with him to where Augustine would be. The P.C. slid away —she could not stop him—to where he could get a ticket or something to enable her to see the prisoner.

The P.C. continued to slide about, but she had him by the arm. At last he had the permission, and they shot away until she stood before Augustine.

'Darling. This is frightful. I will discover if there is any escape. If you can get away I will hire an electric launch. I will advertise for one in the agony column tomorrow morning. We will fly to Africa. We will get away. Darling.'

Augustine was scowling steadily at her.

'Try to stop vapouring. See if an appeal can be any good. Great God!' he suddenly shouted, 'Do you understand what I have lost. A futile little shadow of a man—weak-hearted and weak-witted—and my life ends!'

'Not an end! It will not last long,' said Mary! 'Do not despair!'

The last thing she saw of his face was a grim look of hatred.

The P.C. urged her along, 'Would escape be easy? Could I get my husband away in a launch, fitted with electricity? Could I get him up in a helicopter—are the P.Cs. used to that? What would it cost? How much? How much would you do it for?'

The P.C. was like a block of stone—he could not hear. He just hurried her along, to get her out of the court, collecting a little tip at the end of it.

He got his little tip. She was angry with him for forming into a block of stone, and refusing to get Augustine up in a helicopter. They parted coldly.

When she got outside the court Monica Blunt was hovering for her. They flew in a taxi-cab to a quiet restaurant in Mayfair. They lunched there. Mary was horrified at her husband's attitude. She told Monica that he had shouted at her and seemed to be in despair. Monica did not seem at all surprised. 'He loathes everything, you see, even you.'

But Mary refused to accept that view of it. She was full of talk about her future; and they had a terrible twenty minutes discussing her capital. Monica was more understanding about capital, she was the only woman Mary had ever met who really got excited about capital. After lunch Mary visited Mr Smithers, and they discussed Mary's capital. He had had a great deal to do with the trial, he sympathised with Mary about the result. He also sympathised about the capital. Then she flew, literally, to Paris, and in the week or two spent in that city she thought out very carefully her future life. The trial had not cost so many thousands as she had feared, she was still a rich woman. No friends of hers that she knew of were in Paris. She flew back to London, and rearranged her life in that city. All of Augustine's former expenditure was abruptly terminated; their flat was let, and Mary transferred her residence to a cheaper place. The studio was disposed of, let to an artist. Another Vicar had been appointed to St Catherine and the Angels, with whom Mary communicated on the subject of Augustine's property in the studio, and in his cell at the Clergy House. His books and clothes she took to her new flat. Basil Tertullian, in the competent hands of the

Swiss nurse, was also there. She produced a manuscript of modest size, entitled *The Red Priest*. She made a successful sale of this small book to a well-known publisher, and she also wrote in one of the large Sunday papers a page of reminiscence of the trial, to the annoyance of Mrs Chillingham. The General had been seen at the court, and he remarked, rather cruelly, to Mary that this affair must have cost her a great deal. Mary received a letter from her mother, in which that lady had written, 'You may recall that I told you that a parson was usually an expensive husband to have. If he kills his curates, however, it must really make it very costly.'

Well provided with the spirit of the great Border family to which she belonged, Mary Card was not prepared to admit defeat. She and Basil were determined to face the world with *cranerie*. How she was ever going to manage to live in a quite fairly expensive flat, eventually send Basil Tertullian to Eton, and yearly fight a battle with the Inland Revenue, she could not imagine. These purely material problems were of great importance to her, but beyond that lay the problems under the general heading *Augustine*. If she looked outward upon the world with a brave stare, obviously her husband was expected to do that also. That penniless man, ordained in a profession which would provide the ex-murderer with very little money, could only be a burden to her when he came out of prison.

33

The Plantation

O ne of the first things Mary did was to discover where a colonial territory was to be found as favourably situated as Nairobi in the matter of a little capital. One of the pieces of property that her Aunt Blanche had left her mother to dispose of was a coffee-growing estate near Lake Rudolf. In talking over her problem with her mother, this estate was mentioned; and that none too amiable lady showed a surprising readiness to dispose of this property, and was willing to part with it at so unbusinesslike a price that, in the end, Mary decided to buy it. It was not in the Mau Mau country, though she felt certain, in thinking about it afterwards, that her mother sold it her at a tempting price because she hoped that this would lead to her destruction at the hands of the Mau Mau.

Although Mary possessed considerable aptitude, and an even greater taste for business, she found, when she was at her newly bought estate at Lake Rudolf, that, from a purely business point of view, her coffee plantation was not so promising as she had hoped. Practically all the experienced labour was in the hands of the big companies. But with her usual determination she set out to be a success as a planter, and at the end of a year she had succeeded in making a reasonably good start. Mau Mau ideas had no hold among her work-people.

One or two of the neighbouring settlers had known her aunt. There was one highly unpopular, Lord Bredeset, whom she got to know. He was the son of the Duke of Flamborough. The main cause of his unpopularity was his title, which was too authentic and altogether too grand to please the British settler. Mary got on well with this nobleman, who gave her a few valuable tips, and who was quite good company.

However, the great thing was that she was not losing money, and there was even a prospect that she might make a little. As soon as she had established herself in Africa she returned to England on a visit and went to see Augustine in Dartmoor prison. She told him all about the coffee plantation, and enquired closely into his convict life. The shaven head was so loathsome to her that she determined to do what she could to get him out. In the meanwhile, she said to him, 'Teeny, mind that you're so damned good that they let you out before half your sentence is over.'

Back in London one of the first things that Mary did was to see Monica. Her friend had a relative who lived in Kenya, and she had learned from this man that the settlers had been shaken by a rumour (which of course might be quite a fantasy) to the effect that Mr Butler, the English Chancellor of the Exchequer, was plotting against Kenya. The rumour was that the economic immunity of Kenya was threatened by this terrible man. This sent a shiver down the spine of Mary. She got in touch with an able young economist. She explained her danger, and learned from him the most likely way to keep her capital intact. This plan for the protection of her capital, if the worst came to the worst, was a matter of intense satisfaction to Mary.

She stayed in London, of course, at her flat in Chelsea, which was dominated by Basil Tertullian. She thought he looked more like Augustine than ever. She enjoyed this period very much. Before returning to Kenya she persuaded her father to transfer the lease of her Chelsea flat into his name, her bank arranging with General Chillingham that he should be economically protected. After seeing Augustine again, she flew back to Kenya, leaving Basil Tertullian in the keeping of the Swiss nurse in her flat. She had been back on her plantation for about nine months when a message reached her to the effect that Augustine had assaulted the governor of the prison.

On hearing of these events Mary cabled 'Shall be back London quite soon. Meanwhile behave as well as possible for my sake. All love, Mary.'

She returned to England on the first home-bound ship.

A short while before hearing of this new misbehaviour of Augustine she had received a letter from him. It ran as follows: 'Dearest Mary. I have had plenty of time to gaze at myself from head to foot: and the individual I have been inspecting does not deserve to be your husband. That is so blindingly obvious that it is an insult to tell you; or, since a letter of the same kind is no doubt on the way, this statement will probably look like a device of mine to forestall what I must anticipate. I forestall my congé. If you are not writing something to that effect, it can only be an instance of your invariable kindness.

'But I am not only unworthy to have such a wife as you are—and have proved yourself to be (for when I was about to be hanged as a murderer you came to my rescue, in a manner befitting a heroine of romance)—but there is something else. Nearly all careers are barred to me. I would be a cad and a blackguard to contemplate with equanimity your remaining legally fastened to me. There is nothing awaiting me but a hideous desertic existence. But you understand that in the position in which I find myself I must dedicate myself to a religious life of the most repulsive kind, and I cannot ask you to accompany me. You are extremely beautiful, and still young. Would you prefer to divorce me, or should I divorce you? You must be free at once. Send me a letter by return. I shall go as a missionary to where the world ends.

Ever yours, Augustine.'

34

The Birth of Zero

Back in England, she discovered that what had happened
at the prison was this (rather different from what the
message had conveyed to her). With the best intentions in the world the Governor of the prison had
dropped in to see his distinguished prisoner. Augustine
misunderstood this intrusion. He had, apparently, seized
the Governor by the scruff of the neck, and pushed him
out of his cell. The rudeness of the imprisoned priest was
resented, and it would not count in his favour when the
question came up as to whether his conduct had been good
enough to reduce his sentence, in the usual way.

Mary visited Augustine as soon as possible. What he said
was that the patronising visit of the Governor had occurred
at an inopportune moment, and he had turned him out
unceremoniously, certainly. The Governor appeared to
think that, because Augustine was living in the way that he
did, he was welcome to drop in breezily whenever he cared to.
Augustine said that he wanted to make it quite clear to this
little coxcomb that a visit from him did not cheer up prison
life, as he seemed to imagine it would. This episode had not
improved his standing in this beastly place, he informed Mary.

'Oh, you are a persistent donkey,' was Mary's answer.
'Don't you want ever to get out into freedom?'

In spite of this misbehaviour Augustine was released in
not much more than two years after his imprisonment had
begun—this meant that all Mary had to do was to remain

in England, and not go back, as she had arranged to do, to her plantation. Consequently, when Augustine was released and free to go where he liked, he could come to her at their Chelsea flat. She personally had visited the Governor of the prison, and that official was of opinion that his prisoner had a much more beautiful wife than he deserved. However the Governor most generously confided to her the day of her husband's proposed release. This information she was of course unable to pass on to Augustine. But she arranged with the prison authorities that as soon as the prisoner learned the time fixed for his discharge, he would be able to telephone her, and they would settle together the exact time of his arrival at the flat.

Actually, Augustine Card, as soon as he left the prison, made his way as speedily as possible to where his wife and son awaited him. He reached his destination by three in the afternoon. Mary, holding her child in her arms, met him in the living-room. She and Augustine were both weeping. They pressed Basil Tertullian between them, their son shouting 'Father' and seizing Augustine by the nose.

Augustine was deeply moved; he lifted Basil up upon his chest and hugged his son, not attempting to disguise his tears.

'Mary,' he said, in a sort of whisper, 'we should not have done this. It makes it so difficult for me.'

'Why raise up a barrier between your son and yourself?' she admonished him.

'Only it will make the life I have to live more hard, my dear,' Augustine answered.

'What life? Where?' was Mary's question.

'Where? Oh, the mountains of the Moon,' Augustine said.

'I propose to discuss that with you,' Mary said softly.

She and the Swiss nurse had prepared as good a dinner as could be had in London. They opened a vintage Moët and wept again over their delicious meal. Warmed against the November night by a burning water-bottle where their bed ended, and in each other's arms as never before, the prisoner went to sleep held by Mary as if she had feared his escape. When he woke in his own bed, it was very difficult to return to his harsh plans. But he was bound to tell her what arrangements he had made.

They could, of course, like any other man and woman, he supposed, return now to this personal paradise, as meltingly warm as that bed they had just crawled out of. But there were invisible things which prevented him from accepting those delights. He was obliged to wipe out the murder, which the world believed he had committed, whatever the judge had said.

Mary shrieked. 'Nonsense! What was the use, then, of our dragging you out of all that, if you wilfully plunge yourself back into it again—just as if you had committed a terrible crime after all—which you have not done, of course! You condemn me to suffer too, for an imaginary felony—for murder, which is ridiculous.'

They argued bitterly for days. The position defended by Mary was that he, Augustine, was not a criminal; that the death of his curate was an accident; that the original charge of murder had been proved absurd; that it was ridiculous to go on punishing himself. Against this Augustine argued that if he behaved as if nothing had happened he would be cut everywhere—in the street, in restaurants, in shops. Some insignificant rat of a man would look the other way. What was he, Augustine, to do? Knock him down? No? Just get used to being cut? The Reform Club would probably blackball him. He doubted if even the London Library would allow him to belong—the other members would be polluted—also the staff! Mary just answered 'Nonsense!' Augustine would *not* be cut—he must not think of himself as a pariah. Eton would say that they had no room for the son of a murderer?—Send him to Harrow!—If Harrow refused to take him, send him to St Paul's!—If St Paul's refused him, send him to the nearest Council School. . . . He is going to be a tough baby. Any bus conductor's son who said he did not like sitting next to a murderer's son would have his teeth kicked out!

'Tough' talk enraged Augustine. His voice grew hard.

Mary went to see Monica Blunt, the ex-Ghastly girl. What on earth should she do? The 'Ghastly' answer was straight from the shoulder. 'The man is insane. Secure a first-rate divorce lawyer. Get your marriage annulled—because of his insanity. You rescued him from the gallows. But the refutation of that charge of murder has driven him mad. You must get rid of him. He is dangerous!'

Mary left her 'Ghastly' friend with a black look of disappointment at the failure of this person she had supposed intelligent.

After months of excited argument Mary gave way. She agreed to the course of conduct proposed by Augustine. The good offices of Canon Card enabled his son to secure a post as a missionary—a job which had been refused by a score or two of clergymen. He undertook to go to the habitat of nothing more civilised than an Eskimo—although, even there, to achieve the absolute loneliness he desired became more difficult every day. However, he described as his purpose to plant the Heavenly Standard among the seals.

As to the ultimate Eskimo he would whisper in the ear of this diminutive savage that he was terribly wrong—that there was no God but God. And this enormous man would return to civilised life with the dark soul of this little savage in his pocket.

Augustine sailed for Quebec in the third-class of a small liner. Mary, Basil Tertullian at her side, saw him off, a small white handkerchief in her hand, which she pressed against her eyes from time to time. The tallest and blackest pasenger, Augustine, stuck up in the stern of the ship, waved a long, black arm.

Durrant's Newspaper Clippings delivered at Mary's Chelsea flat any publicity sent by Augustine to what had always been his favourite daily papers.

'The famous Red Priest of former days, Father Card, is to carry the Gospel to the remotest Eskimo, to the Northernmost Man. To reach this practically inaccessible little pagan he will travel across a thousand miles of polar ice in an Eskimo's sled, drawn by those powerful animals, the famous "huskies", with which we are all familiar by seeing the films of polar exploration. They enabled Scott to reach the Pole. They now draw the daring Red Priest to the nearest point to the North Pole inhabited by man.'

From a less friendly newspaper the following clipping made its way to Mary.

'Murderer and Missionary. The main figure in a famous trial, after a London vicar had killed his curate in an access of barbary, has now finished his sentence for manslaughter, and is on his way to carry Christ to the remotest heathen— The tough little Eskimos, who have pushed nearer the Pole than any other man has cared to do, will shortly have this bloodthirsty clergyman whispering to them in a blizzard the Word of God.'

This slap in the face Mary took with a wry expression. But the next message had the effect of a blast from a bomb. It read—'Augustine Card, now polar missionary, arrives at the end of his terrible journey with one of his Eskimos murdered. Strangled it seems. Other Eskimos must have been surprised. But we should not be.'

When Mary had recovered, she proceeded to find someone

in Canada competent to send her accurate messages. The next to reach her was this.

'Missionary murdered. Corpse of Missionary Card arrives at polar terminus. Throat gouged out, apparently by Eskimos. Revenge supposed reason.'

This newspaper clipping filled Mary with such horror that for the rest of the day she was unable to do anything. In a few days there arrived, by air mail, the first of a long series of Canadian cuttings. What came in the middle of these was a mysterious cablegram, signed 'Augustine.' It read—'Had struggle with dangerous Eskimo. He had taken my wallet while I slept. I fear I hurt him. Details later. Augustine.'

Eventually there arrived from the Mounties a wallet, with money and a letter.

'Dear Madam. You are, I assume, Augustine Card's mother or wife. Enclosed is pouch with the money we found in it. Card himself is dead. He was killed by Eskimos, it is supposed, in revenge for his strangling of an Eskimo on first journey up into the ice. Following this we shall be sending you report of doctor, and an account of the trial of the assumed guilty ones. We await your reply, informing us of what your wishes are regarding body of murdered man.' This was signed Sergeant MacBride, at the Vancouver Mounted Police Barracks, B.C., Canada.

Shortly after, there reached her, a little mysteriously, a copy of *The B.C. Forum*. Her attention was drawn, by a bold cross, to an article in this paper. Its title was 'Father Card. Episode in Vancouver' by Kenneth Gilmour. As she read it she saw her Augustine so vividly that she clutched the chair in which she was sitting. She almost heard him speak.

The 'Episode' read as follows:

'I am afraid that this article will not show me in a very advantageous light. But I understand that Father Card was a man of note in England, and I felt that his last hours in Canada, before he started off on his fatal journey, would be of general interest, both in Canada and Great Britain.

'I shall write with great outspokenness, because the indication of the state of his mind which I am able to give would be, I knew, of considerable importance.

'I was staying in the Coronel Hotel in the upper part of Vancouver. It is not a very splendid hostelry, the Coronel, but it caters for people who are *de passage* in Vancouver, offering reasonably priced good plain cooking, a comfortable bed, and the best of service. I am an Englishman, and this is very much to my taste; I always put up at this hotel whenever I am in Vancouver.

'I was surprised, on the occasion of which I speak, to find a man there whom I had never seen before. He was of very striking appearance, a good deal over six foot, and obviously a very heavy man as well as extremely tall. He was cropped like a Prussian. He obviously had no desire for idle chat. But that type of man interests me; and so, without cordiality on his part, I approached him, and led off by saying "You are an Old Countryman, I see, sir. I am, too. That, anyhow, is my excuse for speaking to you." To which he replied, "It is no excuse."

'He was a man of degree, fearless and bluff, and I was not violently displeased at this rebuff.

' "You are right, sir," I replied.

' "Go away," ordered the stranger. "What is your purpose in pressing your company on me? You will deservedly get your busybody nose punched for sticking it in where it does not belong."

'I was, oddly enough, well satisfied at the persistence of this snub. It must mean that this man had something to hide, something, I concluded, that other men would be interested to know about. So I became brazen in my attempt to force myself on this countryman of mine. I recognised that this man belonged to the upper classes, and was no ordinary man.

' "I wish for your acquaintance. Your snubs arouse my curiosity."

'He pointed at his close-cropped head. "I have just come out of prison. This cropped hair has not had time to grow." He gazed stonily into my eyes.

' "That is not the way to repulse a lawyer," I told him. "What was your crime?"

' "Murder," was this strange man's answer.

' "Why were you not hanged?" I asked him.

' "I succeeded in getting the charge changed to one of manslaughter," he informed me.

' "How long ago was that?" I enquired.

' "Oh, two or three years," he answered, almost eagerly, as if this had been a confession that I had been conducting.

' "Was it murder?" I next asked.

'His eyes were fixed on mine. At this point they shut sharply, and opened again. "I should say that it was," said he.

' "I see," I said. "My instinct was right. You are an interesting man."

' "Thank you, you fool," said my countryman.

' "Unusually conceited, aren't you, like many criminals I have met," I told him.

' "You will get your head broken before very long," I was told.

'And, curiously enough, I felt that I should. My legal experience enabled me to guess fairly clearly to what length I could go without getting killed. I could see that this man now wanted to talk to me; but his brain was slightly deranged.

' "A short way from this hotel," I said to him, "you can get an admirable view of Vancouver Island. It is really a pretty view. Should I be snubbed if I suggested to you a little stroll? Just for ten minutes or so?"

'Card, as I now know him to be, rose and nodded his head. "All right—take me for that stroll."

'Not without a tinge of fear I went out with him, and took him a short distance from the hotel, where there was a sort of cliff. There, in the distance, was Vancouver Island as I had told him, and a good deal of water as well. Very beautiful.

' "There, sir, is what I told you I would show you."

'We stood there looking down. I thought I had better go carefully, or this huge man might throw me over the cliff. After a little I said, "How did you come to murder a man? You have not told me?"

' "Oh, you know, he never ceased to annoy me. He was in my employ and then one day we had a fierce argument. He struck me."

' "Did you kill him in a fight?" I asked.

' "Yes. Only I am a trained fighter, and I weighed twice as much as he."

' "You need say no more," I told him. "It was not murder."

'He turned madly on me, thrust me somehow under the chin, and I found myself sprawling on my back, very near the edge of the precipice. I gathered myself together and prepared to rise. He caught me by the arm, and dragged me to my feet. He then began dusting me round the collar, and blowing upon the cloth. Next, continually blowing, he passed over to the other shoulder, and as he did so blew straight in my face. He had two bellows in his chest, this huge man, which were of such potency that I staggered. He nearly blew me over the cliff.

' "I told you you were a fool," Card said. "Why did you say I was not a murderer?"

'He was glaring into my eyes, and I knew, at this moment, that I must be very careful.

' "I know, of course, nothing about your life. You have

not told me anything, really. I daresay you are a murderer, and should have been hanged."

'He took this quite well.

' "Learn another time to mind your own filthy little business, or you will get yourself thrown over a cliff. See!" He said this so fiercely that I said to myself what a fool I was to take this maniac out on to this cliff. And I wondered what was the best way to get clear of it. We were alone, there was no one in sight, and if I had taken to my heels I saw that this madman was quite capable of running after me, and bringing me back to where we were at that moment—I thought of the absolute necessity of showing no fear to a wild animal. I had enough presence of mind to stare back into his face, without showing him (I think) the terror I felt.

' "You have something more to tell me, sir?" I said.

'This woke us from the trance into which we were sinking there together, and I saw him self-consciously waking himself out of it, giving himself a sort of shake. He looked down at the ground. He woke up in a moment and said to me, in a slightly less aggressive voice than heretofore, "My life is over. I am, as it were, upon the edge of that cliff. I am just as ruined as a man can be. I shall always be treated as a murderer."

' "Oh no you won't," I rashly intervened. He turned on me swiftly, with such a blaze of anger in his eyes that once more I knew that my life was in the balance.

'He suddenly seized me by the throat, shook me in a way that only a man of his terrific strength could do, and said, "You . . . poor . . . wormofaman! Will you never learn any sense?"

'He let me drop from his hands, and burst out into a huge laugh. Whereupon he turned on his heel and walked quickly back to the hotel.

'When Father Card, it was announced in the newspapers, had been killed by the Eskimos, I was in no way surprised. I felt that he had just escaped flinging me over the cliff, and probably being hanged for doing so. I thought that my meeting with Card would be of interest to those whose business it is to study the law.'

One of the last things that Mary did in England was to move up Marten's Mews, and, just before she left it, she rang Miss Greevey's bell. When the door was opened, Miss Greevey and Mary stared at one another as if they both had risen from the dead. Jane invited her in, and showed her a number of papers, full of accounts of Father Card's tragic end. Jane was very gentle and pleasant. They both wept as they were looking at the photographs of Father Card and especially those where he was seen as a young man on the battlements of Craigliven Castle. Jane pointed out to Mary passages in an article that gave instances of Augustine's great goodness of heart, quoting acts of kindness, and instances of how he had given a helping hand to a former school fellow and other such things. Mary recognised these as part of the material she had collected for the defence in his trial. But Jane dropped tear after tear over this moving evidence.

Mary asked for news of Hughie, and heard that he was abroad. They parted like two old friends, Mary promising to send postcards from Africa, showing the beauties of Kenya, and Jane said she would write enclosing anything of interest from the London papers.

Mary and Basil Tertullian withdrew to the plantation on the shores of Lake Rudolf, where she gave birth to another child. Her naming was more like a branding; she gave him the fearful name of Zero. She could see that he would look like his terrible father; that he was fated to blast his way across space and time.